THE SISTERS THREE

JAE MAZER

Copyright © 2019 by Jae Mazer & Feathered Tentacle Press

All rights reserved.

No part of this book may be reproduced in any form or by any electronic or mechanical means, including information storage and retrieval systems, without written permission from the author, except for the use of brief quotations in a book review.

Cover art Copyright by Robert Elrod, LLC. The art may not be reproduced, duplicated, or sold without expressed permission from the artist, Robert Elrod, LLC.

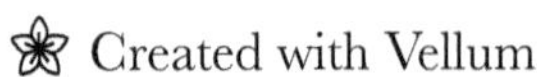

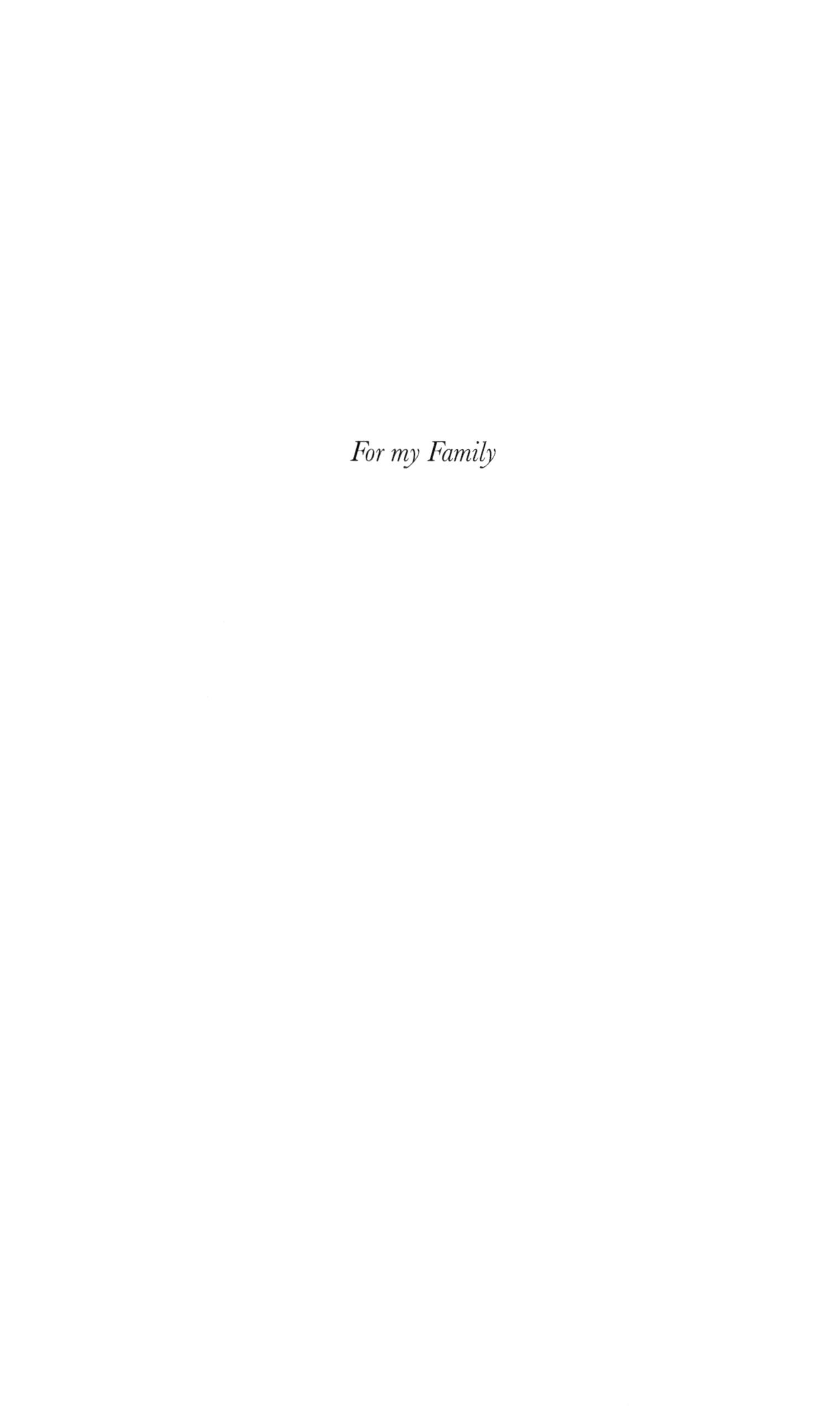

For my Family

The most common form of despair is not being who you are.

— SOREN KIERKEGAARD, DANISH PHILOSOPHER/ THEOLOGIAN

CHAPTER 1

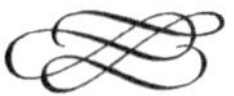

A TATTERED FROTH OF GOSSAMER, the ivory dress flowed like ribbons as Zelda spun the doll in circles, singing, her tiny voice like a blade on crystal.

Below the crystal waves of salt
A pool of tears amongst the drought
A land of beauty down below
Into the depths of life I'll go.

"Zelda!" Willow scolded, looking up from her drawing and clucking her tongue.

Oh, how Zelda hated when her sister scolded her—she had no business wagging fingers or clucking tongues.

She is only a child herself.

"I's just singing," Zelda said, hugging the doll to her chest.

"I know," Willow said, returning to her drawing, "but you sing it too often. It's annoying."

"But it's always in my head."

Zelda twirled the doll's indigo hair through her fingers, humming the song quietly in her throat.

"Still hear you," Willow said, rolling her eyes.

"Nuh uh."

"Do so!"

Zelda furrowed her brow into an angry caterpillar and plunked down on the floor next to Willow.

"Whatcha drawin'?" Zelda asked.

"The woods."

The paper was a palette of browns and greens, a tangled mess of branches and weeds and tiny yellow eyes peering from hidden holes in the white spaces of the page. Zelda stared, admiring her sister's creation, then rose and walked to the window.

A beautiful dusk fell on their little corner of the world. Their large estate was perched on the cliffs of the Haida Gwaii, overlooking the salt waters of the Pacific, framed by thick, deep woods. The scene was a painting, pink sky over black water, the moon dancing on ripples set in motion by fish and insects. A conversation of light flickered between the clouds, the first whispers of a storm starting in the near distance as a rumble rose with the moon.

"Did Mama call us for dinner?" Zelda asked, clutching her grumbling stomach.

"Didn't hear her."

Zelda glanced at the moon, a glowing orb now midway up the darkening sky.

"It's late. Why didn't she call us? I'm hungry," Zelda complained.

Willow sighed and set her pencil crayon down on her paper.

"Fine. Let's go see if dinner's ready."

Still clutching the doll against her chest, Zelda laced fingers with Willow and walked out of the bedroom. The house was awfully quiet, which was unusual for the hour. At the time when the moon was up and the sun dipped below the ocean, pans should have been clanking against pots, Mother's wine-filled speech regaling tales of the day to Father who would chortle over a snifter of brandy. And music. Mother always had music crackling out of the turntable, folk tunes from distant lands. There was soft music playing in the distance, harmonic and calculated. Opera, or classical, maybe?

"What music is that?" Zelda whispered. "Mother never plays that."

The sisters' footsteps landed heavy on the hardwood floor of the upstairs hallway, booming to the levels below. Their steps slowed as they moved farther from their bedroom, the darkness of the hallway swallowing them as they approached the stairs. Zelda's eyes sought the sconces on the wall, usually lit but tonight neglected.

"Mother and Father have the lights off still," Zelda said. Her voice was lower. She didn't know why.

Willow must have felt something, too. She tugged Zelda's hand softly, pulling her behind. Ever the protector, Willow stepped first into the mouth of the stairs, crouching low and peering through the bannisters. Zelda opened her mouth to speak, but Willow raised a hand to maintain the silence.

They waited, listened, barely breathed.

In unison, "Something..."

Willow finished the thought. "Something's not quite right."

Indeed, everything was off. The music, the darkness, the lateness of dinner; Mother and Father were never tardy or neglectful of these very basic functions of home. Fear gargled above the hunger in Zelda's belly, rising like a stone into her throat. And Willow felt it, too. Zelda knew. She knew because what Willow felt, she felt, and Zelda could feel both their hearts beating wild and silent against their ribs and in their temples.

"Can't very well do this for long," Willow said, rising to her feet.

Before Willow chose an action, Zelda lead the way, calling down the stairs, "Mother! Father! Are you there?"

The words cut through the stagnant air, resonating on every surface, louder than they had ever been before. The sisters waited, hopelessly willing a response from either parent, but were greeted by a third familiar yet surprising voice.

"Zelda? Willow?"

Isadora, their big sister, called from the front of the house. Her voice was sing-song and aloof, an indication of nothing awry. Tension melted off the little sisters, unclenching its talons from their throats and bellies.

"I was about to call dinner! Come on down, girls! Table's set and the meal awaits!"

The sisters looked at each other, and the tension struck again, roiling bellies and squeezing throats.

Isadora never called for dinner.

Mother or Father always called for dinner.

Zelda didn't like it, not one bit.

She had never cared much for Isadora. Isadora was in her mid-teens, but acted thrice that, bossing them like an understudy mother. Zelda and Willow gossiped about it at night, about the sly looks Isadora gave them, and the way she glowered at their parents with hatred. Isadora was a stuck-up ninny who was jealous of her and Willow. Zelda and Charlie were close, and their parents gave them the lion's share of the attention because they were so much younger than the first born. Who did Isadora have? Herself and her ego. Perhaps things would be better when they were adults and equal in all eyes.

Regardless of jealousy or trust, disdain or ego, hunger ruled the moment. Zelda was hungry, and dinner was waiting. The strangeness could wait until the food was devoured.

Side-by-side, the sisters descended the stairs, their eyes drawn to the flickering candlelight from the dining room at the back of the house. It was faint, but the rest of the main floor was shrouded in darkness, a sight they were unaccustomed to. Usually the main floor was awash with colour and warmth and light, the glow from many intricate sconces lighting every corner of the old mansion. Though the walls were papered in dark burgundy and chocolate filigree, the prevalence of flame typically brightened the home, showcasing every oak crown molding and vase and photograph. But not this night. On this strange night, normal was interrupted, the halls and rooms coated in the black silk of darkness, shapes and textures revealed only by candle-light reaching from the end of the long hall.

"Girls!" Isadora called, her lyrical voice coming

from the kitchen adjacent the dining room. "I am preparing your plates, now! Take your seats, if you please!"

No sign of Mother or Father. No voices, no clinking of wine or liquor glass, no properly lit passageways. Willow placed her fingertips against the wallpaper, leading Zelda by the hand towards the light. Though ravenous, Zelda hesitated to follow; several times, Willow had to give her a sharp tug. Zelda stumbled, fighting to keep up while holding her doll's hand and her sister's. As they approached the dining room, the kitchen appeared on their left, lit only by a single candle on the stove. Isadora turned to them as they stopped in the entry way. Her face was powdered in flour, her arms elbow deep in Mother's floral cooking gloves, Father's ratty, ember-burnt campfire apron hanging loose off her wiry frame.

"It's fish tonight, girls. Your favourite, yes Zelda?

Zelda's mouth filled with saliva, the aroma of steaming seafood wafting through the house. That fish had been prepared with Mother's special seasoning, a recipe passed down through generations on memory rather than paper. The night might be weird, but with Mother's spice, nothing else mattered.

"Where's Mother?" Zelda asked.

Isadora met Zelda's eye, answering without a blink.

"Why, waiting for dinner! For you to join us so we can get started."

Willow jumped in. "But why are *you* making dinner?"

Hands on her hips, Isadora pursed her lips into a pout. "I can cook just fine. Mother entrusted me to this Friday meal, and I was excited for the challenge. I've had my first blood, I'll have you know. It's time for me to practice running a home."

The sisters looked at each other, then back at Isadora. No one was smiling.

"Look, it's food. If you don't fancy it, there will be something else. You needn't worry though. It's edible."

It does smell amazing, Zelda thought, eyeing the fish on the carving tray.

Hesitantly content with the odd changing of the guard, the sisters left Isadora to her preparations and continued to the end of the hall.

The dining room was bright, dozens of iron sconces on the walls lit with vigorous flame, the colours and textures of the room vibrant, dancing with the moving fire. The table was set as it should be, all cutlery in its place, napkins folded like trumpeter swans just like Mother did on special occasions. A bounty of yams and peas and rolls were laid out, ready to swim in pools of gravy. Most importantly, Mother and Father were there, each seated at their end of the table.

But all was not as it should be.

And the sisters were no longer content with the new routine.

"Isn't this lovely?" Isadora cooed, swooping into the dining room from the kitchen entrance, silver platter in hand. "A right proper feast, this is."

The sound of the platter being set on the table, though gentle, rattled like cymbals in Zelda's brain, loosening tears that poured down her face.

"Isadora."

It was the only word Willow could manage, which was more than Zelda could; she couldn't manage to choke out a single syllable. Her breath disappeared, the wind knocked out of her by shock, the only voice the screaming in her own brain.

What have you done?

"Now girls, sit down. You're already tardy for dinner, but thankfully so was I. The food's still hot, so—"

Isadora's explanation was cut off by Willow's shrill scream, loud and pained enough to strain the crystal goblets at each place setting. Willow tentatively approached Mother, snot and tears running down her face, incoherent ramblings exploding out of her mouth.

Zelda stayed quiet and stared, twirling her fingers through her doll's indigo hair.

Mother's throat was sliced open, blood and vomit spilled over the front of her smock.

A gardening tool was hilt deep in one of Father's ears, poking out the other.

The ivory table cloth—the one with the delicate little flowers Mother embroidered herself by hand; oh how proud she was of that table cloth—was now saturated with a crimson sheen, the life of both parents marring its purity.

"Whatever is the matter?" Isadora said, shrugging her shoulders.

Willow sputtered, "How could you… why did you…"

Isadora waved a hand dismissively. "You wouldn't understand, the two of you. Maybe one day, when you're older and wiser like me."

Isadora grabbed a carafe of water from the liquor cart and started filling the goblets. Willow continued sputtering and Zelda continued staring as Isadora moved on and served up three plates of dinner. When she was done, she walked over to the window and looked out at the ocean, hands behind her back.

"They were going to sell this place, you know," Isadora said, her voice far away. "My home. Can you imagine? There's nothing quite like this place, out here on the ocean all by itself. We are one with the woods and the sea here—"

She didn't get a chance to finish. Willow launched at her, catching her by surprise. With fist-fulls of Isadora's hair, Willow thrashed and tore, ripping out great chunks of the chestnut hair and clawing at her face. But Isadora was older and stronger; she was able to restrain Willow in no time flat.

"You monster!" Willow spat, kicking and biting at the air in hopes of taking a piece—any piece—of her eldest sister.

"Perhaps," Isadora said, "but this is my home. And now it really is. *My* home."

Isadora wrenched Willow's arms behind her back and forced her out onto the patio and down into the backyard. Zelda followed, taking care not to move too close lest her older sister grab her, too.

"Mama," Zelda mewled, weeping quietly. "Mama, help us Mama."

Mother couldn't hear. Neither could Father. But Isadora did. And she laughed, a deep and demented giggle from deep in her belly.

"Ah, wee Zelda, ever the fool. Your flights of fancy won't carry you away on their wings this time, my naïve little dear. Mommy and Daddy are gone, and this," Isadora swept a hand around her, motioning to the property, "is *my* world now."

Willow cried out in anger and protest, struggling violently against Isadora's tight grasp.

What the worst she'll do? Zelda thought. *She wouldn't dare hurt her.*

But she did dare. Isadora let go, and Willow stood, freed and stunned for but a moment before launching back at her older sister with reignited fury. It didn't last long. Their bodies collided with an audible squelch, then both girls fell still and silent. Willow took a step back, and her hands worked their way to her belly where they wrapped around the hilt of the fillet knife stuck in her abdomen.

Zelda found her voice.

"Willow? Willow… no… Mama…"

Willow coughed, bloody drool sputtering from her lips. She clawed at her stomach, her hands slipping off the gore-soaked blade until her eyes widened and she crumpled into the grass. Zelda felt like she was floating as she walked to her sister, kneeling beside her on the soft ground.

"Willow, you're so pale," Zelda said.

Zelda stroked Willow's raven-black hair, smoothing it across the grass. Everything looked midnight blue in the moonlight—Willow's hair, the shimmering grass. Zelda's eyes rose, distracted from her sister by two yellow orbs, a pair of glowing eyes, watching her from the woods, bobbing up and down, growing larger…

Isadora's boney hand grabbed Zelda's arm and

hauled her off the ground just before the wolf pounced, sinking its teeth into Willow's throat and tearing out a chunk. They locked eyes, Zelda and the wolf, as Willow's meat dripped off its lips. It nuzzled its snout into the nape of Willow's neck and clamped down to get a firm grip. Then slowly, maintaining eye contact with Zelda, it backed into the woods, dragging Willow with it. Zelda watched until the soles of Willow's pink feet disappeared into the harsh, mangled brush.

"Willow," Zelda cried.

"Come now," Isadora said, her hand on Zelda's back, guiding her across the grass.

"No! Willow, come back!"

Zelda's voice was below a whisper, audible to only her own mind, but she kept breathing the words, watching the tree line for her sister, even as it moved farther and farther away. She watched the trees, her doll squished into her chest, impeding her breathing. By the time they reached the water, Isadora was carrying her, traversing the rocky shore and submerging them both in the icy water of the North Pacific.

The frigid cold stole Zelda's breath as Isadora pushed her under the water. The waves lapped peacefully against the shore, a cathartic rhythm that moved with the floating gossamer of the dress on the doll clutched to Zelda's chest. Zelda held that doll tight, willing it to bring air to her lungs, to be her mother, her sister, anyone that would still be alive and love her and save her from her watery grave…

CHAPTER 2

The car hit a pothole, and the edge of the can hit Anne's lip. Fizz bubbled out of her nose, and she sputtered and giggled all at once.

"Right mess, you are," Charlie said, shaking her head.

Anne wiped the spittle and pop from her face, then gave her sister a playful punch on the shoulder. "Hey, you're the one trying to hit every bump in the road."

"Little challenge there," Charlie said, scowling. "This highway is more hole than road, I'm afraid."

Anne gazed out the windshield, her expression growing solemn. "I don't remember the highway being this bad."

"When was the last time you were out here? Hell, I haven't been out this way in a decade, at least. Roads deteriorate; they need maintenance, but this one's not traveled much, so…"

"Priorities," Anne said, shaking her head. "Damn NDP party."

The highway, nestled up the western side of Vancouver Island, grew narrower and rougher the more the kilometers passed, but the scenery was phenomenal. Big leaf maples and Garry oaks lined the wide ditches, turning into thick forests of spruce and brush. The grass was peppered with twin flowers, dogwood, and Nootka roses—mangled sprays of pinks and whites and yellows.

It was a wonderland of beach and forest, fresh and rough. Anne had missed it, so much. But once life gets moving, it's a freight train with no brakes coming down the side of a mountain.

Shame we waited this long.

A quick glance in the back seat of the rental car, then Anne faced forward again, trying to keep her eyes and mind on the road. Or her pop can. Or anything else.

"Mom and Dad loved it out here," Anne said, a lump forming in her throat.

"We all did," Emily said. "We'll always have this place."

"Why did we leave?"

"Anne, you know this. Work, family—there's not

much out here other than tourism, fishing and the like. Raising small kids is easier on the mainland. More services, higher pay."

Anne nodded. She had heard it many times when her parents had been alive. Every year they came camping up this way—along both coasts of the island, in fact—and every trip, each night around the campfire, the smell of smoke and salt water thick in the air, Anne could see it. Even as a small child, she noticed the change in her parents when they were out here, breathing the island, its serene pace, the blurred line between civilization and nature. They liked reality, their life in the city, but home was this place.

A dinging halted Anne's daydreaming. The gas light illuminated.

"Need petrol," Charlie said.

"Good," Anne said. "We're just about there, anyways, yes? We can pick up a few snacks and beverages for the hotel."

A SIGN APPEARED through the trees: *THE GOAT'S MOAT*, it advertised, promising gas, food, and souvenirs. The sisters pulled off the road as soon as the glow of the sign beckoned through the trees. The gas station was adjacent to a little convenience store, and a trail led around back to an outdoor restaurant along the edge of a wooded park. Anne slithered out of the car and closed her eyes, tasting the trees, the damp loam, the salt.

"I barely remembered," Anne said. "I haven't felt this in a long time."

Anne savoured the place while Charlie walked around to the pump and grabbed the nozzle.

"I'm gonna take a peek around back, see if the place is fit to dine at. Check out the trails," Anne said, standing on her toes and stretching to the sky.

"Don't go too far," Charlie said.

Always the protector, Anne thought, gazing at her older sister. "I'm just having a look-see. I won't end up pig feed, I promise."

Charlie held Anne's stare, and Anne held it back, resisting the urge to look away, despite the shame. Though brief, Anne caught it, the flicker of Charlie's eyes to the inside of Anne's arms, pocked by old needle marks.

"Anne… are you okay?" Charlie asked.

Anne offered a wane smile and shrugged. "Not okay. But I'm not using, Charlie. Not anymore."

"Promise?" Charlie said.

"Pinky swear."

The sisters hooked pinkies, and Anne looked away, knowing her sister's face would be covered in doubt.

Anne strolled around the back of the building, admiring the Garry Oaks standing sentry for the woods. Though it was still summer, it was the tail end which was the perfect time to visit the island. Fall had splashed itself over the woods, the death of the leaves marked by a pallet of astonishing reds, oranges, and golds. Anne's boots crunched on the ground; the path to the back was no more than a dirt trail with stones to mark the way, and it was covered in leaves, gold and red and orange. But the primitive walkway opened to an expansive patio complete with picnic tables, patio chairs, and a large fire pit. Piles of cut cedar were stacked as high and long as the building.

"We'll need it all, believe it or not. And then some."

A burly man with light blue eyes and a hefty beard hauled another armload of wood from a chopping block offside the patio. His voice was throaty, which was intentionally sexy, or the effects of Canadian flu season.

"I believe it," Anne said. "If this place does any business at all, you'd burn that off in a weekend or two."

"Well, not that quick, thanks be," the man said. "We try to preserve the trees out here, not hack 'em all down in a short span. The fire provides awesome heat, but more for ambience." He pointed at tabletop heaters at most spots on the patio. "We operate year round and don't have indoor seating, so we heat it up like the Caribbean out here."

"It's nice," Anne said.

"Bran," he said, brushing his hands on his jeans before extending one in her direction.

"Anne," she said, giving him a firm shake before tucking her hand back in her sleeve.

"Well, Anne, if you intend on visiting here long, I suggest you pick up some mitts and a toque. It's mighty cool out this way, especially with the breeze off the water."

"I'm not unfamiliar with the island," Anne said. "I'm from Victoria. My family used to come camping out this way."

"A local returned!" Now worthy of more than a handshake, Bran stepped forward and thumped her on the back. "Your blood'll thicken in no time, and this cold won't even phase you. Ridin' the weather here's like riding a bike, they say."

He motioned for her to follow and returned to the chopping block beside the building. "So what brings you home, Anne?"

She hesitated, pushing her toe through a smattering of leaves on the ground. "Family." She couldn't say more and thankfully didn't need to. Charlie came around the corner, rubbing her bare, pink hands together.

"Cold enough to burn," Charlie said.

"Another local come home, I presume?" Bran held out his hand once again.

Charlie took his hand. "Charlie. Pleased to meet you…"

"Bran. I've been chatting with Anne here. You folks are… friends?"

"Sisters," Charlie said.

Anne couldn't help but notice that Charlie's cheeks were flushed, despite the cold.

Pumping petrol a tad invigorating, is it?

A wide, cheeky smile stretched across Anne's face, earning her a scowl from her older sister.

"We offer cabins and a campground out back, if you guys need lodging," Bran said, his eyes glued to Charlie. "Bit cold for camping, this time of year, but if you have the right gear it's real cozy. And I'd let you inside the store to warm up, if need be."

"Thanks, but we're covered," Charlie said, pointing to the highway. "We're staying up the road a short ways. I'm sure you'll see us from time to time. Restaurant open?"

Bran swung the axe, and the crack echoed through the giant trunks of the forest as the blade found its mark. "Like I said, open year round. Kitchen's always open. I live on site, so I can whip you up something anytime. We're steady most nights, what with the tourism. Lots of people passing through."

"Campers?" Anne asked, looking down the dirt road to the campground.

"Not many this time of year but the cabins stay pretty full. And lots of townies pass through on fishing and diving trips."

"We're doing that," Anne said, her voice heightening to a schoolgirl squeal.

"Fishing?" Bran asked.

"Fuck no," Anne said, scrunching her brow. "Diving. We're taking a day trip up to the Haida Gwaii."

"Beautiful diving there," he said, swinging the axe again. "Well, my store is little, but we have everything you need—food, sundries, booze."

"We'll hit you up for all of that," Anne said.

"Go on in and gather it up, I'll come ring you up in a sec."

"No rush," Charlie said. "We drove all the way from the ferry. It's nice to stretch our legs."

"Got much more of a drive?" Bran asked.

"Don't think so," Charlie said. "Waze says it's a dozen or so klicks up the road, then off the beaten path a touch. Never been, so we'll see."

"Ah." The noise came out of him like a stunted laugh. He pulled the wool toque from his head, revealing a mass of brown curls beneath. "Jutland House, B&B?"

Anne and Charlie looked at each other. "Is that a bad thing?" Charlie said. Anne reached out and held her sister's hand. Being a homebody, and always overly cautious, Charlie was a bad traveler at the best of times, let alone when the situation was so full of emotion.

"Beautiful place, Jutland House is," Bran said, looking off in the distance. "Isolated, on the rocks overlooking the bay, backing onto the deep woods. Old house, well-maintained, steeped in history."

"But…" Charlie said.

He smiled, his dimples visible even beneath his thick beard. "No biggie. Just haunted as fuck, they say."

"Fabulous," Charlie said, rolling her eyes.

Anne smirked. "C'mon, Charlie. Let's go grab some chow and hit the road."

Feeling Charlie's hesitation, Anne didn't start towards the convenience store.

"You know, you guys chat a minute. I'll grab the food."

Charlie was staring at Bran, studying him, her face a cooking lobster.

"Charlie?"

Bran was the same shade of scarlet.

"Look, we all know you both want to, so let's just set a date," Anne said, giving Bran the thumbs up. "Tomorrow evening? Say, seven o'clock?"

Charlie and Bran looked at her, and she shrugged. Charlie gave her a firm swat on the shoulder and attempted a non-chalant smile. "Sounds good. We'll pop out for a bite to eat."

"Looking forward to seeing you again," Bran said, sliding the toque back on his head and leaning the axe against the building. "I'll wash up and meet you at the counter."

As he walked away, Charlie's eyes followed.

"Good girl," Anne said, poking her sister in the ribs.

"Fuck off, Anne. That's not why we're here."

"That's not *not* why we're here." Anne embraced Charlie, holding her close. "Relax, Charlie. Let's just enjoy what we can, while we can."

Charlie nodded into Anne shoulder before the sisters linked hands and walked into the store.

CHAPTER 3

TRAFFIC DWINDLED from sparse to nothing; the sisters hadn't seen a single vehicle in over a half hour. The red sun sagged low in the sky, blocked by the fat forest towering at the sides of the road. The purple light of dusk was growing ever darker, and they almost missed the turnoff.

"There!" Anne shouted through a mouthful of ketchup chips.

Charlie slammed on the brakes and the car responded with a mild fishtail that she righted after cranking around the turn. Not much of a driveway—barely a narrow break in the trees—but Anne had spotted the weathered sign hanging on rusted chains between the oak trees, the words faded by age and weather.

JUTLAND HOUSE

Charlie rested her foot on the gas, gently rolling forward through the tunnel into the woods.

"Spooky," Anne said.

"Mhmm," Charlie agreed.

But it's not, Charlie told herself. *We're just spooked.*

"It'll be okay," Anne said, reaching across the center console and taking her sister's hand.

But will it?

Life would go back to normal, they would return to the daily grind, slogging through their routines and going through the motions, day after day, year after year, waiting for an end.

Charlie looked at her little sister, at the smile pulling at the corner of her lip, the fresh life in her emerald eyes. Anne had always been much more carefree than Charlie—too much so, at times. Charlie admired that, but deep in the hidden closets of her mind, stashed away in trunks under lock and key was the dirty truth: Anne was unhappy. Deeply. She hid beneath a mask of peace and excitement, but deep down, she was screaming. Wanting more, searching for something she didn't know she needed. Years of substance abuse, of thrill seeking, a multitude of shallow relationships and dozens of jobs, Anne could never quite find her way.

Just like… her.

The thought terrified Charlie, bringing her to tears.

"You think they'd have this place better marked," Anne said, tossing another chip into her mouth as she leaned forward and looked out the windshield. "It's a wonder anyone finds it at all."

"Uncle Walter mentioned it a few times," Charlie said, pulling herself together. "Saw the building on the cliffs every time he headed out in the bay to fish. The locals say it's a family-owned bed-and-breakfast. Been around for years. Prime location, great views, isolated. Cost us a pretty penny, but I think it'll be worth it, to get away, and so close to the dive center."

"And the Goat's Moat."

"Yeah. The Goat's Moat."

"Yup."

Charlie looked over at Anne, whose smile had spread wide across her face.

"Bran," Anne said, stifling a giggle.

Charlie shook her head. "Ridiculous."

"Oh c'mon, Charlie. It's okay to feel something. No sense in wallowing—"

The trees opened to a massive property, the perimeter marked by thick, deep forest except where the land offered a view of the ocean. In the middle of the immaculate lawn and gardens at the end of the gravel drive was an equally impressive mansion, two stories high, a dark giant lying in wait for visitors. Or prey.

"Well now that's something," Anne said. "Gorgeous. The owners knew we were coming?"

"Yeah," Charlie said. "I mean, I just made the reservation last week."

"There are no lights on. We're not that late—"

The house came alive, flickering light igniting in each window, one at a time as they drew closer. Charlie pulled the car up to the staircase at the front entrance and killed the engine.

"Huh," Anne said, watching the last few windows on the upper floor fill with light.

"Don't see anywhere to park," Charlie said, looking around, trying to spot another vehicle.

"Let's check in, like a hotel. Then we can move the car, right?"

"Right."

They got out of the car, Anne brushing ketchup chips off her sweater and Charlie stretching, despite the fact their stop at The Goat's Moat had only been about half an hour before. Charlie was tense, and the chill in the air made her muscles clench even tighter. Anne was already half way up the stairs when Charlie noticed she had left. She went running towards her, barreling up the stairs and grabbing her by the arm.

"Hey, what's up?" Anne said, rubbing her arm where Charlie had grabbed a little too hard.

"It might not be safe," Charlie said, releasing her sister. "I mean, we don't know the place. I should go first."

Anne rolled her eyes. "Really?" Anne pressed her hand against her forehead, "My Queen in shining armor."

"Stop." Charlie couldn't help but smile. "I just… it's better to go together."

Anne took her hand. "Buddy system."

The front door was beautiful, tall and wide, solid wood intricately carved with scenes and swirls of ocean and forest. A brass knocker shaped like tentacles was posted at eye level. Charlie hesitated, but Anne reached for it, banging hard and loud, four times. While waiting for a response, Charlie took a step back and looked at the windows. Here and there, a curtain rippled, light flickered like air across a flame, shadows floated across the gloom. Charlie hugged her shoulders and looked at Anne, who was stepping from foot to foot, trying to stay warm.

"Try again," Charlie said as Anne grabbed the knocker and gave it another four firm raps.

While Anne continued to dance in front of the door, Charlie walked across the porch, trying to see through curtains, but unable to get a good look at the interior of the mansion. Searching the yard was no help either; the only signs of life were droves of flora.

"I don't hear anything," Anne said.

"But the lights…"

"Let's take a quick peek behind the place, then head back to the rest stop. Bran'll put us up in a cabin for the night."

"Let's do that, anyways," Charlie said, looking up at the house. "I don't like this. Any of this. She knew we were coming. There's something—"

"Look," Anne said, stepping in front of Charlie and resting their foreheads together. "Quick look out back so we don't have to toss those pretty pennies to the wind. If there's nothing, we'll bail. Back to Bran."

"To the cabins," Charlie said sternly.

Anne smirked, and Charlie melted, giving her sister a hug.

The back of the mansion was even more lavish, two-story high windows overlooking a large patio with a view of the yard and ocean beyond. The grass shimmered purple in the dusk, the woods a dark indigo, black as night beyond its borders. While Anne stomped onto the patio, peeping in the windows with no shame, Charlie walked into the yard. She wanted to look over the cliffs to the ocean below. It had been a long time since she had been back to the Pacific, the smell and feel foreign now. The water was calm and quiet, nary a splish from the shore below.

The woods, however, sang a chorus of cracks and whooshes, the breeze blowing through the trees, rustling the brush. A few chitters and chatters from the woodland fauna reminded her of the life on the island that scurried around behind the scenes. As Charlie strolled, her eyes trailed from the cliff to the forest's edge.

She stopped.

Yellow eyes stared back at her, large orbs suspended in the trees a few meters high, deep in the woods. They rocked back and forth, widening, focusing.

"Anne," Charlie whispered, a volume impossible for Anne to hear even if she had been at arm's length. Charlie slowly turned her head to the house. She had walked much farther than she thought and was now a good jaunt from the patio. Anne would only hear her if she shouted, and she wasn't about to do that. She didn't want to alarm the eyes in the woods.

The eyes were glowing, hungry. Charlie decided she could retreat away from the woods, maintain eye contact and creep backwards to the house. The creature would probably scurry off, not wanting to come too close to the structure, to civilization. Executing the plan without another thought, Charlie took a step backwards, but was immediately stopped by a searing pain in her abdomen. She couldn't help but cry out.

"Anne!"

Hot, stabbing pain radiated from just below her belly button to the tips of her toes and fingers, knocking her to her knees. The eyes were all but forgotten as Charlie grasped her stomach, howling in agony. When shock offered a brief respite from the intensity of the pain, Charlie looked up, seeking the eyes. But the eyes had found her first. They were almost on top of her, bobbing though the purple night, a meter from her and flying through the air. A bulk of muscle and fur hit Charlie in the chest, knocking the wind out of her throbbing gut and sending her flying. She flailed, clawing and grasping at a beast who was her size and then some, but her fingers found only solid, impenetrable hide. The massive pelt covered her face, the fur filling her mouth and forcing her eyes shut. Charlie gasped for air, both her covered mouth and the mass on her body impeding even the slightest breath, Lighter, lighter, her head floated though the air, a helium balloon muffling all the sound, the weight, the fur…

"Charlie!"

Thick fur was replaced by cold flesh, a hard slap jerking her head to the side. She opened her eyes.

Anne was crouched down beside her, her red curls dangling and tickling Charlie's cheeks.

"Charlie, what's all this now? You okay?"

"I..."

Charlie sat up and gulped in great swallows of breath, her body aching and spent. Frantically she scanned the yard, then the perimeter, seeking either glowing eyes or thick fur, but found nothing but nature dipped in twilight.

"Talk to me, Charlie!"

"I'm... lightheaded, is all."

"Did you trip?"

Charlie looked down at her body and poked a finger into her belly, which was pain free.

"I passed out, I think."

"What? Charlie, my fuck!"

"Language, Anne."

Anne scowled, her lip falling into a pout. "Seriously?"

A wave of warmth rippled across the grass, blowing out to the ocean. Both sisters noticed, looking at each other then up at the house. The lights were brighter now, giving a clear view of the interior of the mansion. On the patio, leaning on a cane, was a tall, slight woman draped in a long, crimson robe. She was holding a cane with intricate tentacles carved into the shaft, and the head of the cane a small, ivory replica of a wolf skull.

"Guests enter the premises through the front," the woman cawed, a smoker's rattle marring her voice. "Only trespassers loiter on the lawns."

Anne stood. "We have reservations."

"Guests use the front entrance," the woman repeated.

"We tried," Anne said, her voice firm. "Several times, with the knocker. Waited a spell before coming back here."

"I am no spring chicken," the woman said. "Takes me time. Perhaps arrival at such a late hour is not a good idea."

Charlie let Anne hoist her to her feet, and she brushed the grass off her pants.

"If you are quite finished skulking about my yard, perhaps you would like to come in properly, through the front." After banging her cane on the wooden deck, she spun around and walked through the patio doors, shutting them with a resounding thud.

"Pleased to make your acquaintance," Anne muttered, her lip curled. "You good?"

"Good," Charlie said.

Anne led the way to the front of the house. Charlie glanced over her shoulder, checking the woods, her body, and her mind with each step.

CHAPTER 4

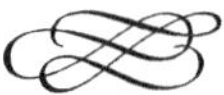

The door shut behind them, the heavy wood slamming closed as if barring them into a dungeon. It was a gorgeous mansion, filled with lavish decor and furniture—clearly antique, some of it exotic. In the entryway, Anne felt insignificant amongst the dark wood furniture, intricate crown moldings, and art adorning the walls. Charlie stood in front of her, head turning from the stairs to the hall to the sitting room beside the entryway, searching for danger.

Ever the mama bear, Anne thought.

"Do come in," a voice called from deep in the house.

Their hostess had not come to the door to greet them, rather, they had found it unlocked; tired of screwing around, Charlie had pushed the heavy handle and walked inside. Anne was relieved. Although she was aloof and brazen, she still looked to her big sister to lead the way most times. *Not so brave after all, I suppose.* Once inside, they stalled in the entrance.

"Go on," the woman called out, a tinge of irritation in her tone. "It's unsightly to linger in the entrance. Go sit in the music room."

Assumedly, the music room was the sitting room to the side of the entranceway. Though it had a seating area, it was also furnished with an upright grand piano and several woodwinds hanging on the wall. Anne opened the double glass doors and helped herself to a seat on the couch. Charlie followed, eyeing all corners of the room before sitting.

"Eccentric," Anne said, riffling through the reading materials on the coffee table.

Sprawled over the table was tourist literature on wilderness excursions like kayaking the Haida Gwaii and deep sea fishing, copies of *Canada Now*, and a tattered old version of Ten Little Indians.

"How old is this?" Anne asked, holding the novel up. Charlie wasn't paying attention; she was lost in some place other than that mansion. Back on the lawn, splayed out on the grass, Anne supposed.

"Don't worry," Anne said, resting a hand on Charlie's leg. "I'm sure it was just a fainting spell. There's been a lot going on, and you were never good with travel or change."

"Yeah," Charlie agreed.

Anne stood and went to the old piano. A beautiful mahogany, like the trees on the island, the keys a tarnished yellow. Anne plinked a key and the old piano sang out, a twang long out of tune.

"Anne, shush!" Charlie scolded, looking out the door for the woman of the house. "You'll get us kicked out of here!"

"This place is lovely, Charlie, but it isn't the last place on the island. We aren't prisoners here. If she has the lid open, and it's in a common space, then she must expect people are gonna tickle the ivories from time to time." Anne played another note, a low A. "And Charlie, lCharlie tell you, I think these keys are actual ivory."

"Indeed they are."

Charlie gasped and Anne spun around as the woman entered the room, a tray of tea and pastries grasped in her old claws. "It was my mother's piano. She and Father got it from the Hudson's Bay Company back east when we immigrated here. Hard haul, bringing that out to the coast."

"I dare say it was," Anne said, running a finger along the top of the instrument. "A big upright grand like this, and heavy wood, at that." Anne looked at the woman. "It's gorgeous. Your whole place is gorgeous. Thank you for accepting our reservation."

The woman stood like a statue for an uncomfortable moment, then a smile cracked across her entire face. She set the tray down and took Anne by the hands.

"Aren't you a lovely young thing," the woman said, cupping Anne's cheek in one hand. "What's your name, darling?"

"Anne Arnold. And this is my sister, Charlie."

Charlie stood and held out her hand. The woman stared at it a moment, reluctant to receive the introduction, but removed her hand from Anne's cheek and gave Charlie's hand a firm shake.

"Isadora Carsten. A pleasure to make your acquaintance," the woman said. "So lovely to have guests out here. I do prefer it quiet, having the place to myself, but solitude is hard on the mind, you know. A lonely mind plays games and tricks, tricks and games..."

Isadora banged her cane once on the floor, and it swished, something rattling inside the wolf skull on the top. Isadora gave it a firm shake, smiling at the sound.

"Okay…" Anne said. "I assume you live out here?"

"Of course."

"Do you live alone? Any family?"

Isadora paused, her eyes glinting. "No, no family."

The smile faded, but quickly formed again. "I'm anything but alone out here, I suppose. There's the help."

Charlie shook her head, trying to silence her sister. As usual, Anne disregarded the implicit suggestion.

"The help?" Anne said. "You mean your staff?"

"Yes, them," the woman said.

"Maids and cooks and yard workers?" Anne said.

"The help." Isadora articulated the word, spitting out the P. "Maids, yard workers—servants."

"Oh no," Anne said.

"No, Anne—" Charlie said.

"Servants?" Anne said. "Please clarify."

Isadora huffed, exasperated. "I pay. I didn't say slaves, now did I?"

"Jesus," Anne said, sitting back down to prevent coming uncunted.

Charlie stepped in. "So, may we check in? It's been a long day—long week, actually—and we'd like to head to our room and get some sleep."

"Certainly. I'll take an imprint of your card and fetch your key."

Charlie handed Isadora her credit card.

"You don't have a servant to do that for you?" Anne asked.

"Matters of money?" Isadora scoffed. "Certainly not. This is my house. I take care of the financials and the business. The help are for cleaning and maintenance."

Before Anne could retort, Isadora spun, clopping out of the room on heavy block heels, her robe flowing behind her like a crimson bridal train. As soon as the heavy footfalls reached a safe distance—somewhere in the back of the house—Anne whispered to Charlie.

"Odd duck, that, but nice enough, I suppose. If you can look past the elitist attitude."

"I'm not so sure about this," Charlie said, wringing her hands.

Anne smiled for the first time since Isadora had spewed her subtle unpleasantries. "This place is amazing. We got a colourful hotelier, but that's no bother. This place wouldn't be the same without her. I mean, I think she completes the ambiance, wouldn't you say?"

Anne wondered if Charlie realized she was trying to placate her—calm her frazzled nerves. Anne was leery of Isadora, but she did like the mansion. It had a rustic magic, cozy and welcoming.

"Look," Anne said. "This place is close to everywhere we have to be and everything we want to do. It's booked. Let's just stay."

Charlie nodded, but looked out the hall, scanning. Always scanning.

"Besides," Anne continued, "maybe she's dead." Charlie looked at Anne, eyes wide. "I mean, old house on the sea, adjacent to the woods, probably a cemetery full of pets and kids somewhere out back. Ol' Granny Haunts-a-Plenty is the cherry on top!"

Charlie's face contorted and scrunched as she tried not to laugh. Once Anne released a squirt of a giggle, Charlie was done, honking out a clap of laughter.

"Well aren't we jovial all of a sudden," Isadora said, coming back into the room with the credit card and a long feather quill.

"Delirious," Anne said, wiping a tear of humour out of the corner of her eye.

"With rest comes sensibility," Isadora said, placing the credit card receipt on the coffee table for Charlie to sign. "Come. I shall show you upstairs to your suite."

"Sounds good," Anne said. "Just let me grab our bags—"

"No need," Isadora said, waving her hand. "The help… my *staff* will take care of that for you."

Isadora rang a sizable brass bell attached to her hip, and footsteps thudded down the hall. In moments, a broad, lanky man appeared in the doorway. He was as tall and wide as the door, with thick white hair shaved almost to his skull and a beard cascading down to the center of his chest.

"Wilfrid, will you fetch these ladies their trunks from that vehicle outside?"

"Suitcases, rather," Anne said. Charlie smirked.

"Their luggage," Isadora said, flashing both Charlie and Anne a glare filled with daggers of ice.

Wilfrid grunted a response Anne assumed was positive because he stomped his way out the door and down the front steps.

"Come," Isadora said, motioning out the music room door with a sweep of her hand. "Your exhaustion is showing in your behaviour. Let's get you settled post haste and begin anew tomorrow."

Without another word, the sisters followed Isadora upstairs to their room.

Isadora led Charlie and Anne to the end of the hall and pulled a large iron key from the deep vortex of her crimson robe. Their door unlocked with a clank, and swung open with a great, howling squeal.

"Wow, can we get a little WD-40 on that?" Anne said.

Isadora paused. "Do you intend to keep late hours? The noise shan't bother anyone during the day."

"We intend to keep the hours we happen to keep," Anne said. "Can't really say what those will be, at this point."

Isadora handed the iron key to Charlie. "Very well.

You are grown women. You are entitled to do what you like."

Anne softened. "We'll be respectful, Isadora. If we happen to come in late, we will do so quietly. I'd just hate for the hinges to wake you."

Isadora softened in return. "You are respectful, I'm certain."

Anne smiled and tilted her head.

"Well without further ado," Isadora said, banging her cane on the ground, "I shall leave you to it. See you in the morning for breakfast. Gwen can give you a tour of the grounds, if you like."

"We'd like that," Charlie said. "Like Anne said, this really is a gorgeous place. We want to soak it all in while we're here."

"Very good," Isadora chimed. "Bright and early."

Another spin, another twirl of the robe, and Isadora was down the stairs, off to some other distant, yet-to-be seen room in the mansion.

"Piece. Of. Work," Anne said.

"Unbelievable." Charlie shut the door and engaged the heavy lock. "She's a right colourful sort, isn't she?"

"She's fine," Anne said. "Harmless. She might even be interesting, once we crack that hoity exterior."

A loud bang drew a gasp from both sisters. Charlie walked over and opened the door a crack to peek out, then swung it wide open.

"Thank you, Wilfrid."

The hulking yeti heaved both suitcases in the room, one on each shoulder, and dumped them on the bed. He snorted some sort of salutation, accompanied by a nod, then exited the room, pulling the door closed behind him. The floor shook as he stomped down the hall and back downstairs to whatever he had been doing prior to their arrival.

"Well then," Anne said.

"Indeed."

Charlie walked over and locked the door, teeth pushed into her lower lip.

"Don't worry," Anne said, taking Charlie's hands and guiding her to the bed. "We're just on edge. It will all be fine."

"Sure," Charlie said.

"Look. Everyone seems like a monster when it's night. In the light of day, this will all feel better."

But Anne didn't believe that. Not really. But she had to stay strong for her sister, and for herself. It was only them now, and they had to stick together.

Tick. Tick. Tick.

Somewhere in the darkness of the mansion, a clock

ticked, amplified by the surrounding silence from every other room

Their luggage is probably tucked away in the closet, clothes organized on hangers and folded in dresser drawers, Isadora thought.

It was hard to tell, but it could be assumed. One of the drawers had been left slightly ajar, the tease of a sleeve hanging out the narrow slit. Isadora moved her cane from side to side, the rattle from the wolf's head soothing her.

The sisters slept hard, Anne gargling with her mouth open and Charlie growling a snore through her nose. They didn't stir when the curtain pulled to the side, revealing the moon hanging long and tired in the 3am sky.

So pale. So pure. Unspoiled.

Though the moon offered sufficient illumination for exploration, there was nothing useful in plain sight. Her eyes moved from the closet to the armoire.

Too risky, opening the drawers. Or sifting through the closet.

Don't be anxious. They won't stay long.

Her silhouette filled the window, her back turned to the world outside.

Why are you here? Isadora thought, a storm brewing within her soul.

CHAPTER 5

"WELL, I'll be damned. It's an honest-to-goodness cock."

Charlie was sitting at the window, reading a book, when Anne woke to the sound of a crowing rooster somewhere down on the grounds. Anne swung her legs out of bed and shuffled to the window.

The sun, though just rising, shone over the lawn, igniting the dew into a million crystals. In the distance, sea birds barked their morning orders as fishing boats headed out for the day.

"Good sleep?" Charlie asked, tucking her bookmark into her book.

"Like the dead," Anne said. "You?"

"Sort of."

"Worried about something?"

"Naw. Well, yes. Unsettled. Something irked me last night, can't say what, really. Just wigged by the room, I guess."

Anne gave her sister a smooch on the cheek and started searching the closet and drawers for an outfit.

"C'mon," Anne said. "Breakfast awaits."

"You've been up for four seconds."

"Must eat. Now. All the food."

Charlie selected her wardrobe from the closet. Each woman took turns in the loo down the hall, relieving themselves and getting cleaned up. Anne, the last one to complete the routine, did a pirouette for Charlie when she came out of the bathroom.

"Good enough to dine with the Countess?"

"It'll do, Donkey. It'll do."

The sisters walked down the stairs, taking care to keep quiet so as not to startle their hostess. They peeked through the banisters, trying to get a look at other rooms, but saw only a long hallway leading to the back of the house. They followed the hallway, Anne adding a cheerful whistle to alert their arrival, but it aroused no signs of life. The kitchen was on the left, they discovered, but empty. Only recently, though. Pots and pans were still on the gas stove, and the aroma of hot breakfast filled the air. Despite being rattled from the night before, Charlie really was hungry. Anne had consumed her body weight in ketchup chips on the road, but Charlie had eaten nothing.

Probably explains my fainting spell.

They continued until the hall opened to a large dining room with a grandiose table set with service fit for the Queen. A slight young woman with straight blonde hair tied in plaits was setting covered platters in the center of the table. Charlie walked a little harder as they entered the room, drawing the woman's attention.

"Oh!" the woman exclaimed. "I do apologize. I should have had this on the table before you appeared."

"Nonsense," Anne said. "You really don't need to fuss over us. This is quite generous of you to even do this much. It's a real treat."

The woman glowed, then offered a deep curtsy. "Penelope," she said, "but you can call me Penny." Dropping her voice to a whisper, she said, "I ain't as formal as the mistress would like to think I is."

Anne laughed and winked.

"Is Isadora around?" Charlie asked, stealing glances of the backyard.

"No, ma'am. She keeps late hours, Ms. Isadora does. She won't be down until after lunchtime, I'm afraid. She did say, though, we were to feed you and give you a proper tour of the grounds."

"Like she said," Charlie said, motioning to Anne,

"everyone can relax. We don't need to be catered to. And also, call me Charlie."

"And I'm Anne."

"Sisters?" Penny asked.

"We are," Charlie answered.

"Pleased to meet you, Charlie and Anne." Again, in a whisper, "Now dig in and enjoy the grub!"

Penny winked before removing lids from platters and leaving the sisters to their feast. It was a buffet of scrambled eggs, smoked salmon, maple bacon, and a selection of freshly baked breads. Both Charlie and Anne gorged themselves.

"You've eaten more in this one sitting than I've seen you eat in the past month," Anne said, tossing another piece of salmon in her mouth and licking her fingers.

Charlie swallowed a massive mouthful of food, then took a break from stuffing her face just long enough to answer. "I suppose so. Haven't had much of an appetite."

For the next few minutes, the conversation died, both sisters chewing and thinking, moving food around their plates and sipping coffee.

Charlie broke the silence. "Anne, we'll be okay. This will all be okay. We'll get through this trip, then move on with our lives."

Anne nodded, sitting up straighter in her chair. "Sure. Yeah. Our lives."

She's so unhappy, Charlie thought.

"I'll always be there for you Anne."

Anne set down her fork and laced her fingers, elbows on the table. "You don't always have to protect me. Even though you're my big sister, I'm pretty big myself, you know. I need you to know I'll be there for you, too."

Charlie smiled. "You know, I pictured you saying that with your hands on your hips in that little dress with the strawberries on it, lips slathered in Mom's red lip gloss, making pouty faces."

Anne frowned, pushing out her bottom lip.

"Hard to take you seriously when all I hear is a sassy lil six-year-old."

"But those strawberries turned to flame, mon soues, and my ginger curls morphed to the snakes of the gorgon!"

Anne stood, flailing her arms like serpents and hissing, tossing invisible hellfire in Charlie's direction.

Their hearty laughter beckoned Penny from the kitchen who couldn't help but get infected with the giggles herself.

"Don't know what's so damn funny, but we ain't had funny here in a while. You girls seem a hoot. Hope you'll keep around a bit."

"Couple weeks," Charlie said, wiping the food off her face. "We have some stuff to do. But we could use some downtime to relax, find ourselves."

"You ain't lost," Penny said holding her arms up. "You's at Jutland House!"

In the light of day, the yard was a palette of rainbows, wildflowers sprayed across the lawn in spurts of reds, purples, and pinks, sprigs of dogwood filling out the natural bouquets arranged by the wind. The air was thick with the scent of sea and wood, and the sounds of nature played a symphony that echoed all around.

Charlie and Anne stood on the patio sipping mugs of hot coffee, steam swirling up their noses and tendrils of white curling from their lips as they exhaled hot breath into cool air. Anne looked over the ocean, the mid-morning sun hitting it just so.

"Can't wait to get out on that water," Anne said, gooseflesh rising on her arms. "It's been so long."

"Few more days."

Penny walked out onto the balcony. "Few more days until what?"

"Dive trip," Anne said. "Up the Haida Gwaii."

Penny grabbed her arms and shook her head. "Aw

hells no! That there is the North Pacific! Save your dives for the Caribbean or the Maldives or Down Under. You'll freeze your nipples straight off in these waters."

"We're prepared," Charlie said.

"We've never done a cold water dive," Anne said. She looked at Charlie, a silent conversation exchanged between them. "But we know someone who has. Did plenty of times, actually."

"Looney toons, the whole lot of ya," Penny said, shaking her head. "Do what you must, but there's good diving right here, too. Better, even. Sea creatures that are spooked by all the tourist companies hide here in our quiet little bay."

"Here?" Anne said.

"Yep." Penny tunneled her hands around her mouth and hollered out to the yard. "Legend has it that these waters hold a rarity in the world of sea creatures. The maiden of the currents, the beast of the deep blue, the—"

"Quit filling their heads with Newfie tales!"

Around the corner came a tall, solid woman with raven hair tied in a knot at the nape of her neck. She was dressed in overalls and a toque, but her arms were bare, save the leather gloves on her hands. She loped across the lawn towards the patio. As she got closer, Anne was astonished at her size. Probably a touch over six feet tall and legs thick as tree trunks, a linebacker would have difficulties taking this one down.

"Folks," Gwen said, tipping her head.

"Pleasure," Penny said, nodding her head to Gwen. "Say, the missus would like them to have a tour of the grounds," Penny said.

"Certainly. Will the *missus* be joining us?"

Penny gave her a hard look.

"Of course not." Gwen released a little huff. "Well, c'mon then. Follow me."

After a quick refill of coffee, the sisters joined Gwen down on the lawn. It was much warmer now, the sun high in the sky, turning the yard and the woods into a rainbow of life. In the daytime, the sun frightened the shadows away for a good portion of the day. Even so, Charlie looked at the woods, her eyes flicking back and forth rapidly, seeking something. Anne touched her sister's arm.

"Charlie. Talk to me."

"What?"

"What happened out here last night?"

"I fell. Passed out, I gue—"

"Nope. Try again."

"What?"

Anne stopped walking. "Something happened. You're nervous, and it isn't just Isadora that has you bothered."

"It's everything. What happened, why we're here—"

"Again, nope." Anne slowed her speech and articulated every syllable. "Last night. Something happened last night."

Charlie said nothing, confirming Anne's suspicions. Anne was going to continue prodding, but realized they were being watched. Gwen was walking towards them.

"Something happen last night?" Gwen asked.

"Not really, no," Charlie said.

"She means yes," Anne said. "She fell. Last night, out here on the lawn."

"It's nothing, really, just stumbled or passed out, or something," Charlie said. "It's been a trying month. I'm just exhausted."

"Mhmm." Gwen looked Charlie up and down and let out a long, hard sigh as she glanced at the lawn. "'Round there?" Gwen pointed to a spot on the grass.

"Yeah, about there," Anne said. "Why? How did you know?"

Anne looked over at Charlie, who followed the line of Gwen's finger to the spot on the lawn, then her eyes lifted, looking off to the woods. Charlie's eyes were wide, and she bit her lower lip.

"I just know," Gwen said, trying to lock eyes with Charlie. Charlie did not look away from the woods.

"This place, this house… there are things. A hunger."

"What does the mean?" Anne asked.

"Let's carry on," Gwen said, walking away.

Anne didn't press the issue, with either her sister or Gwen. She did notice, however, that Gwen avoided the trees, instead choosing to make a beeline for the beach. They walked to the edge of the rocks, and Gwen led them along the short cliff.

"You can rent a boat in town, if you wish. Be sure you's sober and donning a life jacket if you go out. Don't want them havin' to skim the bay for your bodies. Bad for business."

"Penny said there's diving here?"

"Yes." The response was stunted, with no further information.

"Is there diving equipment on site?"

"I don't know why that's any interest to you," Gwen said. "Ocean's a dangerous beast. But if you must, you'd see better sights up the Haida Gwaii."

"That's where we intended to go," Charlie said, looking at Anne. "We'll just stick to our plans. We're set up with a proper instructor up there."

"Lots to see?" Anne asked.

"All manner of plants and creatures. Enough to sate your curiosity, I'm sure," Gwen said.

It was a short jaunt down to the water, trails

offering fairly easy access to the shore. Anne stepped between the rocks, her foot sinking into the light sand of the beach. As Charlie and Gwen carried on, talking about the wildlife on the Haida Gwaii, Anne walked to the water's edge and knelt to the ocean. Water rippled around her slender fingers as she dipped them below the surface. The ocean was chilly and soothing.

"You aren't prepared," Gwen snapped.

"I wasn't going into the water," Anne said. "Only having a feel."

"Watch yourself."

The sharpness of Gwen's words prompted no argument from Anne. She stood and walked back up the rocks, joining Charlie in the yard. Gwen's expression softened.

"I apologize, ladies," she said, running her fingers under her toque. "This place. It has its ways, and if you don't know them…"

Gwen started walking, and the sisters walked with her. Anne resisted the urge to speak, hoping silence would encourage Gwen to open up.

"There is a darkness here. Leave it alone and you will be fine."

"What darkness?" Anne asked.

Gwen looked out to the water. "Death visited here, before its time. An angry death. It lingers here still, watching, waiting."

"Like... ghosts?" Charlie asked. Anne was surprised at how serious her typically skeptical sister appeared.

"No." Gwen considered her next words carefully, her brow furrowed. "Just death."

The women said nothing more of it. Gwen led them along the cliff until they arrived at the tree line along the other side of the house. Charlie seemed much more comfortable along these trees.

"If you have the urge to go exploring," Gwen said, "there are trails through the woods here for hiking; it's a nice little loop, few lookouts for bird watching, great views of the ocean. There are reflective strips on the trees in case you lose your way. Not likely, though. It's a loop."

They continued down a short path where the property branched out into a small, fenced field. There was a red barn tucked against the trees and two horses nuzzling noses nearby. When Gwen's boots crunched the gravel path, the horses threw up their heads and galloped towards the fence. Gwen pulled a couple of carrots from her overalls and the horses gobbled them from her palm.

"This is Whiskey," she said, patting the roan on the neck, "and Jack," patting the dappled grey on the rump. "They are young, but old enough to be tame and quiet. Good for trail riding, if you treat them right.

Gear's in the barn. If you want to take them out, let me dress them. They don't need to be manhandled by no strangers."

Whiskey and Jack munched on the remainder of their carrots while Jack reached his head through the fence and nuzzled into Gwen's chest.

"How long have you been here, Gwen? Working for Isadora?" Anne asked.

A twitch fluttered at the corner of Gwen's eye. "I have worked here for many years. I lived out on T-Souke land, and moved here when my folks passed.

"She pays you, yes?" Anne asked, an edge to the question.

Gwen's expression was stone, but she laughed. "I have everything I need."

"What is she like?" Charlie asked, looking up at the house.

"She's Isadora."

That's not good, Anne thought.

"What about wildlife?" Anne asked, changing the subject.

"All sorts," Gwen said, closing the question.

They walked through the gardens, and Gwen pointed out every local bloom and shrub in great detail before ending the tour at the front steps of the mansion.

"Thank you very much for your time, Gwen," Anne said, reaching out and shaking her hand.

Gwen nodded. "You are smart women. Enjoy this place—its beauty, the wonders it offers—then go home. Be done with it."

She doubled back towards the barn before either sister could say anything more.

"How was the tour?" Penny asked as she came down the front steps with a tray of pastries.

"Good," Anne said. "Gwen is…"

"She's an odd one," Penny said. "I know. I live beside her, in the staff cottages just off the hiking trail."

"She didn't mention," Charlie said, looking at the trail leading into the woods.

"She wouldn't," Penny said. "She's not the social type."

"Fair enough," Anne said.

"So what's on the schedule 'til dinner?" Penny asked.

"Until dinner?" Anne asked, looking at Charlie. Charlie shrugged her shoulders.

Penny smiled. "You don't know?" Penny giggled, rolling her eyes. "The madame is some presumptuous, ain't she? First day of a stay she requires guests to join her for dinner. Thought she'd 'ave told you."

"Requires?" Anne said, her hand resting on her hip.

"Well, do what you want, I suppose," Penny said, moving closer and whispering, "but deal with her wrath."

Charlie intervened before Anne had a chance to speak. "We'll join her, of course."

"Awesome," Penny said. "See you there."

"You'll be joining us?"

"I'll be serving you, silly," she said. And in a heavy, exaggerated British accent. "I don't dine with the royalty."

Penny danced up the steps, singing *Be Our Guest.*

"Well," Charlie said, "I guess we have a dinner date."

"Yeah," Anne said. "We'll give tonight to Isadora. Tomorrow, we're outta here. We'll go do some stuff, blow off some steam."

"There's something about this place." Charlie said.

"There is, yeah. Ghosts, you suppose?"

"I hope it's something cool like that."

CHAPTER 6

Charlie closed her novel with a satisfied sigh—she had spotted the murderer by the halfway point—and levered herself out of the Adirondack chair in the front gardens. Passing through the front entryway, she had a peek in at the hustle and bustle of the kitchen and dining room. A quick look told her they'd be feasting on muscles and caviar, expensive Okanogan wines, and an assortment of venison and fish. A fancy meal hadn't been on the agenda, but that's what they were going to get when they agreed to dinner with Isadora.

Penny was tweaking the decor, replacing white candles with gold ones, the tablecloth replaced with gold linen. Charlie quietly walked down the hall and up the stairs to their room, where she found Anne basking in the sun on their windowsill.

"Quite the setup down there," Charlie said.

"I gather," Anne said. "They've been scurrying around the place all afternoon, like Queen Elizabeth is expected to make an appearance."

"I wonder, does Isadora do this with all her guests?" Charlie said.

"I imagine she does her thing, regardless of who's around," Anne said.

The sisters stared out the window as day waned to dusk, procrastinating until the last minute to head downstairs. Charlie finally gave in, standing from her chair and heading in to get ready for dinner. She grabbed an outfit from the closet—the fanciest she could find, which was a plain white blouse and navy trousers—and went to the bathroom to shower.

It felt good to wash away the grime of the day. Of the past month, in fact. She thought of nothing but the water pelting her skin, each droplet a bead of stress disappearing down the drain. By the time she was finished, the bathroom was thick with steam. She gave her short dark hair a tousle with the towel, dried her body, then swiped a clear streak in the mirror so she could see enough to fancy herself up.

A pixie cut made for simple maintenance; a bit of cream and a few ruffles and she was done. Makeup would be done in a jiffy—just a stroke of mascara on each set of lashes and a touch of gloss and she would call it good. As she held the wand to her eye, her vision dimmed. She blinked hard. In the mirror, the room gathered and darkened. She put the wand down and braced herself on the counter, anticipating the pinhole vision one gets before losing consciousness. But it wasn't like that at all. She had her vision, she could see around her, but the room had somehow grown darker. Faded.

In the mirror, buried in the dark where the shower should have been, were a pair of glowing yellow eyes. Charlie was frozen, a waking paralysis, as the eyes moved closer. Hot breath dampened her back, and a rough tongue pressed into her tailbone, dragging up her spine until it reached the base of her neck. Powerless to stop her own body, Charlie tilted her head, exposing the side of her neck. Sharp teeth dug in, piercing her flesh, and blood spilled over her naked body, a warm, wet heat running over her bare breasts and dripping onto her toes. Unable to scream, unable to move or blink or even breath, Charlie watched as the yellow eyes turned red with blood, and the blood flowing from her neck pooled deeper and deeper on the floor until she was swimming in it, floating up to the ceiling and the room was liquid, her lungs filling with blood, gasping for air…

"Charlie, hurry up! I gotta shower, and my mane takes a hell of a lot longer to wrangle than your pixie."

Charlie's eyes opened. Her feet were on the floor. There were no eyes, no blood, no darkness. She stood, looking at her reflection in the mirror, her naked body devoid of blood or injury. She quickly swiped some mascara on her lashes, pulled on her clothes, and opened the door for her sister.

"Holy shit," Anne said. "I expected an improvement, not death warmed over!"

Realizing she was trembling and panting, but not wanting to alarm her sister, Charlie forced a smile and squeezed by Anne, her heart slamming against her chest. "Get ready. The Madame awaits."

SILVERWARE CLINKED AGAINST CHINA, and the remnants of a lavish dinner settled in satisfied bellies. Anne dabbed her face with a linen napkin. Dinner was delicious. She loved fish, and they had salmon, which was her absolute favourite. Charlie didn't fancy fish, but Anne felt like there was something more than distaste for the meal that kept her sister from indulging.

What is going on with you?

"Did you enjoy dinner?" Isadora asked before placing the last flake of salmon on her tongue.

"It was great," Anne said. "I love fish, especially salmon."

"This is freshly caught, of course. Brought here from the inner island."

"Well, I can easily say it's the best I've ever had."

"You didn't prefer it?" Isadora said, turning her attention to Charlie. Charlie didn't answer, just kept pushing food around her plate.

"She's not much of a fish eater," Anne said, giving Charlie a kick under the table, "and I think she might be feeling a little under the weather."

"Oh dear," Isadora said, eyes focused on Charlie. She was searching, her eyes more prying than concerned.

It took a solid elbow jab to the ribs to get Charlie's attention. She glared at Anne before realizing she was the focus of attention.

"I'm sorry," Charlie said. "Mind's elsewhere."

"Evidently," Isadora said.

There was an edge to Isadora's tone that Anne didn't prefer. Charlie noticed, too, and jumped in before Anne could get riled up.

"So tell me," Charlie said, "this is a beautiful place. How did you come to be out here? You told us the piano in the front was your mother's. That your parents brought it here from out east."

"Indeed, yes, when I was but a child," Isadora said. "They immigrated from Denmark straight to Pier 21 in Halifax. Stayed just long enough to build up some cash before they were drawn out this way by tales of the Pacific."

"Romantic," Anne said.

Isadora's eyes glistened, lost in a far-off memory. She gave her cane a shake and closed her eyes, listening to the sound.

"It was magical, this place. How wondrous it was. A castle surrounded by a moat of wildflowers. To a little girl like myself, it was like living in a fairy tale."

"So you grew up here?" Charlie asked.

"I grew up here, yes. This place was our life. We lived, ate, and breathed this property. Mother and Father wanted us to grow up with nature, appreciate the beauty of the wild."

Us.

"Did your parents run this place as an inn?" Charlie asked.

"No, certainly not," Isadora said. "They were quite taken with their jobs and raising children. They didn't appreciate the beauty of this place."

With a quick flick of her wrist, Isadora rang the bell hanging from her belt. Penny came promptly and started clearing the table.

"They didn't like it here?" Charlie asked.

"Oh heavens, yes they did," Isadora said. "Don't get the wrong idea. They adored it, but as an afterthought. They spent so much time wrapped up in their lives that they didn't truly enjoy the magnificence of this place. One could never leave these walls and still live a perfectly happy existence."

"Us," Anne said.

Both Charlie and Isadora cocked their heads.

"Pardon?" Isadora said.

"You said *us*," Anne clarified. "You said your mother and father 'us' to grow up with nature."

Jaw clenched, wine glass grasped in a bony hand, Isadora drew a deep breath in through her nose.

"Yes," Isadora said.

Charlie and Anne stared, waiting for more. Isadora took a slow sip of her wine, swishing it around her mouth and swallowing hard, but offered no more.

"Yes?" Anne said, refusing to let it drop. "Yes, there was an 'us'?"

Another sip.

"Yes," she said, her eyes dark. "There *was* an us."

Another ring of the bell summoned Penny to come with a refill of merlot, fuel for this particular conversation, Anne supposed.

"I had sisters, long ago."

"Sisters?" Charlie said.

Anne watched as Charlie's face tightened, her teeth clenched.

"Yes, two of them, Isadora said. "Zelda and Willow. Younger than me."

"Did they move away?" Anne asked.

"Sadly, no," Isadora said. "They passed."

"Oh!" Charlie exclaimed.

"I'm so sorry," Anne said.

"It's all right," Isadora said. "How were you to know? Besides, it's been many years. I've had plenty of time to grieve."

Silence.

Anne waited for Isadora to continue, to give them something more, but she did not. It probably pained her still, the loss of her siblings. She was all alone.

"Do you often have visitors?" Anne asked. "It must get really lonely, out here all on your own."

"I prefer it," Isadora said. "I can enjoy the tranquility and beauty with minimal bother besides the help."

Penny, who had been clearing the rest of the dinnerware, shot Isadora a brief but scornful look, quickly excusing herself to the kitchen to hide her disgust.

"Besides," Isadora continued, "I have lovely guests like you ladies to keep me company from time to time."

Anne and Charlie smiled, and Isadora returned the favour, a warmth they hadn't seen much of since meeting her.

"This place," Charlie said, looking around the

grand dining room that overlooked the yard and ocean. "It's phenomenal. You are very lucky to be out here."

"Oh luck has nothing to do with it," Isadora said, her tone sharp. "I've worked hard to keep this place alive."

Anne was about to respond, but Penny came in with a tray of luscious desserts. Never able to turn down sweets, Anne accepted the fresh crème brûlée, savouring it in small nibbles.

"So tell me, girls," Isadora said, swirling her spoon around her dessert cup. "What brings you out this way?"

Anne looked at Charlie, who looked back at her, stunned.

It's okay to say it out loud, Charlie.

"Just a vacation," Charlie said. Eliminating the opportunity for elaboration, Charlie stuffed a huge bite into her mouth.

Anne knew it was avoidance, and used the opportunity of Charlie's full mouth to respond.

"We came out here with a purpose," Anne said, matter-of-factly.

Charlie coughed, nearly spitting out her food. Isadora's cocked a brow and looked over at Anne.

"Do go on," she said.

"We are originally from the island," Anne

explained, "well, the other side. Victoria, but close, and we used to come around here as kids…"

Anne sighed and placed her dessert spoon down on her saucer.

It's okay. It's time to start facing this.

"We're here to spread our sister's ashes."

Like she had been punched in the gut, Isadora's breath escaped her in a gasp, and all the colour drained from her face. For a moment no one spoke—Anne wanted to speak, but the words were caught in her throat—then Isadora broke the silence.

"Why, what ever do you mean?"

Her eyes hostile—accusing, almost—she looked back and forth from Charlie to Anne, and then to Penny who had come into the room with a spot of tea. Charlie dissolved into her dessert, shoveling it all in her mouth in three heaping spoonfuls as Anne tried to form an explanation out loud.

"We lost our sister a little over a month ago," Anne said, sorrow gurgling in her throat.

"Oh my word." Isadora's eyes welled with tears. "What was her… tell me about her."

Anne drew a deep breath, steadying herself. "Emme. Her name was Emme."

Charlie winced at the name, both times Anne said it, and Anne wondered how long she could blather on before Charlie said anything. Perhaps Charlie would say nothing at all. They hadn't spoken of Emme since the funeral, and even then, it was procedural and cold. Anne would have loved to see a tear, nervous laughter, anything at all. The pain was bubbling below Charlie's surface, ready to boil over, and would tear her remaining sister apart if that pressure found no release.

"Was she older?" Isadora asked.

Charlie's face had become a grey shade of pale.

"Oldest child," Anne said. "Few years older than us."

"Bloody shame, indeed," Isadora said, shaking her head.

"It's been… difficult, to say the least," Anne said. "Emme had been planning to come here on vacation. She liked to dive off the Haida Gwaii, swim in the unique ecosystem of the North Pacific. It'd been a recurring trip for her."

Anne remembered Emme, on her knees at the beach, sifting through the sand for anything that might crawl or wriggle, her stringy blonde hair tied back into a tight ponytail on the top of her head.

"She was cremated," Anne said. "We decided this was the best place to bring her. To spread her ashes off the Haida Gwaii, so she could rest in the ocean, close to home."

"It's the perfect place for her," Charlie said, barely a whisper.

Though it was quiet, Charlie's voice silenced the room, piercing through Anne's heart and startling Isadora. Anne smiled and reached for Charlie's hand. The sisters looked at each other, both sets of eyes threatening to spill tears. Anne nodded, encouraging more.

"It's what she'd have wanted," Charlie said, swiping away a tear with the back of her hand, "to be here, where the ocean and land meet. She always loved nature. It's where she belongs."

"All of us, I think," Anne said. "We need more nature in our lives."

A guttural cough escaped Isadora; it was a sharp, angry sound. Charlie and Anne startled, and Anne jumped to her feet, ready to assist. The old woman sputtered and gagged, pressing her napkin over her mouth. Anne went to her side and patted her on the back.

"Isadora, are you okay?"

With a sharp slap, Isadora struck Anne's arm, swiping her away. "Do not touch me!" Isadora snapped, "I am quite fine."

A few more coughs and sniffles later, Isadora had calmed. She dabbed a napkin on her lips. "I do apologize, girls. Went down the wrong pipe."

In the brief confusion, Penny had hustled out with a pitcher of water, and poured a glass topping it off with fresh lemon. Isadora looked at her, then picked up the glass and hurled it at the large window overlooking the bay. The sisters braced themselves at the tinkling waterfall of broken crystal. Thankfully, the window itself stayed intact.

"You imbecile," Isadora hissed, standing from her seat and grabbing Penny by the face. "My throat coughed raw, and you try to sting me with lemon? What were you thinking?"

Anne couldn't quite decipher the look on Penny's face; was she going to punch Isadora or slink away? After a few seconds of what seemed to be intense contemplation, Penny bowed her head.

"Of course. I'm sorry, ma'am. Don't know what I was thinking. Out of habit, I guess."

"You weren't thinking," Isadora said, draping her napkin over her half-eaten cup of crème brûlée. "Now do be a dear and clean up that glass, will you? I shall take the sisters to the drawing room for a snifter of brandy and some cigars.

Anne and Charlie looked at each other, horror and emotion contained beneath sealed lips.

CHAPTER 7

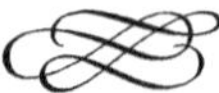

Isadora sucked on her cigar, the smell nauseating, causing Charlie's stomach to flip. The taste of dinner had been fresh on Charlie's palate until Isadora had lit that god awful thing, coating everything in her presence in a veil of smoke. Charlie thought it a shame that such a gorgeous sitting room should be drenched in such a stench.

"This is amazing," Anne said as she walked around the room, eyeing the furniture and artwork.

The sitting room was adjacent to the dining room. It had two glass walls—one overlooking the backyard and one overlooking the side of the house. It was night, and cloudy—so quite dark outside—but Charlie could still make out the shimmer of the ocean and the tangled claws of the woods.

Old and regal, the room was dressed with antique furniture upholstered in burgundy velvet, and the two walls were covered in black and gold filagree wallpaper. Every surface had some sort of trinket on it, either a small sculpture, pricey vase, or First Nations figurine. The art on the wall was astounding, oil paintings of all manner of nature, along with portraits of what Charlie assumed was Isadora's kin.

"This is your family?" Charlie asked.

Isadora didn't answer right away. She breathed the cigar in deep, then left her perch at the window and stood in front of the array of portraits on the wall. The first portrait was of a man and a woman, both handsome and fresh with youth and love, and another, two smaller girls, a brunette and a redhead, hands linked.

"Zelda and Willow?" Anne asked softly.

Isadora nodded.

"How old were they when they—"

"Young," Isadora said. "The eldest, Willow, was barely eight."

"Oh," Charlie and Anne answered in unison. Charlie went to the portrait and examined the small girls.

"Like two peas in a pod, those girls." Isadora smiled briefly before her face went dark and she took another drag of her cigar.

Charlie touched Isadora's arm before returning to the couch. "I'm sorry."

Isadora cleared her throat. "Don't be. It was long ago."

"But still—"

"So your sister. Emme."

Anne was examining the pictures on the wall and didn't turn when Isadora said that name.

C'mon, Anne, Charlie thought. *You opened this can of worms.*

"Emme." It was all Charlie could say before sorrow wrapped its hands around her trachea and squeezed. Isadora stared at Charlie, studying her face.

"Tough times," Isadora said. "I am not unfamiliar."

Charlie nodded.

"Well, best to get it done with, move on," Isadora said.

"I don't think it's that easy." Anne had turned away from the paintings, and now stood beside Isadora, staring her down. "But we'll do our thing. I don't know about moving on, but we'll do what we have to do."

The glare from Isadora could have frozen molten lava. Charlie winced as Anne clenched her fists.

"So tell me," Charlie said, standing and walking to the window. "You call this place Jutland House. Where does that name come from?"

Isadora held Anne's combative glare for an extra moment before succumbing to Charlie's question. "Ah, Jutland. The homeland. My parents were from Denmark—South Jutland, specifically. They moved here when they were young, wild teenagers with the whole world in their hands. They used to regale us with tales from across the pond, showing us pictures of the old land in Denmark, the rock and sea. It was magnificent, houses that looked like castles, the fuzzy definition between nature and habitation. When they moved out here, they were just trying to stay afloat. Mother saw this place, and it reminded her of home. She called it Jutland House, and the name stuck."

"That's a lovely story," Charlie said, perusing the pictures. "Did you grow up with a lot of the Danish culture? And do you still adhere to it?"

"I do," Isadora said, her mood considerably lighter. "I celebrate Christmas on the twenty-fourth, I use real candles on the tree, I prefer snack of small fish and delicate pastries… and I do love old folk tales around the fire."

"Vikings," Anne said, smiling at a painting of the Snekke, a Danish Viking War Ship.

"Yes, and folklore. Fairy tales. The Little Mermaid, the Mara."

"The Mara?" Charlie said, her voice louder than intended.

Isadora stopped, hesitating. "Yes, well, all silly childish tales are concocted around campfires and in the shadow-lit corners of little girls' bedrooms. Nonsense, but every culture has them, don't they? Nessie and Ogopogo, the Yeti and the Bumble."

The Mara.

Charlie's bones grew chilly at the word. She walked to the window and looked out into the dark, her eyes scanning the yard, the trees…

"Do you have any problems with animals around here?" Charlie asked.

"Problems?" Isadora said. "We do have animals around here, if that's what you're asking. Of course we do! I mean, you know this."

Slender fingers wrapped over Charlie's shoulders, Anne's tender hand both ensuring she was doing all right and telling her she was there. For her.

"Yes, but any significant problems?" Charlie asked. "Bothering the guests, I mean, or the horses."

"The horses are quite safe, I assure you. As are you, if you exercise common sense." Isadora walked between the sisters and the window, standing directly in front of Charlie. "I mean, you should know better than to stroll into the woods or enter the water at night. That's when the creatures come out to feed and play."

A laugh both jovial and terrifying exploded from Isadora's throat, pushing both Charlie and Anne a step backwards. Isadora doused her cigar in a nearby ashtray and floated towards the door, her crimson robe trailing behind.

"It's time for me to retire, ladies. Do what you please—go mingle with the fauna, if that's what tickles your fancy—just don't disturb me after I turn in."

"We'll probably just call it a night," Anne said. She turned back to the window and rolled her eyes at Charlie.

"Dear, that glass is reflective," Isadora said as she rounded the corner towards the staircase. "I can see your sass."

As soon as she was gone, Anne covered her mouth, holding in gales of laughter. "Fuck. Old crone busted me."

Charlie laughed too, but it was forced. Her mind was elsewhere, down on that lawn, in amongst the trees where she could feel something watching her, waiting…

As white as a ghost, barely breathing through pale lips, Charlie slept, a restless, fitful sleep. Anne sat on the windowsill in their room, sipping a warm milk and Bailey's, watching her sister toss and turn.

What is going on with you?

Emme's death had hit Charlie quite hard. It hit everyone like a freight train—of course it had, sudden as it was—but Charlie was a brooder. Always on edge, always doom and gloom. Closest in age, Emme and Charlie had experienced life's up and down together—the playful imagined worlds of childhood, the tumultuous teenage years full of tears and hairspray and unwelcome blood.

Emme had died long before her heart stopped, but that didn't lessen the blow. She was never really whole, only a wisp of the woman she wanted to be. A manifestation of chaos, a quiet desperation hidden behind a stoic, lying mask, a false joy often manic and misunderstood. Depression and suicide are the most stealthy of beasts.

Anne touched a finger to the window, drawing wriggles over the ocean. It was cathartic, being there by the water, watching it glisten in answer to the moon. Anne moved with it, feeling the cool wetness on her skin, thinking of nothing but the icy caress of the salt water to cleanse her mind of the memories of Emme and her sickness.

A ripple.

A splash.

A disturbance moved the water, distorting the mirror of the looming forest. Anne held her eyes open and pressed her nose against the glass, trying to catch a glimpse of what moved below the surface. She hoped to see a fin, a nose, anything at all. She loved what lived beneath, whether it be in the ocean, a lake, or even an aquarium.

A loud snort from across the room stole Anne's attention from the Pacific. Charlie moaned and tossed in her bed, pushing the blankets off her chest.

"Heavy," Charlie muttered as she curled up into a ball. "Can't breathe..."

Bare legs and arms woven through clumps of blanket, Anne could see goosebumps rising on her sister's flesh. She left the window and tugged at Charlie's blankets, freeing them from her limbs and tucking her in again.

"It's okay," Anne whispered as she kissed her sister on the forehead. "We are going to be okay."

CHAPTER 8

"How do these look on me?"

Anne strutted in front of Charlie, twirling on her toes then holding her leg out to model the new hikers on her feet.

"I dunno," Charlie said. "They're kind of wild."

Anne looked down, admiring the glittery, aqua-coloured boots on her feet. "They're different. And so perfectly me."

"They are that."

"Done deal." Anne didn't even take her new kicks off to pay for them. She took the box to the counter and told the clerk she would wear them out.

It had been a wonderful day perusing the local boutiques, picking up a few items for back at Jutland House, and splurging on souvenirs. As they loaded their treasures into the car, Anne clutched her growling stomach. "Wanna grab a bite to eat?"

"Yeah," Charlie said. "Let's get something out. Not that I don't want another dinner with the Lady of Jutland House, but…"

Anne nodded with vigor. "Somewhere else. Anywhere."

Charlie laughed. Anne was pleased that Charlie seemed to have relaxed. The shopping helped, as did the small town atmosphere and being away from the suffocating confines of Jutland House. Though big and beautiful, it was claustrophobic, and the mood that hung over the place was somehow menacing.

"I think we should stop at The Goat's Moat," Anne said, trying to hide her smile.

"You do now, do you?"

Anne smiled and slid into the car.

Charlie didn't put up even a smidgen of protest. They passed a dozen restaurants on the way, but not once did Charlie suggest something different.

Good. It'll be good for you, Anne thought.

When they pulled up to The Goat's Moat, it was very different from when they had stopped for gas that first night. It was suppertime, only a sliver of sun casting light over the trees, and the place was hopping. Patio lights illuminated the back porch area, and every table was full and then some; people were standing around the blazing fire pit, lined up at the bar, and milling around a live band.

"I don't know about this," Charlie said as she parked.

"Why? This'll be good. Take our minds off things for a night." Anne reached out and held Charlie's hand. "Besides, regardless of Emme, you need to live a little. You're wound so tight, Charlie. Live. While you can. That's what Emme would tell you."

Charlie stared out the window at the crowd. Anne knew it could go either way. Either Charlie would ball up the emotion that undoubtedly swelled at the mention of Emme, and go home and let it fester in another fitful sleep, or she would say fuck it and get out of the car.

Fuck it, Charlie. Get out of the car.

And, to Anne's surprise, she did just that.

They found themselves a spot on a large log near the woods, and Charlie sat there while Anne fetched them a couple of drinks. When she returned, Bran was next to Charlie on the log, his big brown eyes staring into hers as she spoke.

"Hey, Anne! Nice to see you again!" He jumped from the log and grabbed Anne, squeezing her in a hug tight enough to lift her new boots off the ground. Before he lost his spot, he quickly sat down again next to Charlie. "Charlie was telling me you were flitting about town today."

"Yep. Just wanted to get out and about."

"That Jutland House," Charlie said, "Nice spot, but pretty isolated, you know?"

Bran looked at Charlie and shook his head. "The stories that come out of that place are something else."

"Such as?" Charlie asked.

"Oh you know, old ghost stories, folklore, Texas Chainsaw Massacre kinda stuff. The owner out there… Isadora? I hear she's something special."

"Oh she's special, all right," Anne said, laughing.

"Well I'm glad you're here," Bran said, gazing at Charlie. "I'll come hang out in a bit. Gotta make sure the wolves are fed and the drunks aren't thirsty."

"Yeah, sure thing," Charlie said.

After Bran disappeared into the crowd, Anne sat next to Charlie. "You, girl, are glowing like a full moon."

"I am not."

"Are so! And who gives a shit if you are? You are a grown-ass woman and can do what you like. And you deserve to do something you like, Charlie. Forget about everything and be here. Right now, right here. Not tomorrow, not six months from now, not a month ago. Now. Here."

Charlie looked at Anne, then grabbed her glass and chugged it back in three hefty gulps.

"And that's how it's done!" Anne said. "I'll go get us another."

THE BAND HAD long since called it quits, and the herd had thinned to a few straggling card players and marshmallow roasters finishing the dregs of their Molson Canadian. Charlie and Anne danced by the fire, Anne's red ringlets twirling in the light from the flame and Charlie's sleek black pixie cut shimmering like the dead of night. They laughed, stumbling over each other and spilling their drinks on the ground while they belted out Celine Dion tunes to the waning moon.

"Ladies, please," Bran said, a slight stumble in his own step as he wrapped his arms around them and led them to a nearby picnic table. "I can't have you falling in the fire."

"Hey," Anne said, poking a finger in his chest. "We know fire. We aren't strangers 'round these parts, mister."

"You don't say," he said, grinning.

"We know the woods and the water better than you

could ever dream to," Charlie said, placing a hand on his knee.

Charlie felt her face flush as soon as her hand touched his leg, but she didn't move it. She looked at Anne, then down at their empty solo cups.

"I'll get us a refill," Anne said, taking the hint and rising from the picnic table.

Charlie watched as her sister's red curls bounced away, her feet skipping a little jig as she passed by a few dwellers by the fire.

"She's full of spunk," Bran said.

"Sure is. Too much, at times," Charlie said, turning her face to Bran. She hadn't realized how close he was sitting to her. She could feel the warmth from his body and turned away.

"I admire her," Charlie said. "She's such a strong woman. So resilient."

"You are both a force to be reckoned with, I'm sure."

"I don't know about that," Charlie said.

Before realizing she was doing it, she leaned into Bran and pressed her lips against his. He pressed back, his tongue finding the part in her lips, gently rolling around her mouth as she weaved her fingers through the back of his hair. She breathed harder, faster, pulling herself closer to him until they were pressed together, but he put his hands on her shoulders and pushed away.

"Fuck, you taste good," he said. "But I'm working, and you're drunk."

He's flushed, she thought, manic butterflies fluttering in her stomach. *He likes me, too.*

"I'm not that drunk," she said, looking into the woods. The trees were bent, bowing towards her, reaching their fingers out to grasp her throat and squeeze the life out of her. She looked away, up at the almost-full moon that was bearing down on her, growing larger, brighter, closer…

"Yeah, never mind," Charlie said, nodding in resignation. "I'm blasted."

Bran laughed, deep and throaty, and put his hand on her cheek. "You are. And I'm not. And we aren't doing things that way."

She leaned forward and kissed him again. "Yeah, we aren't. Good call."

He hesitated, stumbling over words until Charlie spoke for him. "I'll come back soon. We'll hang out."

"That'd be awesome," he said.

After sneaking one more kiss and lingering on it for a moment, Bran left to make his rounds of the patio, checking on the patrons and offering final refills. Anne, who had been lurking in the shadows with their drinks, hopped over and plunked down beside Charlie.

"So?" Anne said, taking a swig of her drink.

"So what?"

"How did it feel? How does it feel?" Anne set her drink down and hugged Charlie. "Are you okay?"

Charlie started crying. She didn't know why—she felt good, lighter and more relaxed than she had in a while—but the tears came, regardless. The sisters sat there and hugged it out, each of them crying until tears turned to giggles, and they fell off the bench and rolled around on the forest floor.

"And what in the all holy hell is going on here, ladies?" Bran said, standing overtop of them. "Do I need to kick you drunks outta here?"

"Probably for the best," Charlie said, brushing herself off and reaching for his hand.

Though Bran was beautiful, Charlie's eyes were drawn away from him to a looming presence standing sentry at the edge of the woods. Eyes of a hungry predatory, dark and deep and hungry, hovered a good four meters in the sky. Charlie couldn't look away, even when Anne rested a hand on her shoulder.

"Phenomenal," Anne said.

"Haunting," Charlie said as heaved herself off the ground and walked towards it.

"That's one of the things I love about the Island," Bran said, standing beside Charlie and looking up at the stagnant behemoth. "These totem poles speaks volumes about culture and history."

The totem pole loomed above them, whittled intricacies of feather and fur, talon and claw.

"This totem stood and watched as the forest was carved out around it to make way for the highway."

"It's quite stunning," Anne said, gazing up in wonder. "I've seen plenty, especially around Victoria, but none so detailed. And more animals on this one, yes? Not just the usual frogs and beavers and ravens."

"Our legends and fables span the globe," Bran said. "An artist in the late 1800s erected this one to celebrate creatures from the nooks and crannies of worldwide legend."

Bran took a step back, his finger pointed to the sky. "Perched at the very top is the Sluagh, a spirit of the restless dead, welcome in neither heaven nor hell. She's a crow-looking lady, said to steal souls of the dying before their last rites are read."

As if on cue, a murder of crows exploded in a chorus of caws and gargles from the deep reaches of the forest.

"A Sluagh sits atop a tangle of snakes, the tresses of medusa tangled in trees. The snakes are perched upon the shoulders of the elusive Sasquatch, and he rides the back of the Wendigo. At the Wendigo's throat is an overseas version of the werewolf, and the base of the totem is our island treasure, the Giant Pacific Octopus. See here?"

Bran fingers caressed the totem pole, outlining the carvings of tentacles and suckers.

"Her tentacles wrap all the way to the top, connecting all the creatures."

"But that…" Charlie trailed off, her eyes firmly in the place they started, on the werewolf tearing at the Wendigo's throat. Though only chiseled wood, the sheen of moisture and sap made the werewolf's jowls appear like they were slick with blood and dripping with gristle. The Wendigo, a formidable force of its own, looked paralyzed by fear, its eyes screaming in terror.

"Le Loup Garou, of sorts," Bran said.

Anne said, raising a brow. "So not just a French-Canadian werewolf?"

"She's a werewolf," Bran said.

"I'm aware of the legend of the Loup. But you said *of sorts*. Meaning…"

"Meaning she's not quite Le Loup-Garou. Le Loup-Garou is temporary, a werewolf whose change can last up to a hundred and one days. And Le Loup isn't always a wolf. She's sometimes a calf or small ox, perhaps even a cat. This totem? She is all wolf, all the time. This is another legend entirely."

Finally, Charlie turned from the totem pole, facing

Bran so suddenly he jerked back.

"What legend is this?" Charlie asked.

"Female werewolves, always in the form of the canine unless taunting and luring their prey."

Charlie and Anne stared at him until he broke, a goofy smile spreading across his face.

"Jesus, so serious!" Bran said. "These are campfire tales, nothing more. I'm about as close to a Sasquatch as you'll get, and the old farm dog here's as close as you'll get to a werewolf. Not to disappoint, but the tooth fairy ain't real either. Santa, the Easter Bunny. All bunk."

The women did not smile. Charlie looked back at the totem pole, at the eyes of the wolf, and Anne watched Charlie. A roiling panic swelled in Charlie's stomach, and she could almost taste the fur in her mouth.

"Well then," Anne said in her best English accent. "That's plenty of unsettling tales for one night. Call us an Uber, will you good sir?"

Though the tension dissipated, Anne's laughter was forced, and Bran watched Charlie with a wary eye. Charlie tried to smile, to feign a laugh of her own, but the eyes of the totem bored into her, swelling her throat with suffocating fear.

THE HEAVY OAK door slammed with such force Anne was sure it would rattle the portraits off the walls and drive that old bag of bones clear out of her bed.

"Shhh!" Charlie shushed through stifled laughter.

The sisters stood still, listening for the waking of the witch, but were soon content that their boisterous entrance hadn't been loud enough to wake the beast.

Stumbling past the music room, they made a pit stop in the kitchen to load up on armfuls of snacks before making their way up to their bedroom.

We sound like a bloody herd of elephants, Anne thought as they pounded up the stairs.

But she didn't care. It was the best, most carefree night they'd had in a while. Aside from seeing her sister loosen up and allow herself to enjoy both beverage and Bran, they had bonded more as sisters. Although close, adulthood had driven a wedge between them. Through jobs, responsibilities, and subsequent geographical distance, they had become distant background noise in each other's lives.

But we can start new. Here. Now.

Charlie sprawled out on the bed, tossing a handful of cheese in her mouth and reminiscing about their night.

"He was…" Charlie said, munching away. "Respectful."

"Jesus blathering Christ," Anne said. "Booooring."

"He was not!" Charlie said, stuffing more food in her mouth. "He was kind."

"Also, hot." Anne dropped her bag of chips on the bed and headed right back out the door. "Gonna have a piss. I want the juicy stuff when I get back."

Anne stumbled to the bathroom and sank down on the toilet seat.

You never really realize how drunk you are until you're sittin' on the shitter, Anne thought.

With her head rested in her hands and her elbows driven into her knees, Anne swayed back and forth as she relieved herself. The room spun and heaved, and the motion made her stomach do the same.

"Oh lord, no."

She flushed and stood, attempting to ignore the brewing storm, but it came with force. After dropping to her knees in front of the toilet, every bit of booze and food she'd consumed in the past few hours reappeared in a violent surge. Her stomach purged itself until her chest and belly ached and she was damp with sweat. She rested her forehead on the toilet seat and reached up, groping for the handle to give it a flush. The sound of the swirling water was refreshing, and purging her stomach had lifted a burden from her body. With her cheek pressed against the cool seat, she listened to the water filling the tank, enjoying the cool splashes that hit her cheek. The water droplets ran, dribbling down her collarbone and between her breasts. She focused on the sensation, allowing the water to cool and soothe her.

Soon she was submerged, her hair floating above her, the pressure of the water heavy on her skin. She tried to open her eyes, to draw a breath, but she couldn't; water filled her mouth when she strained to scream. Tendrils of her hair wrapped around her like tangles of seaweed, slithering over her skin, vining through her bra and coiling around her limbs. She struggled to break free, but the tendrils were strong, pulsating, suctioning onto her flesh…

She vomited again, this time against the back of the toilet lid, a projectile stream that splashed back on her face. After a minute, her system was sufficiently purged enough for her to crawl into the bathtub and douse herself in the spray from the shower. With the cold water came reality, washing away the hallucinations and sensations of moments before. She scrubbed, lathering herself in heavily scented soap, then toweled off and cleaned up the bathroom enough for it to be passable until she could deal with it in the morning.

Damn, girl. Limits. Learn them.

Though amused by her drunken shenanigans, the reflection in the mirror looked scared. Haunted. Anne looked down at the toilet, imagining phantom tendrils on her skin. Her heart stopped when she heard something from the other room. A feral bray. A scream. A… *howl?*

Charlie?

Her heart in her throat, Anne threw open the bathroom door and ran towards the howl coming from their room. When she burst through the door, the room fell silent.

"Charlie! Oh my fuck, what was—"

Charlie was standing by the window, looking out at the lawn. As if in slow motion, she turned to the sound of Anne's voice, her mouth open wide, an unnaturally large cavern.

"What are you doing?" Anne asked, breathless.

After a moment's hesitation, Charlie's mouth snapped shut. "What are you on about?"

"That noise? I heard a scream… well, no, more of a… howl?"

Charlie laughed. "You're more fucked up than I am, if that's possible."

Charlie stumbled to the bed and pulled the covers up to her chin, her eyes so heavy they were already closed. And Anne would have believed it, that nothing was wrong, had she not seen Charlie open one eye and look out the window.

Anne crawled into her own bed and pulled the covers over her head, trying to ignore the phantoms crawling over her skin and the fear in the room.

CHAPTER 9

THE MORNING WAS fresh and crisp, a generous coating of dew shimmering on the lawn. Charlie rose with the sun and decided she had two choices. Go for a gentle run to work off her hangover, or suffer all day long. She decided the fresh air would do her a world of good.

"You're insane," Anne said, poking her mass of curls out from beneath her cocoon of blankets.

"Sure am," Charlie said. "But I'm also going for a run." Charlie hauled the blankets off Anne and threw them on the floor. "And if you know what's good for you, you'll at least come sit outside, get some fresh air. When I get back, we can have a heavy breakfast. Some grease will settle our stomachs so we can get through the day."

"Don't suppose there's a McDonald's around here?"

"Probably," Charlie said. "But we don't have the car."

"Ah shit," Anne said, remembering that they'd taken an Uber home from The Goat's Moat.

Charlie pulled on a pair of leggings and tied up her runners as Anne bundled her hair in a knot on the top of her head. They went downstairs together, but Anne collapsed in a chair on the patio, wrapped in the duvet off the bed.

"Have fun," Anne said, pulling the blanket over her head.

"I smell coffee," Charlie said. "Penny will bring you some, I'm sure. Just holler out."

"Or toss something against the window, I suppose."

The sisters smiled at each other, and Charlie took off in a jog towards the woods.

Charlie had no intention of entering the woods; she just wanted to run along the forest, breathe in the smell of the maples and the spruce. But as she circled the property, the sun rose high enough in the sky to illuminate the nooks and crannies of the wooded areas, at least as far as she could see. She picked the widest path, where the trees overhead were spaced far enough apart to let the sun drip through.

It was refreshing, her runners on the rugged path, the squirrels darting up trees as she approached, the wind through the leaves, swaying the branches. The path went deep into the trees then curved, enough to seclude her from the property but still allow her to see the house through the brush. As she ran, she wondered if there was a property line. She imagined traipsing on someone else's land, even running all the way past the Goat's Moat and beyond.

Along with the thought of the Goat's Moat came the image of Bran, his goofy smile, the way he made everything else in her brain fade to background noise. On top of the heat from her pounding heart, she felt herself blush, a flutter bringing a smile to her lips.

Stop. You aren't a girl anymore.

It was better, though, this feeling of lust. Better than wallowing in death and self-examination. Since Emme died, Charlie thought far too much about her own mortality, looking down the line instead of right in front of her face. There, in those woods, running with the squirrels and flying along with the birds, shadowed by branched giants all around, she felt a certain sense of hope that had eluded her for quite some time.

It's good for us, this place. Nature, freedom… a healthy road forward.

Darkness fell, just a smidge, but Charlie realized

that in her daydreaming the path had led her away from signs of human life and deeper into the trees where the branches grasped tighter and the path squeezed narrower. She could no longer see Jutland House. Charlie's heart beat faster, pounding harder than her soft jog should have caused. She could feel eyes all over her body, even on the flesh beneath her snug clothing. Panicked, she swatted at her skin, the feeling of spiderwebs clinging to her, gluing her to the ground beneath her feet.

She tried to increase her speed, sprint away from the restraints, but her feet would go no no faster, carrying her at a snail's pace towards…

Back. I need to go back.

Charlie turned back down the path from which she had just came. But she didn't head towards Jutland House, or move even a centimeter. Stuck in place, jaw agape, she stared down the cavernous forest trail.

She wasn't alone.

Standing in the middle of the trail, erect, was a creature, a horrible conglomeration of human and beast. At least nine feet tall and a meter wide, the beast was a rippling mass of muscle and fur. Thick black fur grew in patches over its contorted body, thinning especially around its belly, eyes, and snout. Its hands were long claws, humanoid, with bony fingers a good thirty centimeters long with black, jagged nails. *It* was a *she*, her defined labia etched with rough, course fur. The she-wolf stood still as stone, canine jowls open, drool glistening off razor-sharp teeth.

"No," Charlie said, as if scolding a dog. "No."

Bears could be frightened off by noise, so could mountain lions. But Charlie wasn't entirely sure that this biped hell-wolf could be run off by anything short of a flamethrower, if even that.

Locked in a standoff of inaction, they stared at each other, Charlie and the wolf beast, until it clicked its nails together. Its mouth stretched into a wide, blood-soaked smile, tattered meat stuck between its teeth.

"No." This time when Charlie spoke, it was much quieter, more to herself than to the thing in front of her. She was frozen, paralyzed by fear as it moved, its long, muscular limbs carrying it towards her in bulky, heaving movements. Crossing several meters in only a few steps, it stood snout to face with Charlie, the stench of rancid meat blowing off its hot breath directly into her mouth. Its lips pursed together, its tongue coiling and rolling around its mouth as it formed an awkward, guttural word.

"Sistah."

In an explosion of movement and sound, leaves

whirled up from the ground as the beast tore off through the trees, blazing a path of its own in a flurry of broken branches and shredded brush. After the destruction in the creature's wake stilled, and the song from the smaller creatures of the forest reignited, Charlie coughed out an exhale, unaware she had been holding her breath. Her breathing came out in sobs and screams as she collapsed to her knees, head in her hands, the taste and smell of the creature still fresh in her mouth.

THE OCEAN WAVES they sing to me
White and wispy, so they be
And down below the surface green
Is the loveliest life I'd ever seen.

The song played in Anne's mind, a folk ditty from her childhood. They had always loved the ocean, her entire family, for different reasons. Charlie liked the woods, Anne liked the cold, fresh feel of the water and the grit of the sand between her toes. Emme had liked the unknown. They all liked folklore and legends, of what lay beneath, of the vast unexplored territory that humankind could only dream of.

Water lapped the shore, a gentle whisper, the tide saying good morning to the rising sun. Anne breathed in deep, the scent of the salt water settling her rolling stomach. Penny was off doing other things somewhere else, so Anne took it upon herself to prepare an especially strong coffee with an obscene amount of maple creamer.

If only I had a good feed of McDonalds to murder this hangover, I'd be good as gold.

The island was home to a plethora of exotic marine life. Anne was most fascinated with the Orcas, their playful personalities, the savagery that could take down a great white shark for sport. But deeper than that, not frequently seen, were the more elusive types of marine creatures. Cold-water fish, deep water flora, the Giant Pacific Octopus. Anne couldn't wait to see the alien planet that was beneath the surface, but more than that, she wanted to see what no one had, experience that which no one could understand.

They were taking Emme up to the Haida Gwaii, to a stretch off the island where kayakers liked to go out at night and paddle amongst the luminescent jellyfish. Emme would have loved that, a natural parade of lights to see her off to the other side, if there was such a thing. Anne didn't believe in heaven or hell, Jesus and all that, but there was something, for sure.

We don't just return to dust, star or otherwise. There's something out there. We just don't understand it yet.

Eyes closed, she turned her face to the dawning

sun, letting the warm glow tingle on her fair, freckled flesh. So peaceful, so simple, so quiet…

Panting and pounding drew her attention. Opening her eyes and tilting her head to the yard, she saw Charlie approaching at a sprint, her face a white beacon through the trees.

"Charlie?"

Something about the expression on her sister's face told Anne this was no joke. Charlie wasn't just winded from a run or sick from drink. Something had happened. And from the look of terror on her face, it was the same something that had happened that night they arrived.

"What the bloody hell, Charlie?" Anne shouted. She dropped the quilt to her feet and ran to meet her sister in the center of the yard. Charlie bent over and put her hands on her knees, gulping in breaths, tears streaming down her face. Anne eased her to the ground, where Charlie rested her head in her hands, taking slow, calculated breaths until she could manage to speak.

"The woods," Charlie said as she swiped the tears off her cheeks. "There's something in the woods."

Anne looked towards the trees, her eyes searching down the path. "Yes, there are lots of somethings in the woods, I suppose. Birds, rodents. I imagine you ran across something more substantial. Cougar? Bear?"

Anne always worried about Charlie's jaunts into the wilderness. The backwoods of the island were notorious for black bears, mountain lions, and the occasional wolverine to put a kink in someone's hike. Animals flourished here, with the small and dwindling population and strict regulations on tourism. It was a haven for those of fur and feather, so creatures might be unaccustomed to human visitors on their territory.

"No, not that. Nothing like that." Charlie was shaking her head, making large gestures with her hands. "It was… so big. Too big. And how it stood…."

The colour was slowly returning to Charlie's face, a soft pink now glowing on her damp cheeks.

"Charlie—"

"Never mind," Charlie said. "It was a… wolf."

"Bloody fuck!"

"Yeah, no, it's okay. Just a wolf."

"Okay? A wolf is not okay, Charlie. We have to let Gwen know."

"I'm sure they know," Charlie said, rubbing her temples.

"How fucking big was it, Charlie?"

"It was…" Charlie looked up, seemingly measuring something that stood way taller than a wolf should have. "I'm just tired. Hungover." She looked at Anne, offering a shrug and sideways smirk. "I'm being ridiculous. There's no gargantuan fucking wolf running around the woods on two legs."

"On two legs? Like what? A werewolf?"

Charlie shook her head. "I'm being ridiculous. Let's go inside, see how much grease Penny can cook us up for breakfast."

CHAPTER 10

The tension in the dining room was thick as molasses. Isadora's face was twisted and sour as she sipped her breakfast tea. Anne and Charlie kept stealing glances at her as they wolfed down their breakfast—bacon and toutons, a treat Penny was eager to cook up.

"This is delicious," Anne said, grabbing another touton from the platter.

"Obviously," Isadora said, glaring down her nose at Anne. "It's your fourth one."

Anne chewed hard, defiant. "Yeah, well," she said through a stuffed mouth, "cures a hangover."

Charlie smiled. "And they really are quite delicious. Where did you learn to make these, Penny?"

Penny took a break from refilling coffees to beam at Charlie. "Me mudder taught me."

"Mudder?" Anne said, grinning. "From Newfoundland, are ye, b'y?"

"Indeed!" Penny said with a proud smile. "Woody Point, if you please. Best damn fish and chips on the island."

"You make them here?" Anne said, her mouth watering.

"Sure do! Not quite like our North Atlantic Cod from back on the rock, but delicious, nonetheless. Want me to cook some up tonight?"

Despite the remnants of alcohol still sitting high on her belly, Anne couldn't wait to gorge herself on a good feed of traditional Newfoundland fish and chips. "That would be awesome."

"Anne adores fish more than oxygen," Charlie said. "Always has, even as a picky little eater."

"This is not an a la carte restaurant!" Isadora snapped, slamming her fist on the table.

Like a shock wave through the room, everyone fell still and silent, all eyes watching Isadora's every twitch.

"I… I jus' figured, I don't mind cooking up some fish 'n chips, ma'am," Penny said.

"And who shall buy the fish?" Isadora said, her sharp eyes boring into Penny.

Penny voice grew very quiet as she looked down at the coffee carafe in her hand. "We have fish, ma'am. Gwen's got a huge haul from Edvard—"

"*My* fish," Isadora stated.

"Well, Gwen brought it here, free of charge, so—"

Isadora pounded her fist on the table a second time, making the cutlery jump and rattling the sisters' already sensitive nerves. Isadora leaned on her cane as she walked to Penny, then stood over top of her like a gargoyle.

"Who owns Jutland House?" Isadora sneered.

"You do, ma'am," Penny said, cowering.

"Who employs those who walk these grounds?"

"You do."

"And the refrigerators and freezers where we store the fish? The pans in which we cook them, and the stoves we use to heat the pans?"

"You own them, Ma'am."

Isadora dipped her head in a decisive nod. "If the fish is here—cooked here and eaten here—it is mine." Isadora tapped her cane on the floor to punctuate the statement.

Penny opened her mouth, but shut it very quickly when Isadora fired her another unblinking glare. Coffee carafe in hand, Penny disappeared into the kitchen, releasing a string of expletives as soon as she was through the doorway. Shocked as Anne was at Isadora's behaviour, she snickered, drawing Isadora's attention.

"And you girls," Isadora said. "Your behaviour

should be considered as well."

"I mean, she offered the fish, it's not like we were demanding it—"

"Stumbling in drunk at all hours of the night is behaviour more suited to harpies and drug addicts. Is that what you are, women of ill repute?"

This time, Charlie spoke up. "That's ridiculous."

Isadora's mouth fell open, and she glared at Charlie. "Pardon me?"

"This isn't the dark ages," Charlie said, stirring creamer into her coffee with such force that Anne thought she might very well break her mug. "Women can stay out after dark," Charlie continued, "wear what they like, and do as they please. This may shock you, but we have sense enough to keep ourselves safe and proud, but also have a little fun like the rest of the humans on the planet."

Mouth drawn tight and lines scrunched deep on her forehead, Isadora stood once more, this time throwing her napkin down on her plate.

"Well, if that's the kind of women you'd like to be—"

"Are we bothering you?" Charlie said, tossing another piece of bacon into her mouth. "I mean, really, we're just renting a room. If we've broken any rules, or are bothersome, we can shift over to a motel in town. You can keep our money."

Isadora studied their faces, considering them and the question until her shoulders lowered and she closed her eyes.

"Yes, I suppose you're right," she said, her words tinted with disgust. "I am just offering a place to stay. Keep in mind, however, that breakfast is included, nothing more. Please do enjoy the rest of your stay, and I'll keep out of your way, provided you stay out of mine."

Anne sighed. "And we will be more mindful of our conduct. We apologize if we woke you."

Isadora looked at her and nodded. "Very well."

With her robe flowing behind her, Isadora walked towards the door, but Charlie stopped her with a question.

"Do you have wolves in these woods?"

Though Isadora was back on, Anne could see tension stiffen the old woman's spine and muscles. Her hand clenched her cane until her knuckles were white, and her shoulders scrunched to her ears.

"Yes, of course. The Vancouver Island wolf. Lots around here, but I can't say I've seen any in the area in… years."

"I was out for a run this morning," Charlie said, "and I think I saw… well, I'm not sure. I've seen wolves in the North when I was a kid, but this was much larger, and up—"

"Probably a coyote," Isadora interrupted. "If we had a problem, Gwen would know about it."

"It was no coyote—"

"It was no wolf." Isadora's tone communicated, clearly, that there would be no further discussion on the matter.

"Be that as it may, I don't think I'll be running in the woods anymore," Charlie said. "Whatever it was, it was… unusual."

"We are all a little unusual, aren't we girls?" Isadora's face cracked, and a laugh wheezed out of her throat. "Instead of flitting about the forest and getting intoxicated, why don't you partake in some sightseeing elsewhere? Wasn't that the plan?"

"We are heading up the coast tomorrow," Charlie said. She hesitated, then, "Going on a dive."

Isadora stopped in the doorway and looked over her shoulder. Her expression softened, her eyes moist. "*The* dive?"

Charlie's lips parted and her eyes closed. "I…"

"We'll see," Anne said. "We'll take… her with us, but we'll have to decide if the moment and the place is right when we see it."

"Her," Isadora said quietly. Anne couldn't quite read Isadora's tone; the old woman's voice was a confusing dichotomy of sad and wistful, or harsh and accusatory. "You mean, Emme is here? In my home?"

Charlie looked like she might vomit, her hand finding her throat and her skin turning a grey shade of green.

"Yes," Anne said, "we have her ashes with us. Where else would they be?"

Still in the doorway, Isadora's eyes searched the ceiling. "I'm not entirely sure I'm comfortable with that."

"Excuse me?" Anne said, standing from the table. Isadora spun on her heels to face Anne, her fist clenched around her cane, the shake of her hand igniting the rattle inside the wolf's head.

"A dead body in my home is a little unorthodox."

Charlie jumped from her seat, positioning herself between Anne and Isadora but facing the old woman.

"Listen," Charlie said with surprising strength in her voice, "we've only told you as a topic of conversation. What we have in our possession, short of illegal substances or items, is none of your damn business. And certainly, calling our sister's cremated remains a dead body is both heartless and disrespectful."

"I mean no—"

"You mean every bit of it," Charlie said, her voice crescendoing to a volume that made even Anne wince. "Since we arrived, you've been condescending and arrogant, judging us as if we were delinquent schoolgirls rather than professional adults. We are customers,

Isadora, and we are paying for lodging. That is all. You will respect us as such, or we'll be on our way."

With her face scrunched—in anger or shock, Anne wasn't sure—Isadora nodded once.

"And to make us feel this way?" Charlie said. "With everything that's happened, everything we're having to face? I'm done."

Shouldering by Isadora, Charlie stormed from the room and up the stairs. Penny stood in the doorway of the kitchen, mouth open, smiling. Isadora stood in shock, watching after Charlie until the upstairs door slammed and all was quiet.

"Quite the scene," Isadora said, brushing at her dress as if to wipe away the embarrassment. "I do apologize. I forget myself. Please tell Charlie… again, I do apologize."

With her cane tapping the ground, Isadora retreated into the house to a lair Anne could only imagine, but she turned to say one last thing.

"I know it's hard, dear Anne. Don't think I don't know. I've been through it myself, remember. Hardens a soul, it does."

And with that, the tail end of her crimson robe slid around the corner, and Isadora dissolved into the house.

Isadora did not appear for dinner.

Charlie opted to stay in her room as well, a cocktail of Xanax and merlot lulling her into a much needed rest. Anne considered protesting, but left well enough alone, knowing the day had been a bust from the moment brunch had gone south.

A large meal of crab and Pacific fish seemed overkill for just Anne, but shortly after dinner had been laid out on the table, Penny and Wilfrid joined her.

"The madame shan't be joinin' us, I dare say," Penny said. "Not after a row like that."

"Bit dramatic," Anne said, taking a piece of fish off the tray. "Wasn't really a row, more of a heated exchange."

"She's not used to that. Being stood up to," Penny said. "And Charlie gave it to her good."

"Charlie will only tolerate so much before putting her foot down," Anne said, feeling a sense of pride. "She's always been protective, more of me than herself, but Isadora was challenging all three of us, really. Since the moment we came, treating us like that. It's the last thing we need."

Penny pushed the food around her plate. "I'm sorry. Emme…"

"It's okay," Anne said. "Well, it is, and it isn't. It's a thing, and we need to deal with it, and I think we're doing that the best way we know how. At least we're doing something, and not just sweeping it under the rug."

"How do you mean?"

Anne took a sip of her wine and sat back in her chair. "I loved my sisters, and they loved me, but we drifted. Which, I mean, people do, families especially. We got jobs in different parts of the country, me in Okotoks, Charlie in Saskatoon… Charlie ended up in Edmonton, though she travelled all the time."

"Any families of your own?"

"No. Emme was single when she… Charlie's a bit of a loner, had a few relationships but nothing ever stuck. Hopeless romantic, though. If she can get herself together, find herself again, a match will find her."

"And you?" Penny asked, reaching across the table and pouring another wine.

Anne searched the young woman's face, looking for intent, judgement, a hint of anything.

"A romantic as well, but of a different flavour."

Penny's head cocked to the side and her brow furrowed, nearly touching in the middle of her forehead. "You one of them party girls, likes all sorts of dudes at once? Or the whips and chains and latex, all that?"

Anne nearly choked, and her wine dribbled out of her nose, her eyes watering down her face.

"Oh gosh!" Penny said, jumping up and coming to Anne's side with a serviette. "You okay? You ain't choking, are you?"

Anne shook her head. "I'm fine. Just a lesbian."

"Ah," Penny said.

Sniffling and wiping her face with the serviette Penny handed her, Anne tried to gage her reaction, and the reaction of the lug across the table. She had got Wilfrid's attention, his eyes wide as the moon and mouth hanging open, but Penny's face was expressionless as she sat back in her chair.

"I never know," Anne said. "I don't always get a warm reception…"

Both women turned to look at Wilfrid, whose face was a blank slate. All he cared about was the bacon hanging off his lip as he chewed like a moose chews on on cud. Penny clucked her tongue and tossed a serviette at his face as she took her seat again. Anne thought her face might explode from shock and embarrassment —she could feel the deep crimson pounding in her cheeks. Penny pulled one of Anne's ringlets, letting it bounce down over her face.

"Don't be 'shamed," Penny said, reaching for Anne's hand. "Love's a beautiful thing, and you won't find no haters 'round these parts."

Anne breathed a sigh of relief, and the fire in her cheeks cooled. "I never know."

"Suppose you don't, the world the way it is these days." Penny stuffed another bite of food in her mouth. "So you have a special missus at home then?"

"Naw. Lots of them, but no one special." Anne's fingertips found the ghosts of needle marks on her arm. "I just can't seem to get my shit together. Can't seem to find what I'm looking for."

"Good on you. You're young. Don't fall into it too soon, or you don't get to see what else is good up the buffet line." Penny paused, glancing at Anne's arm. "How long?"

"I'm sorry?"

"You've been clean how long?"

"What makes you think I'm clean?"

Penny laughed. "Spritely thing like you? Vibrant, energetic, rosy glow. Ain't nothin' in those veins weighing you down."

Anne swallowed hard and looked down at her lap. "Four years."

"That's wonderful." Penny took a swig of her wine and her voice grew quiet. "And what took its place?"

Startled, Anne looked at Penny, her mind rushing over her life—skydiving and rock climbing and traveling and spending. She had a plethora of thrills and debt and sexual partners…

"Nothing. Nothing took its place."

"Can't find what yer lookin' for, eh?" Penny set her

cutlery down.

"Maybe there's nothing to find." Anne couldn't bear to eat anymore. The tears swelled in her eyes and the lump throbbed in her throat.

Is that what Emme felt?

"Oh love, no. There's always something. Maybe it's just not what you think."

Anne laughed. "Perhaps. I hope it's not a dude. Don't fancy those ones."

They laughed, and Penny took Anne's hand.

"You gots three jobs, girl. Eat, sleep, live! The rest is icing."

They laughed, even Wilfrid, who grunted a chuckle through his hairy nose.

The rest of dinner was lovely, full of small chat about the world and lifelong dreams. Anne loved the company; she had missed being around other people, just enjoying herself without worrying about the what ifs and the treachery of the next step. For now, she was here, at Jutland House, time stalled just long enough to restart a new chapter of her life.

"You should have seen their faces," Anne said.

Charlie finally smiled, a pleasant break from her day of brooding and drug-intoxication.

"Well, I'm glad you weren't lynched," Charlie said.

"Me too."

Anne coiled her finger around a curl and sat down on the windowsill beside Charlie.

"Charlie, you ever think about what will happen when we go back?"

"What do you mean?"

"I mean after this, when we drive home, go back to our jobs and our lives."

"Well, just that I suppose. I have a caseload waiting for me, and you have your studio—"

"Yes, I know the mechanics of what will happen."

The grass on the lawn was shimmering, the moon now high and bright in the sky, twinkling of the ocean and grass in equal but unique splendor. Anne rested her head on the glass, watching the water, feeling its serenity as she continued, talking as much to herself as she was to Charlie.

"I'm in a rut, Charlie. So are you. Out there, trudging through life, day after day, punching clocks and going through the motions. That shouldn't be how we live out our days."

Anne didn't turn to look, but she could see Charlie's face in her peripheral, the way she looked out the window, her fingertip coming to her mouth so she could bite her nail like she always did when she was anxious.

"We are fine. Safe. Stable," Charlie said, a slight tremor in her voice.

"We are Emme," Anne said.

Anne took Charlie's hand, and the sisters turned to face each other. Silently, Charlie was crying, fat tears rolling down her face.

"I loved Emme," Anne said. "Always will. But let's not be her, okay?"

Charlie cried harder, her lip quivering and eyes blurry with tears.

"Let's learn from Emme," Anne said. "We've fucked up our lives, but we have time to fix them."

Anne was crying now, too, though she hadn't realized she'd started. She tipped over and put her head on Charlie's chest, and the sisters held each other and cried.

"I miss her," Charlie said.

"Me too."

"I want things back the way they were."

Anne breathed deep and pulled away from Charlie. "No. I want things better than they were."

Charlie sniffed. "I can't… think beyond the next few minutes, the next day."

"Then don't. Let's just be here, while we're here. When we get back, let's not go back the same. Let's claw our way out of our ruts, really start living."

"It's not that easy, Anne."

"Why?" Anne looked out the window at the calm ocean. "There are plenty of excuses to stay stagnant, to just get by, but why? Will we be worse off if we quit our jobs, take the chances?"

"We need to survive, Anne. To pay the bills. And we could get hurt—"

"So fucking what?" Anne placed her hand on the cool window. "What we are hurts, too, but we're just numb to it." Anne turned and looked into her sister's eyes. "Charlie, we are intelligent, capable women. We will always pay the bills. We will always survive. Let's do better than mere survival."

Anne watched her sister's eyes focus out the window, on the lawn below. And the forest.

"But you know," Anne said, sliding off the windowsill and patting Charlie on the shoulder, "you're right. We needn't worry about this today. All we need to worry about today is resting up. Big day tomorrow."

"Big day tomorrow," Charlie said.

Charlie looked out at the world like it was a predator waiting to devour them whole. Anne felt that way too—she was always moving, always running.

But they would be fine. They would follow the light, find their way to the surface of life before drowning.

"Love you, Charlie."

"Love you, Anne."

CHAPTER 11

The cool spray from the waves was refreshing. At least Anne thought so. Charlie, on the other hand, hung her head over the side of the boat, spewing offerings to some Pacific Poseidon as the boat heaved through the water at a lolling speed.

"Little green around the gills, are ya, big sis?" Anne asked.

Anne laughed and slapped Charlie on the back. Charlie answered with a belly-deep belch.

"Nice," Anne said, waving her hand in front of her face.

The drive had been long, and they had been ready to hit the ocean as soon as they saw the Salmon Arm bobbing at the dock. Not a huge vessel by any means, but relatively new and modern, with all the comforts and tech required for a safe and cozy dive.

"You birds have obviously dived before," Captain Miller said.

"Not much, but yeah," Anne said. "Her less than I, but we are both certified."

"Here?"

"Caribbean."

Miller laughed, sea water and caffeine in her chortles.

"Well, this is a different kettle of fish, so to speak. Ain't gonna be able to take a dip in your bikinis 'round these parts. And you won't see the glittering turquoise of the warmer waters, that's for sure."

Rolling her eyes, Anne flipped the woman a solid bird.

"Atta girl. Thick blood in your veins, I see," Miller said, then tilted her head towards Charlie. "Her?"

"Probably sitting this one out," Charlie said, hanging over the rail.

"The sea life is beautiful up here," Anne said. "Unique, fascinating—"

"Emme adored it here," Charlie said, pulling her head up from over the edge and wiping her chin with the back of her hand. "She dove here lots."

"Huh," the woman said. "Emme Arnold?"

"Yes," Charlie said, sitting on the bench and taking a sip of water. "Did you know her?"

"Met her a couple times. Loved to dive round the circuit of boats. She was up here on the regular. I see it now."

"See what?" Charlie asked.

"You," Miller said, pointing at Charlie. "You's sisters with Emme."

Charlie winced as if she had been slapped. "Yes. Both of us."

Miller looked over at Anne, then back at Charlie, and a smile spread across her face. "Yes, I see it in ya both. The sisters three, ye be! Where is Emme holed up these days? Haven't seen her around for the better part of a year."

Charlie gazed out at the sea, and Miller's face dropped. "How long?" the captain asked, her voice now soft.

"A month," Anne said.

"Ah shit," Miller said, pulling her ponytail through the back of her cap. "So young. Cancer?"

"No," Anne said. "Suicide."

"Ah," Miller said, shaking her head. "Makes sense."

"Pardon?" Anne said.

Captain Miller tugged at her ponytail once more,

then looked out at the water. "Always lost, that one. Never found, I guess."

Silence enveloped the trio, allowing the splashing water and cawing of the sea birds to dominate the conversation.

"Well fuck that, Emme. Hopes she found what she was looking for."

The captain had no more words. She gave both Anne and Charlie a quick pat on the shoulder, then muttered some tasks to the deckhands and went below. Anne tightened her diving gear and adjusted her dry suit, making sure the cold grasp of the ocean wouldn't cut the dive short before she was ready to surface. The crew helped her, checking her tank and her gear before she took her place on the edge of the boat to wait until they reached a spot off the northernmost coast of the island.

When the boat's motor whirred to a stop, Charlie went over to Anne.

"I'm sorry," Charlie said, "I just can't. Not today."

"Hey," Anne said, cupping her hand on Charlie's cheek. "It's cool. I'm only diving because we paid for this."

Charlie laughed. "You love it. But that's not what I meant."

"Oh." Anne said.

Both sisters glanced over at a cabinet on the deck,

the one they locked their stuff in when they first came aboard.

"I'm not ready to let her go," Charlie whispered.

"Me either," Anne replied. "And we don't have to. There's no rush."

Charlie drew a quavering breath.

"I'll ease up on the booze, take some Gravol," Charlie said. "We'll try again in a few days, another spot, maybe."

"I suppose you could convince me to go again," Anne said.

"Ready, m'loves?" Miller said, coming back upstairs.

"Just me today," Anne said.

"Figured," Miller said. She held a can of beer out for Charlie, who scrunched her face into a grimace.

"No hair of the dog?" Miller said, smirking.

Charlie pantomimed a puking motion, and the crew laughed.

"So you," Miller said, pointing at Anne, "my crew went over the diving procedures on shore?"

"Sure did," Anne said.

"Hand signals?"

"Yes."

"Rules?"

"Yup."

"Animals you might see down there? Plants? What to watch out for, not to touch and whatnot?"

"All the above."

"Good. Any questions?"

"May I go?"

Miller looked stern, then pulled Anne's mask on her face, securing it with a tug. Anne gave the thumbs up, and Miller pushed her backwards off the boat.

THE DEPTHS of the ocean were like an alien planet, the kelp and sea grass moving, suspended in heavy rippling motions, the water tinted a dark emerald blue. It had been forty minutes, so Anne knew her time was up. The frigid waters of the North Pacific were unforgiving, and regardless of how much protective and insulated gear they had on, they could only spend so much time in the cold beneath before hypothermia took hold.

The wildlife was phenomenal, the startling blues and greens of the deep water plants, the shapes and movements of the fish in these waters. Though not as colourful as the schools of rainbows swimming in the tropical waters Anne was used to, the fish here held a certain appeal: earthy, hardy, mysterious. Life under these waters was rustic and powerful, a foreign land rarely breached by human invaders.

Water fizzed in Anne's peripheral, a frantic waving from one of the guides. Anne looked, catching the thumbs down hand symbols and frantic hand flapping that told her there was something of interest to see. She followed pointed fingers to a grove of brush and rock. There were a few fish swimming around, but nothing out of the ordinary. She kicked her flippers, diving deeper until she was at the grove, then rooted around, gently parting the foliage and checking the nooks and crannies of the rock pile for exotic fish or rays. She rested her hand on a flat rock, giving it a push, but it was firmly lodged in place. The divers above were watching intently, waiting. Anne shrugged and decided to surface, when she felt a tug on her finger.

An appendage, soft and pale pink, toyed with the tip of her gloved finger. Anne breathed slow and even as a tentacle emerged from beneath the rock, coiling around her hand and wrist, feeling its way up her arm. Then another tentacle appeared, and another, until the entire creature had wriggled its way out of its hidey hole on the bottom of the ocean deep.

Holy fucking shit.

One of the more elusive creatures that called these waters its home, the Giant Pacific Octopus was a sight to behold. Arms throbbing and gyrating, suckers moving in different rhythms and patterns, feeling Anne's limbs and body. It was beautiful, the pale pink turning to bold red, moving through her legs to explore her equipment. Anne floated as still as she could, bracing her body against the rocks so the octopus could check her out without getting spooked. She closed her eyes and felt its movement over her body, imagining what the creatures grasp must feel like on bare skin, all those suckers tasting and touching independently to explore this new visitor. The tentacles pressed against her mask, and she watched, transfixed, as the suckers moved across the lenses and the other tentacles played with her equipment.

In a flurry of movement, the tentacles stiffened, pulled her, pushing her, dragging her down to the ocean floor as the octopus's mantle slid beneath the rocks. It yanked, trying to bring Anne with it to its ocean home. Anne felt its intensity, but she wasn't scared. She was entranced. Curious. Regardless, the divers were on top of her, peeling away tentacles and pushing off the ocean floor, trying to get enough leverage to pry Anne out of the creature's hold.

Anne knew she was in danger, and that her safety rested in the hands of her very experienced dive guides, but she fought them off. She wanted to be there, under that water; she wanted to forget everything and everyone above and just live in the ocean where it was quiet and slow and peaceful. She imagined staying there, her body adjusting to the cold until it felt like nothing, her body changing to accept its oxygen from the water rather than a steel tank, her eyes clearing to see the world around her.

Anne looked up, up to where the land was, where her life awaited. She saw Emme floating there, her body rotting, black vomit covering her pale breasts. The doctors had charcoaled Emme's stomach at the emergency room after Charlie and Anne had found her passed out in the motel room, empty pill bottles strewn about everywhere. And here it was, that scene, floating in front of her in living colour, a reality waiting for her above water.

Stay.

With Emme's voice came a black purge, charcoal vomit swirling through the water like oil, slithering towards Anne like hungry eels. Anne tried to dive deeper, to crawl under that rock with the octopus and never, ever see the light of day again…

Without realizing what she was doing, Anne's fist came up, making contact with one of the diver's cheeks, gashing it open and spilling tendrils of blood that floated up with the bubbles. Anne clenched down on her regulator, unable to gasp, and the tentacles released her, the octopus retreating to its home beneath the rocks. Anne watched it go, focusing on the sand and the darkness, watching for a tentacle to poke out as the divers pulled her towards the surface.

WITH MOST OF breakfast and part of her stomach lining offered to the waves, Charlie sat on the deck, watching the tree line in the distance. It was a good idea to watch the horizon, a focal point that was still and static and could calm her equilibrium. She always got more sea sick than both Anne or Emme, but it happened more frequently with age. She could manage it, though, she just hadn't planned well.

Next time I will have less alcohol and more Gravol.

Anne had always loved the ocean more than Charlie had. It made Charlie jealous, watching Anne and Emme frolicking in the waves, but at the same time she loved the woods while they didn't care for being amongst the trees. Where Anne found boredom, Charlie found beauty—a stray golden maple leaf, a squirrel-pile of acorns, the tracks of fallow deer. Charlie longed for the musty smell of the forest, the darkness of tree cover, and the chitter and chatter of insects and rodents.

Though thoughts of the woods soothed her roiling

stomach and soul, a disturbance in the water below distracted her from her reverie.

"Haul up!" Miller's voice cut through the calm, followed by a frenzy of activity, pulling and hauling and yelling until one by one, the divers surfaced.

Anne's red hair billowed around her as Miller grabbed her straps and hoisted her aboard. The other divers climbed the ladder, the first one up being assisted by the one behind. One diver's cheek was spewing blood, his hand held to the side of this face. Charlie evaluated him only briefly before dropping to her sister's side.

"Anne, what the fuck?"

Charlie yanked Anne's mask off her face, pulling masses of red hair to the side to see the damage. Anne was fluorescent white, as she always was, but no worse for wear.

"Damnit!" Anne said as she pushed Charlie away. "I'm fine!"

"Fucking lucky is what you are," one of the divers shouted as he tossed his mask on the deck.

Miller stood in front of Anne as the diver came towards her, fists clenched.

"Mill, she clocked Des! Right in the face!"

"That was her?" Miller asked, evaluating the bloody crew member seated against the wheel house.

The diver continued yelling. "The octopus got her,

wrapped her and tried bring her down. She got too friendly with it, gave it its chance, then fought us off when we intervened."

Miller turned and faced Anne. "This true?"

The bloody deckhand shouted, "You could have killed us! It's no fucking joke down there!"

Miller put her hand on the man's shoulder and gave him a little shove. He retreated to his partners on the deck and started peeling away bloody clothing. Miller knelt down to Anne.

"Really?" There were so many questions in Miller's tone.

"Anne, what did you do? What happened?" Charlie said, speaking softly and moving between her sister and the captain.

"I..." Anne trailed off and looked at the water. "I'm sorry. It was just so beautiful, I..."

Miller pushed Charlie aside. Charlie was going to retaliate, to jump in and defend her sister, but Miller's stern expression had softened considerably. "M'lady, the deep is a wonderful, exotic place," the captain said. "But it isn't ours. It is many times our strength, and the beasts have home team advantage down there."

The captain stood and reached out her hand. Anne took it and allowed herself to be pulled to her feet. Charlie stood on her own and put her arm around her sister's shoulders. After lighting a cigar, Miller continued.

"The Giant Pacific Octopus is a sight to behold, for sure. Not many divers get to meet one, not up close anyways. They like the deep, and the cold."

"It was incredible," Anne said.

The emerald fire in Anne's eyes raised the hair on Charlie's neck.

"The GPO is a magnificent creature," Miller said as she leaned over the edge of the boat. "Changes colour with mood, highly intelligent. More so than the lot of us, that's for sure. Central brain, but also cerebral cortex in those tentacles, too. And each of those suckers moves independently, often with different functions."

"Damn," Charlie said.

"Impressive, sure," Miller said, looking at Anne, "but bloody strong. And dangerous. If that there animal wanted to keep you under, not much you could do to stop it."

"She seemed so kind," Anne said. "She was checking me out as much as I was her."

"Certainly," Miller said, "but you need to be cautious. That's her world, and she calls the shots. The world belongs to the beasts."

Miller turned from the rail and faced Anne. "You put my crew in danger."

"I didn't mean—"

"But you did. Curiosity is one thing, but you broke the rules. I was pretty explicit about the ins and outs of a dive."

Charlie came to Anne's defense. "But you didn't specifically mention the octopus."

Miller looked at her, eyes dark and angry, but nodded her head. "Aye, I did not. I assumed common sense might run in your DNA."

Like she'd just suffered a punch to the gut, tears welled in Charlie's eyes.

"Hope you enjoyed your trip, nonetheless," Miller said. "It will be your last with me and my crew. Now get yourself changed, or you'll catch your death out here."

Anne was shivering, Charlie noticed, her skin an impossible shade of white. Charlie led her sister below deck and helped her into her clothes before wrapping her in a blanket.

"You're managing okay," Anne said.

"I am now. Your fuckery has me distracted me from my puking. I'm sure I'll resume if I'm down here long enough."

Anne tucked a curl of hair behind her ear and looked out the window.

"Anne, are you okay? What happened out there?"

Long ago, when Anne was a child, they used to go

to the beach every weekend; it was a short jaunt from their house in Victoria. Charlie remembered her sister wandering off, only to return with buckets full of creatures, shelled or clawed. Even a mouse, once, that she'd somehow trapped in that plastic beach bucket. Her arms were constantly covered in scrapes and pinches and bites, but Anne never shed a tear. *They are friendly*, she'd say. *They were scared*, or *they were defending their territory*. One time, she came back to her and Emme, her arms decorated with Hermit crabs pinched to her skin. But instead of wailing, she was glowing, excited for her find. *Isn't it wonderful?* she'd exclaimed. *I can paint their shells*!

No such enthusiasm was present this time. Anne was sullen, not a hint of glee on her face. Eight-year-old Anne would have been giddy about the experience.

"What happened down there, Anne? Did it hurt you?"

"No," Anne said dreamily. "Not at all. And she didn't want to hurt me."

When Anne turned her face away from the window, Charlie noticed her eyes were their normal bright green.

"She was pale, almost peach. That's a relaxed octopus. Had she been fiery orange or red, that'd mean she was pissed. She liked me."

Anne stood and went to the mirror to preen her wild curls.

Ah, Charlie thought. *That's better. There's my girl.*

But there is something odd…

"What did happen down there, Anne?"

Anne stopped fussing with her tresses but didn't look at Charlie. "What do you mean?"

"Well, there's a bloody dude up on deck, so…"

Anne twirled a curl away from her face. "I didn't want to go, that's all."

"You knew the rules. You shouldn't have touched it."

Anne rolled her eyes. "You know me."

"I do," Charlie agreed. "But it wasn't safe."

"It didn't matter," Anne snapped.

Both sisters were still and quiet until Anne shrugged and slipped into her coat. "Let's go up. I want to watch the trip back, not waste it down here stewing over my disobedience.

Before Charlie could argue, Anne was up the stairs and out on deck, offering soft apologies to the crew. From the sounds of it, they'd had enough time to simmer down, and all was well again.

But Charlie knew something was up. She thought back to her episodes with the biped wolf, and how she'd hidden that from Anne.

What are you hiding, little sister?

CHAPTER 12

The night was glowing pink as the sisters pulled up the driveway of Jutland House. The day had slipped away in the blink of an eye. Anne suggested they go to the Goat's Moat, but Charlie resisted, a flush of pink in her cheeks. Though Anne had wanted to chide her sister for her cowardice in regard to Bran, she didn't. The day had been exhausting in so many ways, and Anne couldn't wait to flop down in her bed and get some sleep.

"Tired?" Charlie asked.

"What gave it away?" Anne said as she put the car in park. "Was it the eight times I fell asleep on the boat after the dive, or the two times I slept driving back here?"

"Though I prefer you not sleep while you're

driving," Charlie said, "I'm glad you got some rest. Also, we haven't eaten all day. We should grab some chow before we collapse."

"This is not a diner," Anne said, feigning her best accent and crunching her face to imitate Isadora.

Charlie cringed.

"Yeah," Anne said, looking up at Jutland House. "Maybe we should have gone down to Goat's, and not just for the beef cake."

Charlie gave her a slap on the shoulder, but didn't unlatch her seatbelt.

"We still can," Anne said. "I promise I won't embarrass you or push you at him. In any way. Just grub and go."

Charlie seemed to consider the trip, but a hard rap at the window startled them both to attention. It was Isadora, her fingers curled into a fist over her cane, rattling it with every movement.

"Ladies!" she shouted through the closed windows.

Anne opened the door and slid out. "Hey Isadora."

"How was the water today?"

"Lovely," Anne said.

Isadora studied her, then ducked down to look through the window at Charlie, who was fumbling with her buckle.

"Well, do come in," Isadora said, her tone jovial. "Supper will be ready promptly."

"Ah, thanks," Charlie said as she stood out of the car, "but we're really tired. I think we're just going to call it a day."

Isadora stopped moving and honed in on Charlie with such ferocity that Anne wanted to step between them.

"You must eat," Isadora said, her words sharp.

"And we will," Charlie said, equally firm. "We've got food in our room."

"Nonsense," Isadora said, breaking her glare and walking towards the house. "You need a proper meal, not ketchup chips and donuts. Come on, then. You may change your attire if you wish, or just dump your stuff at the bottom of the stairs and come have a quick bite."

Isadora did not wait for a response. She clopped up the stairs in her square heels, her crimson cloak flowing behind her.

"I'd rather eat glass right now," Charlie said.

"Jesus," Anne said. "We don't have to obey her, you know. This is a fucking hotel. We can do whatever we want."

"I don't want to be rude—"

"You know what's rude?" Anne said, her voice rising with her irritation. "What's rude is this subtle bullying and presumptuous behaviour. We aren't her little sisters..."

Anne's thoughts trailed off into the air, and Charlie looked uncomfortably towards the house.

"Bollocks," Anne said as she sighed. "That's it, isn't it? She's missing her sisters."

"Imagine so," Charlie said.

"Right then," Anne said, giving a curt nod. "Suppose we should join her."

"Suppose so."

"But just tonight. A quick bite, then to bed. We have a good excuse for keeping it short—the dive today, and you puking up your guts."

Charlie held her stomach as if remembering the experience.

"You gonna be able to eat?" Anne asked.

"Dunno," Charlie said.

"Well, you'll have to try," Anne said. She shut the car door and linked arms with Charlie, guiding her towards the steps. "You hurled your breakfast overboard and had nothing to eat since. You need to get something into you, even if it's only a biscuit."

As they closed in on the house, Anne pulled Charlie along as Charlie's feet slowed, her attention directed towards the yard. Anne looked at the grass, and at her sister's strained face, and thought about her experience with the octopus. The emotion, the urge to stay down there, the fear of rising back to that boat. She had been entranced by the creature, by that underwater world. And terrified of what was above.

Did something like that happen to you, Charlie?

"Charlie—"

"Now now, ladies." Isadora was standing at the top of the stairs, a dark silhouette against the warm glow of Jutland House. "Hurry along. Penny will have dinner on the table in five minutes."

Charlie walked up the stairs, leaving Anne at the bottom full of questions and confessions.

"Amazing. Truly ethereal."

It was difficult for Anne to describe her experience beneath the water—the rippling, emerald beauty, the touch of the octopus.

"Should you have been touching it?" Isadora said. The purse of her lips suggested she disapproved of the whole thing. A wicked smile played at the corner of Anne's mouth.

"Evidently not," Anne said. She stuffed a shrimp in her mouth so she didn't have to say more.

Isadora watched Anne chew for a moment, then directed her glare at Charlie.

"What does that mean?" Isadora said.

The mouthful of shrimp was suddenly a regrettable

choice, Anne decided, as Isadora's eyes bored into her sister and Charlie's eyes sought help.

"Anne chose not to follow the rules," Charlie said with a shrug. "She touched and interacted with the octopus, and…"

"And?" Isadora said, her voice high and tight. "And what?"

Anne swallowed, the food sliding down her throat like a clump of thick mud. "I didn't want to get out."

Isadora cocked her brow and waited.

"I… I wasn't thinking clearly. It was just so beautiful, and that creature was amazing… I touched it, and let it hold me, and it pulled me down... When the crew tried to pull me up—"

"Save you," Charlie interjected.

"Yes," Anne said, glaring at her sister. "When they tried to help, I resisted them."

Both of Isadora's brows were now raised.

"Gave one a good wallop, actually," Anne said.

Anne couldn't help but laugh, and Charlie followed suit with a nervous giggle. They were both stopped abruptly when Isadora pounded cane on the floor, the head rattling. Both sisters looked at her, shocked. Isadora placed her hands on the table, drumming her fingertips on the hard wood, slowly, one by one.

"Disrespectful." Isadora clucked her tongue and stood from the table. "Immature, dangerous…"

Anne wanted to speak, to fight back, to put the old woman in her place, but as Isadora walked over to the window and paced like an animal in a cage, Anne's bravado shrank, pity taking its place.

"What were you thinking?" Isadora scolded. "I mean, I guess I can assume what you were thinking. Same thing you think here, prancing around, entitled and spoiled. You can do whatever you please, whenever you please, that's what you think."

Isadora stabbed a bony finger towards Charlie.

"That's what you both think."

"I'm not sure this is called for," Charlie said.

"You," Isadora hissed, "lurking about in those woods. *My* woods, thinking you know better than me, than the creatures that call the forest home. You were trespassing, the both of you, and your disrespect got you in trouble, now didn't it?"

With both sisters standing, and Isadora pacing back and forth in front of the window, Penny came in the room, tray in hand.

"Tres Leches?" Penny said in her sing-song tone.

"You fool!"

Isadora screamed and grabbed a vase from the bookshelf. Penny managed to duck as Isadora flung the heavy object through the air, the fine porcelain smashing against the wall just above where Penny was crouched. Like the air had been sucked from the room, the sisters stood breathless, Anne hesitating which way to move, and Penny's face contorted in shock. After a moment, the tension from the outburst settled, and Charlie quietly went to Penny's side, helping her stand and leading her back into the kitchen. Once out of the room, a string of colorful profanity flowed from behind the closed kitchen door. Anne turned her attention to Isadora. Isadora had gone back to the window and was looking out over the lawn and water. Her hands fumbled with her skirts, smoothing creases and wrinkles that weren't there.

"I do say," Isadora whispered to the window. "That was unfortunate."

"Isadora?" Anne voice was soft, and she kept her distance.

"Child," Isadora answered. She did not turn.

"I'm sorry about your sisters, Isadora."

In the reflection of the window, Anne could see Isadora's fumbling slow down, but her fingers still trembled, and now her lip did, too.

Isadora spoke quietly. "I'm not sure why that matters."

"Are you lonely, Isadora?"

Isadora didn't answer.

"Nobody is ever going to replace your sisters."

Anne walked to the window and stood beside

Isadora. The ocean was beautiful, the starlight glimmering off the soft surf.

"No one will ever be Emme," Anne said. A swell of emotion made her words quiver. "I know that. As much as I want her back, I know no one will replace her. All I can do is appreciate the people who are still in my life and cherish the memories."

Isadora's head had turned, and she studied Anne's face. Anne kept speaking, talking to release the words rather than communicating to Isadora.

"We'd grown apart, the three of us, after Mum and Dad passed. Not because we didn't love each other or get along, but just, you know, life."

Anne hugged herself as Isadora watched her like a hawk.

"I don't quite know when it happened. We saw each other on occasional holidays, Skype now and then. But we'd lost that connection, you know?"

Anne had never felt quite right, always sailing through life, looking for purpose, seeking something that felt right. Nothing quite hit the mark. She knew Charlie had been doing the same, but her fear kept her grounded, kept her nose to the grind. She had always been that way, Charlie. A worrier, a planner. She had it in her head that she needed to be professional, married, 2.5 children and a golden retriever.

"They were not good girls."

Isadora's voice cut through the air, cold and harsh. Anne met the woman's steely stare, and a chill hardened her bones.

"What?"

"My little sisters. Not good."

After pulling an album off the bookshelf, Isadora glided to the music room. Anne hesitated but followed, and sat on the loveseat when Isadora patted the cushion beside her.

"I wasn't happy when I found out Mother was with child. Then it happened a second time. The day she and father brought them home, I couldn't understand. Wouldn't. There were two of them, and Mother and Father loved them dearly."

Isadora placed the photo album in Anne's lap and flipped it open. A family photo, a couple—presumably Isadora's parents—glowing with pride, seated on a stone bench in the garden, a small child in each lap.

"They look like you," Anne said.

Isadora smirked. "Not a compliment, I think."

"It's…"

Isadora waved a hand. "Not to worry, my dear. No offense taken. Of course I've aged, but my personality remains. Stoic, firm, strict."

Hooking a finger under the cardboard page, Anne flipped to the next photos, the girls playing in the garden, hand in hand.

"They had each other, the girls," Isadora said. "They felt things in each other I could only see, had secrets between them, unspoken jokes; their childish laughter cut me like a blade."

The picture accentuated the differences between Willow and Zelda. Unique individuals. One had long hair tied in plaits, the other a shaggy pixie cut. The one with long hair wore flowing dresses and bangles on her arms, and the other wore overalls and grubby logans on her feet. The photographs showed them playing barefoot in the yard, building castles out of mud and sand, and playing ball in the grass.

"It was a constant state of energy in our house after they arrived. First it was the crying and the eating, sucking Mother and Father dry of all their attention and emotional stores. Then they became children, full of curiosity and raw intelligence, a endless bank of energy and moxie."

Knuckles white, fists clenched, Isadora looked off into a distant yesterday, her eyes hot with anger.

"You didn't get along with them," Anne said quietly, evaluating the emotion in the old woman's face.

"They were them and I was me. Our family was never the same. This place was never the same."

In that face, the grey skin sketched with deep wrinkles and those dark eyes filled with so much anger,

Anne found. something terrifying. Raw, violent hatred. She knew the old crone was unpleasant—crazy, even—but she had never imagined this.

"Well I'm sorry to hear that," Anne said. "You must be quite relieved to have this place all to yourself."

Isadora's face melted to a smile. "Yes. It's lovely isn't it?"

As if introducing Anne to Jutland House for the first time, Isadora talked about the gardens, about the old oak floors and beautiful burgundy window treatments. Anne flipped through the pictures, little girls at play, a happy family. The sisters did many things, planted flowers in those gardens, played the instruments in that very room—one on the piano and one on the violin. Had it been just the parents and the sisters, it would have been the picture perfect family. But that third wheel, the darkness hovering unseen in the background, marred the fairytale.

CHAPTER 13

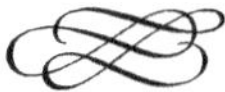

THE WORD HUNG in the air, suspended by disbelief.

"Murder?" Charlie said.

Anne shushed her sister, moving to the window where Charlie sat and lowering her voice to a barely detectable whisper.

"Yes, Charlie, I think she murdered her sisters!"

"Oh Anne, I don't know about that. I mean, she's kooky, but—"

"No. She's not just crazy. She's a psychopath. She basically admitted it, talking about how jealous she was, how her sisters ruined the family and this house."

Charlie shook her head, unconvinced.

"Charlie, seriously, the way she talked about them, her expression when she was telling me about their childhood. It's not normal, Charlie. Not okay. Something happened here."

"Did you ask her?"

"Hell no, I didn't! What was I gonna say? Accuse her, right after she pitched that vase at Penny? The woman is dangerously unstable, Charlie. We need to get the hell outta Dodge."

"This is insane, Anne."

"*She* is insane! Charlie, you need to trust me."

"I do trust you, it's just that… I think you've had a long day, and you're tired."

Anne huffed and crossed her arms. "There's something wrong here. Very wrong."

"Yeah, the woman is set in her weird old ways, but—"

"What are you hiding from me, Charlie?"

Charlie looked startled, her jaw dropping open and her eyes wide. Anne half regretted bringing it up, but she would have had to, eventually. Now seemed the time to lay it all out.

"What the hell do you mean, what am I hiding?"

"You know exactly what I mean," Anne said.

"I don't—"

"Don't bullshit me! I'm not a little girl anymore."

But she was that angry little girl, frustrated when her older sisters tried to shelter her, to keep things from her when all she wanted to do was know everything.

"Something happened to you out on that lawn when we first arrived. Then again in the bathroom. That same something keeps happening, and you need to tell me what it is."

"I…" Charlie trailed off, her eyes looking out at the lawn below.

You can tell me.

But when Charlie's teeth clenched together, Anne realized the drawbridge had been closed and locked tight.

"If there was something going on, I'd have told you," Charlie said.

"Liar," Anne said, her voice no longer a whisper.

"Pardon me?"

"You're lying. Just like you did when we were growing up, just like you did when you knew Emme wasn't okay."

"I didn't tell you about Emme because I wasn't sure. I didn't want to overreact, to see something that wasn't there."

"Why? Because we couldn't handle it? Couldn't face it? Were you embarrassed? See, this is the problem with you, Charlie. Never assertive, never facing things head on."

"Jesus Christ, Anne, it's not that."

"Then what? And what now? Why aren't you telling me what happened to you? Are you protecting me, or protecting yourself because you're worried I'll think you're as fucking insane as Emme was?"

Standing from the windowsill, Charlie threw her book at Anne. "Fuck you, you skag!"

Charlie grabbed a black cardigan and slipped on her runners before turning back to Anne.

"It's precisely what I said it was. I felt faint, passed out. I've been a little woozy on and off. It's stress. Because of fucking Emme!"

The tears were rolling in great gushes down Charlie's face. Anne wanted to reach out, to hold her and apologize and tell her they would leave this place and everything would be okay and things would go back to normal once they lulled into their routines again.

But Anne was done lying to herself. And to Charlie.

"I'm sorry to have upset you. I'm tired, but we've gotta face some stuff. We have to acknowledge what happened to Emme, what she did. And what is happening to us."

"And what is that?"

"We're depressed too. Just like Emme was. We knew she was. We all saw it, everyone! But it made us uncomfortable, so we didn't talk about it. Didn't want to hear the dark thoughts brewing in her head because it scared us. Because we were embarrassed, ashamed, uncomfortable."

Anne grabbed Charlie's shoulders and gave her a single shake.

"Time to fucking be uncomfortable. Talk about it, or we'll suffer the same fate, one way or another." Anne sobbed, her body heaving. "Awkward, angry, and uncomfortable is better than dead. Talk to me, Charlie."

"You don't get to tell me what we've got to do."

Charlie stormed out of the room, slamming the door behind her. Anne listened for the downstairs door to slam as well before crumpling to the bed and sobbing into her pillow.

Rocks sprayed from beneath the tires of the sedan as Charlie fishtailed out of the driveway, trying to leave some of her anger with the rubber on the road. Tensions had been high since Emme had died—long before that, even. It was bound to come to a head, and who better to lose your shit on than the ones closest to you.

Anne meant nothing by it.

And besides, she's not wrong.

Charlie had lied to her sister. Repeatedly. Lies of omission, direct lies, too, when she claimed that nothing was wrong. Everything was wrong. Emme's death was traumatic enough, let alone serving as a reminder of Charlie's own mortality, and the futile efforts of her adult life.

And now there was some sort of werewolf business to add to the fuckery.

The Goat's Moat was very much alive, a sizable crowd drinking and dancing, the band blaring folk tunes into the night. Charlie rolled the car into one of the sparse spots in the gravel lot and killed the engine. With her hands on the steering wheel, she thought about the door handle. Should she reach for it, go out into the world and face people after the exhausting day she'd had? Seemed like the last thing she should do. An introvert by nature, Charlie found people exhausting. That being said, they were also distracting. It would be difficult to think of wolves and dead sisters while trying to maintain small talk with strangers.

A few deep breaths later and Charlie was out of the car, walking towards the bar, her heart beating in her chest and lower lip threatening to tremble, signaling the tears to flow. By the time she had reached the building, she wanted nothing more than to turn around and jump back into the car, drive down the highway, and keep driving until she hit the trees or the ocean, whichever came first.

"Charlie!"

Bran's voice made it all melt away. So casual and

blissfully unaware of the turmoil within, he was a welcome ray of light.

"Hey," Charlie said.

He both surprised and thrilled her, wrapping her in a tight bear hug before setting her down on her toes.

"Flying solo tonight?" he asked, looking behind Charlie towards the car.

"Uh, yeah. Anne's tired. We went for a dive today."

"Oh right! Your dive! Cool. How did it go?"

"Ah, well, she dove. I vomited."

A hearty laugh exploded from deep within in Bran's chest. "I hear ya. I can't do ocean. Only axes, fires, and forest animals for me."

"Anne had her hands full with marine animals, that's for sure."

Charlie regaled Bran with tales of the deep, Anne's struggle with the Giant Pacific Octopus and the cold cock to the diver's cheek. She found herself animated and relaxed, and quite regretful about her heated exchange with her sister. Emotions were high, and Anne wasn't wrong. Charlie had just been sensitive about her own bullshit. Once she got back to Jutland House, she would apologize to Anne and come clean about her experiences since they'd arrived.

"Tequila?" Bran asked, pointing to the margarita machine.

"I'm thinking no," Charlie said, her mind on her sister.

"Classy tonight, are we?"

"As fuck."

Bran smirked and disappeared into the store. Charlie stood and stretched, the crisp air refreshing her. She strolled through the crowd, breathing in the smell of the campfire and the nearby pines. It was so beautiful, this outdoor oasis on the side on the woods. Within minutes, Bran was back, handing her a glass of wine.

"Merlot. Not the best there is, but a nice finish. From the Okanogan."

Charlie sipped it and nodded her approval. The chill was reaching her bones, so a glass of red would warm her just fine.

Charlie and Bran visited for hours, though to Charlie it felt like minutes, his story-telling and good humour providing the escape she so desperately needed. Every so often, Bran would lean against her, his shoulder against hers, the side of his hand on her outer thigh. When she made eye contact after a sly touch, he flushed a particularly glowing shade of red beneath his beard and suddenly found reason to examine his shoes.

Cute. Soft, funny, harmless.

Charlie hadn't wanted anyone in a very long time,

but she found both her body and mind responding to Bran.

The crowd thinned, the smattering of tourists filtering out into Ubers and hotel shuttles. Charlie polished off the bottom of her glass and set it on the bar.

"Thanks so much," she said to Bran, who was wiping down a picnic table.

"For what? Serving is my job."

She smiled, and felt her cheeks glow.

"Spending time with you is kinda cool," she said. "So thanks for that."

His hand was warm on her cheek. She leaned into it, closing her eyes and feeling his rough flesh. The soft brush of his beard tickled her face as his lips met hers, his tongue parting her mouth. Her chest heaved and breathing quickened, and she wrapped her arms around him, pulling him against her body. His chest was hard against her breasts, and she felt a throbbing between her legs; it was an ache she hadn't felt for quite some time.

When they pulled apart, Charlie was nearly out of breath. Reaching out, she ran her finger along his collar then down the middle of his chest, stopping on the button of his jeans.

"Charlie," he said, his voice trembling. "You've had a lot of wine."

"I have," she said, pressing her palm against the firmness in his jeans. "Hold this thought?"

"I'll hold it," he said.

After brushing his lips against hers again, he grabbed his phone and summoned an Uber.

"Don't worry," he said, reaching around and teasing the hair on the back of her neck. "I can swing by and get you or Anne tomorrow, bring you back to the car."

"I'm not worried," Charlie said, pulling him in for one last kiss.

She wanted to linger there forever, against his body, his warm breath in her mouth, but she knew she couldn't. She had to make decisions like this when she was sober.

Don't fuck this up, too.

"Look, I gotta take care of the stragglers," Bran said, hooking his thumb over his shoulder at the few drunks flopping around the fire, "so I'll say goodbye now. Uber'll pick you up at the road."

"No problem," she said.

And it wasn't. There were no problems now, no problems she couldn't tackle. She just needed to get out on her own, blow off some steam. And she had done just that, regret free.

But I will be back for more, she thought, watching Bran.

Giggling, she stumbled towards the road, the light of the patio disappearing behind the building as she dragged her feet up the gravel drive. Night was beautiful out here in the woods. Just like Jutland House, The Goat's Moat was isolated enough that the meager patio lighting didn't interfere with the stars and moonlight. Charlie closed her eyes and breathed deep, the taste of Bran still in her mouth.

She took another breath, the humidity thick in the air, and she coughed from the moisture. She coughed and coughed, sucking in air that wasn't so pleasant as Bran and the forest; it was the taste and stench of rot and decay—old, rancid meat.

It can't be.

After Charlie got the coughing under control, she scoured the parking lot behind her and the edge of the woods. There was very little movement, just the rustle of the trees and the soft arguments of drunken dilly-dalliers behind her. She stepped out onto the highway and looked towards the town, then down the road towards Jutland House.

There it was. The biped wolf, crooked and huge, standing in the middle of the dark highway. Its yellow eyes were larger than she remembered, and darker, but they still glowed like a full moon. The creature stood at an awkward angle, one shoulder drooped and the corresponding knuckle scraping against the pavement as the beast wavered from foot to foot. It was too dark to see it clearly, but Charlie could tell that its mouth was open, thick fluid and chunks of something pouring from its loose jowls.

Bran.

Her voice had no volume, though. In her mind she was screaming, her legs sprinting back behind The Goat's Moat and to the axe that Bran had stuck in the log. In reality, though, her feet stayed cemented in place, her voice choked off by terror. Even when the wolf dropped to all fours and stalked towards her, she couldn't will sound from her throat or movement from her limbs. Only once the slow pad of its feet became a faster lope did she start backing away, speeding up until she stumbled around and ran for the trees.

Why the trees? You fool! Stay on the road! Go back to the patio!

She circled around towards the fire, but there wasn't a soul to be found, only flankers in the air and Bran's voice echoing from the inside of the store. She spun around, intent on sprinting for the back door, but the wolf-beast pounced between her and the building, its hackles up and drool pouring from what looked like several rows of sharp, jagged teeth.

Into the woods Charlie ran, veering off the path into the thick brush, hoping the density of the trees would slow her predator, grab its fur at hold it at bay.

But the sounds of snapping and cracking behind her told her this thing was a freight train that wouldn't be stopped.

Faster and deeper she ran, the trees overhead blocking out what little light the moon was trying to spill. The chill had reached her bones, and her joints screamed in agony, the tension of fear and the exertion of the run slowing her pace. The trail was gone, only heavy underbrush and towering oaks in its place.

BOOM. BOOM. BOOM. Her heart pounded in her ears, crashed against her chest, and throbbed behind her eyes.

Why didn't I call out for Bran?

Why didn't I go straight for the building in the first place?

Why didn't I just stay at Jutland House, and be honest with Anne, and face my demons?

Charlie stopped running.

Because I'm a coward.

The sounds of the chase had ceased. There was no breaking and cracking ringing through the trees. The only sound Charlie could hear was her own laboured breathing, the frantic throbbing of her pulse in her ears, and the rustling of the leaves. Branches like claws reached out all around her, their sharp fingers threatening to cut her, but there was no sign of teeth or eyes or fur. Charlie held her breath, to tame the alcohol and fear in her system, trying to hone her senses to the world around her, to the slightest minutia of forest life. The twitter of a bird, a small hiccup of wind, the soft brush of fur against the back of her neck…

Like Bran's beard, she thought as the scruff brushed over her flesh, gentle but firm. She turned into the fur, and came face to face with the eyes, as bright and glowing as the harvest moon.

Meat dripped off its lips, a recent kill still lingering between its teeth. A low rumble quaked in its belly, a combination of rage and laughter.

"What are you?" Charlie whispered.

It tilted its head, its large ears perked at the sound of Charlie's voice.

"How can you be?" Charlie asked.

It huffed, barking low, and ran its nose over Charlie, its rough tongue pulling over her collarbone, down between her breasts, and along the seam of her jeans. When it rose to her face again, Charlie was convulsing —from fear, from the bitter cold… from all of it.

"I can't die this way," Charlie said, so upset she couldn't even cry.

"*No die.*"

The creature's jaw moved in unnatural, jarring motions, its throat strained by the formation of the words. Out of shock, Charlie's trembling ceased, and she tried to process what she'd just heard and seen.

"What?" Charlie said.

"*Sayfe.*"

The creature poked Charlie several times in the chest and repeated the word.

"*Sayfe. You. Sayfe.*"

Is that compassion in those eyes? Charlie pondered.

It didn't hurt when the creature's teeth sank into Charlie's throat.

Who are you? Charlie wondered.

It didn't scare Charlie when hot blood flowed from her severed neck, pouring down her shirt and soaking her clothing.

She means me no harm, Charlie thought, as the creature ripped her to shreds and left her carcass on the forest floor.

CHAPTER 14

"I'M SURE 'TIS NOTHIN'," Penny said as she tried to hand Anne another cup of coffee. Anne waved it away, watching the driveway and pulling at a single curl until her head hurt.

"But we're out here, together, and she's gone," Anne said, anger and worry rising in her throat like acid.

"She's banging a dude," Penny said. "Or drunk and sleepin' it off in the car."

Anne glared at her, then resumed her watch of the front yard and driveway from her perch in the music room. When Anne had woken at the crack of dawn, she hadn't realized straight away that Charlie wasn't there. Not until she had used the bathroom and came back to the bedroom did she notice that Charlie's bed was still made from the day before, and her runners were gone. After throughly grilling both Gwen and Penny, Anne realized that Charlie had not returned after her angry exit the night before.

"What did you fight about?" Penny asked.

"Oh, stupid shit," Anne said. "Sister stuff."

"Ain't no stupid stuff, if it was worth fightin' about."

Anne stared off, trying not to cry.

"It'll all be fine," Penny said. "She'll be back."

"Yeah."

Anne didn't know whether to believe it or not.

Where would she go? Would she really just leave me here?

Anything was possible. She and Charlie had both been in emotional turmoil since Emme's death, and both of them seemed to be at an impasse in their own lives. But would Charlie really kill their relationship, stranding her here on the island?

No. She wouldn't do that. Something's wrong.

"What's all this about, then?"

Isadora came around the stairs in her crimson gown, the train flowing behind, as always. Her mood seemed much softer, her question a simple inquisition.

"Charlie stayed out last night," Anne said, studying the woman for disapproval, ready to pounce.

"Hmm," Isadora said. Her scowl told Anne that

she was passing some serious judgement, but she kept her opinions to herself. "You look worried."

Anne nodded. "I am. Despite what you think, this is unusual for Charlie. And we had a fight last night—"

"Oh dear," Isadora said. She sounded concerned, but looked secretly delighted. "What about?"

The fact that you're a murderer.

"Oh, just sister stuff."

Isadora considered it, studying Anne's face before looking out the window. "Well, I'm sure once cooler heads prevail, she'll resurface. Then you can sort out these petty differences and go about your business."

Train swooshing behind her, Isadora walked down the hall towards the dining room, summoning for breakfast as she passed by the kitchen. Anne looked back out the window, determined to remain on surveillance for the day, when Isadora called out.

"Oh my!"

Anne ran down the hall to the dining room, and Penny burst out of the kitchen, looking around to see what was happening. Isadora was standing at the window, looking out at the back yard. Anne joined her at the window, trying to see what had elicited such a reaction.

"Oh," Anne said.

Walking up the lawn, tattered shoes in hand, was Charlie, looking like she's been put through the ringer.

Her clothes were caked in dirt and partially shredded, and her short hair was a matted crumple on top of her head. Her skin was waxy and grey, her eyes dark and sunken into her head.

"Charlie, oh my god!"

Anne ran out the patio doors to greet Charlie as she reached the patio steps. Though looking like the reanimated dead, Charlie smiled, her eyes bright and clear.

"Anne, I'm so sorry about last night."

Charlie threw her arms around her sister, holding her close and stroking her hair. The smell off Charlie was horrid, a combination of dank forest and spoiled food.

"Jesus fuck, Charlie, what in the hell happened to you?"

Charlie pulled back and surprised Anne with a smile as wide as her face. "Had a rowdy night."

With a wink, Charlie passed by Anne, Isadora, and Penny, and disappeared into the house.

"Well then," Penny said, hands on hips, "she had quite the bender, didn't she?"

A shiver walked like fingers up Anne's spine. She looked over at Isadora and saw something she hadn't seen before on the cold-hearted bitch's stone facade: terror.

Eight slices of bacon, four sausage links, and two eggs later, Charlie let out a huge belch into her serviette and laughed.

"'Scuse me," she said, then helped herself to more scrambled eggs. "Seems I've worked up quite the appetite."

"Huh," Anne said.

Charlie had spent half an hour in the bathroom, showering and freshening up. Instead of returning to their bedroom when she was done, as Anne had expected—they had stuff to hash out, after all—Charlie had gone straight downstairs and dove into breakfast.

"I was worried about you, Charlie."

Charlie huffed. "Worried? Why ever would you be worried?"

Anne gave her a hard look. "Charlie, where the hell were you?"

"Blowing off some steam."

"So I gather. Where did you go?"

"The Goat's Moat."

"For the whole night?"

Charlie lips curled into a cheeky grin. Anne did not smile with her.

"Seriously, Charlie?"

Another piece of bacon found its way to Charlie's mouth, despite the fact that her cheeks were already stashed with food. With exaggerated enjoyment, Charlie savoured every morsel, slowly, her gaze occasionally drifting to Anne as she devoured her breakfast. Charlie looked at Penny, and nod towards the kitchen was all the request Penny needed.

"Seriously?" Anne said.

There was no answer, other than the squishing and grinding of bacon between Charlie's teeth, and the occasional groan of indulgence through a mouthful of greasy breakfast fare. Charlie's odd behaviour was unsettling enough to make Anne's stomach gurgle in disgust. Anne pushed her plate away and looked towards the window where Isadora hovered like a carrion over death, watching Charlie's every move. Anne could almost taste her discomfort, her scrutiny, her... *fear?*

"There ya go, missus." Penny set a fresh plate of sausage and hash in front of Charlie, who promptly stabbed her fork into the mass of food, shoveling it, consuming it without much chewing. Shifting from foot to foot, Penny looked over at Anne, then at Isadora, who released her with a nod. Without hesitation, Penny disappeared into the kitchen, looking over her shoulder at Charlie who was hunched over her plate, chewing and smiling.

It was awful. Weird. Uncomfortable. Anne could take it no longer. The heavy wooden chair squawked beneath her as she pushed away from the table, and Isadora jumped from the sound. Charlie did not. She just kept eating and smiling, smiling and eating. Anne stormed from the room, up the stairs, and down the hall until the house shook from the slam of her bedroom door.

LIKE A TONGUE, abrasive and irritating, dragging up the ridgesof her spine and niggling inside her eardrums, the sound of Charlie's consumption tinkered with Isadora's nerves. Not one to be easily rattled, Isadora detested the sensation, and hated this woman who had slithered directly beneath her skin.

What has gotten into you? Isadora wondered, her eyes glued to her ravenous guest.

With the younger woman gone in a tantrum that had carried her to the bedroom above, and Penny dismissed from her duties, Isadora and Charlie were alone in the room, stuck in a speechless stasis.

Isadora didn't like it, not one bit. These strange women, coming in off the highway, not a simple vacation or rest stop, but an unusual and macabre purpose. *A dead sister? How morbid.* And now this, a sudden shift in the eldest one, some tomfoolery that crept into Jutland House like venomous ivy.

A heavy clip, a clop, and another clip carried Isadora across the hardwood floor, banging and rattling her cane to draw Charlie's attention away from her gluttony. But it did not. No matter how hard Isadora struck her cane on the floor, Charlie's attention did not waver from the food, even when Isadora came to a stop directly behind her chair. Shimmering chocolate, with the occasional wisp of white, Charlie's hair gleamed in the overhead lighting. Isadora bent down, admiring the thickness and youth of those tresses, breathing deep the rose and honey conditioner. But beneath that feminine perfume, there was something. Something else. The woods, but not the trees. Not the loam or the fungus, or the damp dogwood and cedar.

With a sudden jolt, the top of Charlie's chair struck Isadora in the ribs, knocking the wind out of her with a little huff. Isadora stumbled back, grasping her midsection, steadying herself on her cane.

"I do say!" Isadora said.

"I do say you's in my way," Charlie said as she dabbed her mouth with the serviette folded in her lap.

In a fluid, sensual motion, Charlie slithered out of her chair and turned, moving gracefully until she was nose-to-nose with Isadora.

Those eyes, Isadora thought, her mind jumping,

clawing through recent memory. *Were those always her eyes?*

The amber fire that flickered in Charlie's glare emanated a heat—real or imagined—that caused Isadora to wince. And Charlie's breath, ripe with coffee and thick with meat, blew directly into her mouth.

"Something to say, old woman?" Charlie said, head cocked.

Is that... you?

Isadora smoothed the front of her robe and puffed out her chest, holding her head high. The posturing inflated her ego and confidence back to a distended state. "You shan't talk to me that way. You are a very rude woman, and not so young as to not know any better."

Charlie moved forward, but Isadora did not back off. She didn't even lean back on her heels.

She will not intimidate me, this brute.

Contemplation held Charlie in place for a moment, and Isadora held her breath. It was the kitchen door that deflated the standoff, when Penny burst through with another pot of coffee.

"Oh, I's sorry to bother, I jus' figured..." Penny held up the pot, then looked at the empty cups on the table.

"That's fine," Isadora said, not taking her eyes off

her opponent. "Breakfast is finished. You may start clearing."

Penny hovered in Isadora's peripheral for a moment before scurrying along the table, gathering plates and silverware, as quiet as a mouse. Charlie took a step back, but kept her eyes trained on Isadora all the way to the door. Even as Charlie passed out the door and out of sight, and even as Isadora could hear her footfalls carry her up the stairs and down the hall to the bedroom, she could still feel those eyes bearing down on her.

"Everything all right, ma'am?" Penny stood by the table, worrying the tea towel in her hands, watching Isadora.

"Fine, yes. Fine. Rude woman, is all. Now shoo, get your work done."

"Yes ma'am."

Isadora walked to the window as Penny moved around her, cleaning and clearing. She barely noticed though. Her mind and thoughts were trained on the forest beyond the perimeter of the yard, and those yellow eyes.

"What's your problem?" Charlie said.

Charlie closed the door behind her with vigour—

not quite a slam, but loud enough to get Anne's attention.

"I might ask you the same thing," Anne answered.

"Why? Because I was eating breakfast?"

"It was how, Charlie. And you know it."

"What I know," Charlie said as she flopped down on her bed, "is that I am stuffed and exhausted."

It was unnerving, the way Charlie's mouth was fixed in a crooked smile, the way her cheeks were flushed and her belly bloated from an uncharacteristic overindulgence. Even her hair was different, a gleam and a fullness that hadn't been there before.

"Where did you go?" Anne asked.

"The Goat's Moat."

"So you said. How did you get back here?"

Charlie opened her mouth to answer, but it snapped shut again. Her brow furrowed and her smile faded.

"I… walked."

"Walked?"

"Suppose so."

"Bullshit. It's too far."

Charlie fluffed her fingers through her hair, looking surprised at the thickness herself.

"Charlie, did you see Bran last night?"

"I think so."

Charlie held her head and laid down on the bed on her stomach.

"Jesus, Charlie, what happened to you?"

Charlie didn't answer. Not really. Her response was a growl, a rattling expulsion of air as her breathing slowed and her lungs heaved out a gentle snore.

"Charlie?"

But she was out, her hand dropped off the side of the bed, her fingers grazing the floor as soft, rhythmic snores passed over her lips. Anne watched her hands, those pale pink nails brushing the hardwood. She moved in closer, close enough to see the thick, black dirt and dry blood caked under Charlie's sharp nails.

"What did you do?"

Glowing embers littered the ground, radiating heat to the stormy sky. The stench of burning flesh was wet and dank, filling Anne's nostrils and coating her tongue. On the horizon she saw movement, a heaving, pumping mass in the blackened tress atop a black mountain peak. Though her flesh peeled off, melting onto the embers, she pushed forward, needing to know what manner of beast lurked in the distance. A feral howl blasted in her ears as the beast raised its head, wet globs of sinewy flesh drooling from its jowls.

Still she walked. The stale stench of blood and old sex

marked the trail to the beast, evidence of its path strewn about the landscape. A Wendigo lay screaming on the side of the road, its own antlers impaled through its eyes, freeing a stream of pus and eye jelly that flowed violently over the landscape in rapids that crashed over boulders of bone and ruin.

A few more steps and she came upon the Sasquatch, scalped, blood spurting from every pore. More than the pain, the anguish of being scalped bit by bit, Anne could feel the anguish of its humiliation. A creature long since protected by mystery lay here exposed, naked, vulnerable. And utterly unremarkable.

A Sluagh flapped by, sprays of blood misting from the tips of its clipped wings as it careened to the ground, crashing in a ball of flames.

A Gorgon writhed in the center of a lake of blood, being eaten alive by her own snakes, each forked tongue licking off bits of flesh as if they were fluttering, swiping razor blades.

When Anne reached the peak, it was there. Howling, braying a feral cry of pain, of victory, of pleasure. The front of its massive chest was coated in bits of blood and bone, its fur matted with all manner of gore.

It was hot and horrible, all that death and pain. But behind Anne came a radiating chill, a wash of refreshing pleasure that soothed her soul and aroused her body. Behind her, in the distance, the crimson hellscape faded to an ethereal indigo, green waving foliage and emerald air swirling in an icy, glittering mist. And tentacles, long and sliver, pulsating, reached for her, beckoning her, longing for her. Anne reached back, her fingers grazing the tips of the tentacles, and her flesh turned, crackling and splitting, revealing silver flesh beneath. Her vision wavered, rippling like water, then this new world became clear.

They weren't suffering, these beasts of myth and lore. They were flourishing, drunk on the spoils of horror. There was no land, only mounds and pillars of feather and flesh, scale and shell, talon and bone. It was horrible and beautiful.

"They belong. You belong."

Emme's voice startled Anne awake. She shot out of bed, her shirt front soaked in sweat and tears. A quick inspection of the room assured Anne that all was as it should be. Charlie was on her back, groaning in a fitful sleep, and the room was still and devoid of any creatures of the night. Or dead sisters.

Anne walked to the window and looked over the indigo water, a slice of the moon casting silver over the gentle waves. Each heave and splash carried with it a note, stringing together a tune both melancholy and serene. Anne touched her cheek to the window, listening carefully to test the reality of the melody. Like the cracking of a whip, the glass against Anne's face split and she jumped back. A crow sat on the windowsill, its eyes red, a wet streak of crimson on its beak.

"What…"

The crow tap, tap, tapped its beak open and shut as

if speaking, and Anne noticed tufts of black hair on its tongue.

Charlie's hair.

A scream brewed in Anne's throat, but a blink washed away the horror. The window was intact, the crow was gone, and the song was silenced. All that remained was Charlie's soft snores and the whisper of a breeze outside. Anne slid back under her covers, pulling them to her chin, eyes wide and mind racing.

CHAPTER 15

The sun went from low to high, and Charlie slept away the remainder of the morning and half the afternoon. Anne watched Charlie breathe as she half-heartedly read a book in the windowsill while focusing on every little movement from Charlie's bed. It was a fitful sleep; at times Charlie would moan and cringe as if there was a heavy weight on her chest, and once she even lashed out, clawing at the air over the bed at some invisible hanging assailant.

Many things scrolled through Anne's mind:

A head injury?

Trauma?

Is this mental illness? A reaction to the pressure?

Was she attacked? Did she attack someone?

Anything was possible. The stress had been bottled

up, forced down to the bottom of their guts and crammed all the way to the tips of their toes. Emme's death, their own mortality, their own lives weighing them down into the bowels of their own anxiety. And it was at a fever pitch. Until this trip was over, and Emme was really gone, they would exist in this state of limbo, unable to move on, to take the next steps, whatever they may be.

And that was part of the problem, if not the problem itself. Saying goodbye to Emme meant not lingering in their grief anymore. It meant that they would have to each press play on their lives again, get moving, make decisions, start living. But neither Anne nor Charlie knew how to live.

Anne stared crying, softly, silently, watching her sister's contorting face as she tossed and turned and mumbled on her bed. As horrible as it was, lingering in their grief for Emme, Anne wished they could stay there, where they were permitted to be sad and unreasonable, far removed from the expectations of everyday life. The thought of moving past it was worse, having to function again on a foundation of grief that would always be there like a basement, a gaping hole beneath everything in their lives.

Before Anne's despair could spiral out of control, Charlie shot straight up in bed, a wet gasp bursting from her mouth.

"The hell?" Anne said.

Anne ran to the bed and took Charlie's hands.

"Where am I?" Charlie asked.

Charlie was panicked, her eyes darting around the room and her pulse visible on her neck. Anne rested a hand on her cheek, gently stroking her face.

"Jutland House, Charlie. The island. For Emme."

Charlie's breathing slowed and her eyes glazed with tears. They were wild, those eyes, examining the room and then Anne. After a few moments of silence, Charlie drew some deep breaths and hung her head.

"Oh fuck."

The words came out on a sob. Charlie collapsed forward into Anne, wrapping her arms around her sister and shuddering.

"It's okay," Anne said, stroking Charlie's hair, which was soaked with sweat. "It's been a stressful year, and this trip is just fucking surreal."

Charlie nodded against Anne's chest and her breathing calmed.

"Tell you what," Anne said. "Why don't we head into town, grab some food, hit the boutiques and spend money on shit we'd never buy."

Charlie sniffled and swiped the back of her hand against her snotty nose.

"Do you hate me?" Charlie said.

"Never!" Anne said, holding Charlie's face. "We will get through this. We will be fine."

But as Charlie hugged into Anne again, Anne caught sight of those nails, of the debris caked underneath, and caught a whiff of that smell, raw and rotten and horrible.

How will we ever be fine again?

LUNCH WAS DELICIOUS, but Charlie was shocked she didn't feel like a bloated mess after the breakfast she'd downed. Though it was late by the time she and Anne jumped in their Uber, close to three in the afternoon, Charlie figured she still should have been full from breakfast. She hadn't arrived back at Jutland House until midmorning, but the amount she ate should have kept her stuffed until nighttime.

It was troubling, the loss of time. On the drive into town, Charlie racked her brain, trying to recall how she'd arrived at that breakfast table from deep in the woods, after being absent for an entire night in the wilds of the island. But that's the thing. She figured she wasn't lost in the woods, and hadn't hoofed it home from the Goat's Moat. Probably, likely, she had never made it away from that campsite, that she and Bran had...

"What are you thinking about?" Anne asked.

Did I have that much to drink? Would I really have just…

Never one to be flippant about her sexuality, Charlie couldn't imagine simply getting plastered and falling into bed with a man she had just met, at a time when grief poisoned her desires.

I have more sense than that. Don't I?

"Not much," Charlie finally answered. "Just thinking about last night."

Anne didn't respond. She stayed very quiet, and Charlie wondered if she was holding her breath. It was almost comical. Anne wanted so badly to know what her sister had been up to, no doubt hoping for a raunchy rendezvous or drunken stupor. Anne had always accused Charlie of being uptight, of holding back and not living life to the fullest. But Charlie had no regrets, not really. She had stayed safe, quiet, comfortable.

But not happy. Happiness takes a certain degree of risk. Charlie was satisfied with content.

Am I?

The drive stayed quiet for several minutes, until Anne gave up and asked the driver to turn on the radio to suffocate the silence. When they arrived at the Goat's Moat, Charlie strained to see signs of life behind the building or into the campsite. Anne laughed.

"Shut up," Charlie said.

"Whatcha looking for?"

"Wildlife."

Despite her best efforts, Charlie couldn't help but smile. Anne smiled back and gave her a pop on the shoulder. Bran sidled up to the sisters as the Uber pulled out of the lot.

"Ladies," he said. He gave Anne a brief hug before turning to Charlie and giving her a soft peck on the lips. "I have your keys behind the bar. No troubles getting home?"

Charlie felt her neck, caressing a phantom pain tingling on her skin. "Would appear not."

"Geez, really?" Bran said. "You seemed okay when you left. Were you that drunk?"

"I guess the day caught up with me."

"Happened to me before. Fell asleep in a cab, and couldn't remember getting home," Bran said.

"Yeah," Charlie said.

After an awkward pause, Bran started towards the building. "I'll, uh, grab your keys then."

"Thanks," Charlie said.

As Bran walked away, Anne linked arms with Charlie.

"Yeah. You guys hooked up," Anne said.

"I don't know. I really don't think I was that drunk."

"He's not that bad."

"That's not what I mean! I'd remember."

"You don't remember the ride home?"

Charlie looked at the highway, then out into the woods. She could feel the crunch of the forest floor beneath her feet, the branches as they dragged along her skin as the forest got thicker and thicker. Anne looked out into the woods as well, dropping Charlie's arm.

"You came around the back of Jutland House, though. Not the road…" Anne said, trailing off. "Well, I dunno what happened to you, Charlie," Anne said, "but I hope it was good."

"So do I."

THEY ROLLED into town around dinnertime, but neither of them were hungry. To fuel the remainder of the day, they popped into a coffee shop and got a couple lattes to go. In the window next door, a burlap model was draped in a stunning, aqua blue dress trimmed with green embroidery. Charlie thought it would look very lovely on Anne, with her fair skin, red curls, and dusting of freckles.

"I think you should try that on," Charlie said,

linking arms with Anne and guiding her to the boutique.

Anne didn't resist. "I certainly will! If you try on something, too."

Charlie groaned, but agreed to find something to appease her sister.

The little bell hanging from the door jingled as they entered, and a portly woman with large hair popped up from behind the counter.

"Welcome to Vera's!" she chimed, sharp as the bell. "You ladies just having a gander, or are you looking for something in particular?"

"Just browsing," Charlie said, avoiding eye contact.

Anne, ever the socialite, moved in for a handshake. "My sister here, Charlie, saw that dress in the window. I'd love to give it a try."

"Oh that one would look amazing with your ginger locks," Vera said. She went to the rack and started sifting through blues until she found the size she deemed appropriate for Anne.

"You too," Anne said, jamming an elbow into Charlie's ribs.

"Yeah yeah."

Charlie ran her fingers over the clothes, walking up the aisles, perusing the colours and sparkles and textures. Once Anne was settled away in a fitting room,

Charlie stopped the charade, and stood waiting at the counter.

"You trying something too?" Vera said as she waddled behind the counter.

Charlie opened her mouth to answer, but was struck by a heavy odour that stole her breath. She gagged, not because the smell was bad, but because of its potency—a thick aroma that assaulted her mouth and nose. The source of the smell became clear when Vera bent down and took a hefty bite of Pho from a take away container behind the counter—lemongrass beef from the smell of it.

Charlie wanted to answer her, or at least walk away and select some outfit to appease Anne, but she couldn't. She was cemented in place, saliva pooling under her tongue, her stomach roaring in want of the food.

"Everything all right dear?"

Vera closed the lid of the takeaway container and wiped her chin with a serviette. Charlie turned her head and closed her eyes, trying to rid her mind of the smells, but she was overcome. She stumbled away from the counter, clutching her belly as it protested leaving the proximity of the food.

After reaching the other side of the store, Charlie was able to gather herself and offer Vera some reassurance that she was, in fact, not insane.

"I'm fine," Charlie said, her voice shaking.

With the food out of range, she felt better. Energized, even. She started looking through the racks with purpose, all the colours and textures, sensitive to the richness and brightness of the plethora of clothing. Vera came around the corner, holding up a soft silver dress with embroidered yellow flowers.

"This would look lovely on you, that dark pixie cut of yours. And you're so slender."

Charlie huffed in the direction of the delicate dress and pulled a different one off the rack.

"I'd like to try this."

Vera raised a brow but maintained her smile, taking the garment from Charlie and leading her back to the fitting room. As the door to the fitting room shut, Charlie heard Anne's door open.

"Charlie?"

"Be right out."

Anne was surprised that Charlie was actually trying something on. Her sister was a tomboy, and getting her to shop for clothes was like pulling teeth. When the door to Charlie's fitting room opened, Anne gasped.

"You don't like it?" Charlie asked.

Charlie's voice was wrong. Flat. Monotone. Deep.

A long, slender leg stepped out of the fitting room, followed by a shimmering, muscular body. Charlie sashayed over to the three-way mirror and spun around in a circle. The blood-red fabric of the sheer dress fanned out, teasing a peek of her muscular thighs.

"What do you think?" Charlie asked.

Your breasts are full, swollen.

You are taller.

Where did those muscles come from?

"Anne?"

"Yeah, uh…"

Anne's mouth hung open, words caught until Vera touched her on the shoulder.

"It's, lovely," Anne said. "Well, no, lovely isn't quite right… Charlie, this isn't you."

"What?"

"It's not you. It's risky, it's provocative, it's—"

"Everything I want," Charlie said.

The way Charlie punctuated her words with a sharp glare chilled Anne to her core. A smile spread across Charlie's face, her lips pulling back from her large, white teeth.

Anne nodded. "Yes, it looks amazing on you, though. I'm just not used to seeing you…"

"That's right," Charlie said, nodding at the reflection in the mirror. "You aren't used to seeing me."

With a final twirl of the fabric, Charlie was in the fitting room, door shut, whistling a merry tune. The red dress spilled over the top of the door like a waterfall of blood.

"Be a dear and ring that up, would you?" Charlie said before continuing to whistle.

Vera reached for the dress, wincing as if the fabric might scorch her fingertips, and hurried it over the register. Charlie appeared a moment later, credit card drawn and cocked at the till. With the transaction complete, Charlie strutted out the door like a proud lion carting its kill.

"The fuck was all that?" Anne demanded.

The car hugged the curve, pushing Charlie back in her seat as she pressed her toe on the gas pedal, her heart pounding.

"What do you mean?"

"Charlie, c'mon. That dress. Your attitude."

"What's the problem? You've been preaching about living life and letting go. I'm just lettin' my hair down."

"Yes, but—"

"But what? It's a nice dress, isn't it?"

"And the way you… Charlie, something's wrong. You're different."

"Because I'm not moping?"

"Because you're strutting around like cock of the walk! Because your skin is different, you… you're… bigger. Taller. Something's fucking up, okay? I know it doesn't make any sense, but—"

"You're jealous."

"I'm fucking what?"

"Jealous."

"Like hell, I am!"

"You can't stand for me to be happy. You never could."

"Happy over a fucking slutty dress? It's odd, don't you think?"

"You've never been satisfied, Anne. Always trying something new, always the risk taker. Now ol' Charlie is taking a few risks, and you can't stand it."

"What in the bloody hell are you—"

"Anne, you can't hold down a job. You've moved five times in as many years. You leap from relationship to relationship, using friends and lovers like kleenex. You are an addict, Anne, even without the fucking drugs."

"Goddamn you!"

Charlie felt like laughing and crying all at the same time. The words were hers, but they flew out of her mouth at a rate and pitch she had little control over. She didn't mean to hurt her sister, but she liked it.

"You," Anne spat. "Miss play it safe. You are stagnant, stuck in the same, roach-infested apartment in your safe little bubble, at your boring little job, trudging away, day after day, waiting to die."

"It's stable. I'm a responsible adult."

"You are purposeless. You are going nowhere. Waiting. Nothing more. Just like Emme, though she had the initiative to do something about it."

The car screeched to a stop.

Silence swelled. Anne's hands were over her mouth a moment too late to silence her cruel words.

A lump swelled in Charlie's throat, a tumor thick with rage, with devastation, with adrenaline.

"Get out."

Anne didn't argue. She threw the door open with force and stumbled into the ditch. The door had barely slammed shut before Charlie pinned it, throwing a spray of gravel as she whipped a u-turn and sped back towards town.

CHAPTER 16

IT FELT good to blast down the highway with the windows open and the wind ruffling her hair. Everything was a haze, the forest flying by in Charlie's peripheral, the glowing center line reflecting the headlights in the dusk. Out of the corner of her eye, Charlie spied the red dress peeking out of the bag on the back seat.

With a sharp yank, Charlie pulled the vehicle onto the shoulder.

Everything was odd, wrong.

The metal of the door handle felt heavy and cold under Charlie's fingertips. The night air stole her breath, seeping into every pore, every organ. She walked around the car to the passenger side, sliding her t-shirt and jeans off with every step, then her bra, a pointed toe tossing her panties into the woods. The red fabric slid over her flesh like butter. Her hands slid down her body, tracing the lines of newly developed muscle and plump, supple skin…

"Need a hand there, missy?"

Charlie turned towards the voice.

It was a man, slender and gangly, face gaunt and smug. He had but four yellowed teeth in his head and a greasy, grey mullet that gathered on the shoulders of his stained, navy jacket.

"I's good with cars, if that be yer problem. I gots a farm up the way. Do all sorts of tinkering."

He dragged his tongue across his chapped lips as he looked Charlie up and down, no doubt imagining her inside and out.

"Now there, little honey. Don't be shy. Name's Robert."

With a hand extended, he took a step towards her. She could smell those fingers, his nails caked with grime and pig leavings, the stale aroma of woman lingering on his saggy body.

"That's a real purdy dress, there. Definitely shows off your… assets."

With his eyes locked on her chest, he stepped closer, his hand hovering above her erect nipples. She took a step back, and his other hand snapped around her forearm.

"Now now, sweetie. Play nice and you might just enjoy yourself. We can stay here, or you can come back to the farm."

The look of surprise on his face was almost comical, Charlie thought, as she licked her own lips and pinched his fly between her fingers. With a sharp tug, his pants were around his ankles, and his shaft squeezed firmly in her hand.

"Like that?" Charlie cooed.

His answer was a thin ribbon of drool dangling from his lower lip and a feeble nod. His head tilted back as she squeezed and stroked.

"Or like this?"

With surprisingly little effort, Charlie's nails pieced Robert's scrotum until they tapped each other. Then, in one violent but smooth motion, she ripped his entire package off his body and held it in front of his face.

He didn't scream.

He didn't breathe.

He stared, slack jawed, eye wide in horror as Charlie licked the blood from the severed manhood before tossing it into the woods. His hands fumbled at his crotch, his only concern as Charlie took her sharp nails and swiped them across his throat. One hand on his crotch and one on his neck, Robert wavered on his feet, his mouth moving but no words coming out.

Charlie kissed him on the cheek, leaving a splotch

of blood, then gracefully ducked into her car. As she pulled away, she caught the satisfying image of the man crumpling to the ground, and heard the agonizing mewls of a neutered animal reverberating through the woods.

THE NIGHT WAS CHILLY, too chilly to be walking such a distance outdoors, Anne thought as she stomped towards Jutland House. The conversation screamed in her mind. Charlie's behaviour, though odd, was nothing compared to Anne's own callous remarks.

Guilt and panic worked itself to a boiling point the farther from her sister she walked, and by the time Anne reached Jutland House, not even its beauty could calm her frazzled nerves. Anne tried to focus on the flowers shimmering in the moonlight, the blue grass beckoning her to linger. She walked around to the backyard and sat on a stone bench overlooking the water. The last thing she needed was to be inside, the claustrophobic confines of the house a boa constricting her. It was a still night, the water silver glass beneath the glow of the moon. She stared, hoping for a ripple, but it remained an unbroken reflection.

Then she heard bells.

A crystal ringing through the air.

Looking out over the water, Anne tried to spy a boat or campers across the way. But the water remained undisturbed, and the woods stood silent.

The sound continued, a gentle crescendo, a haunting lilt. Someone was crooning a ballad in a minor key, throat open, projecting over the ocean. Anne was drawn to the sound. On bare feet she shuffled through cool grass, across sharp rocks, and sunk into wet sand as she waded into the water.

It was beautiful, the song, wordless but full of stories, a high yet guttural melody that sounded like diamonds. In the distance, Anne saw a stain of white floating on the midnight water. No amount of squinting or straining would sharpen the image, so Anne walked out. The water lapped against Anne's shins, then her knees, thighs, and upward until she was submerged to her neck, the surf nipping at her face. She reached, her slender fingers white as bone in the moonlight, and grasped the specter floating on the surface.

It was a doll, weathered and waterlogged, its ivory dress tufts of shredded gossamer. The paint on its eyes was gone, leaving it with a blank, hollow stare.

A wave heaved and splashed Anne in the face. With a lick of her lips, she was overwhelmed by the salt of the sea, a bitterness that took her breath away. Sputtering and coughing, she turned back to land, gulping in great breaths. She wasn't standing, but treading water, the shore a panorama of lights in the distance.

Panic. She bobbed below the water, poking her toes down like a ballerina, trying to touch sand but finding only the abyss. Floundering and flailing, the darkness below threatened to swallow her, its gaping nothingness an overwhelming vacuum of dread. Anne's screams filled with water that weighed down her belly, dragging her beneath. The harder she fought, the faster she sank, a thousand grasping hands pulling her down, down…

Something wrapped around her calves, a slippery snake, suckling her skin, pulling and speeding the descent. But with that rubbery touch came peace, warmth, calm. As the snakes caressed her, running up and down her legs, more snakes coiled around her arms and neck, kissing, pressing.

Tentacles.

Anne opened her eyes.

The darkness was gone, replaced by glittering pockets of amethyst and emerald, indigo and sapphire. The world beneath the waves was alive with light and beauty, fish of every colour darting this way and that, kelp swaying with the surge like clusters of hair.

And her.

The most beautiful… *woman?*… Anne had ever seen. And also the most horrible.

Skin glowing white, long, thick tendrils of indigo hair swaying in the currents, eyes solid silver. Her body was curvaceous, shimmering flesh accented by violet nipples and a tuft of indigo hair where her… *labia?*… was.

But this *woman* had no limbs. Not as Anne knew them. In place of each human limb this woman had two tentacles, long and slender, peppered with silvers suckers that flexed and contracted with the swell of her breath.

Her black lips curled into a smirk, and her mouth opened, revealing a hollow cavern framed by several rows of sharpened teeth. Anne opened her mouth to scream, but only bubbles blew out. The woman mimicked the scream, but her breath carried sound, a banshee wail that boomed through the ocean like a sonic blast.

Anne squeezed her eyes shut and covered her ears. The sound was terrible, the sensation overwhelming. She was heavy but floating, drawing in water but full of air. A soft touch coaxed her eyes open. The woman was closer now, close enough to caress Anne's arms and legs with the tips of her tentacles.

Hello.

A knee-jerk reaction, Anne opened her mouth to speak, forgetting she would not project any sound. But, to her surprise, she did.

"Help me," Anne said, the voice from her belly belonging to a child, alone and scared.

Help you?

"Where am I?'

In the Pacific.

How?

You came from the surface.

"But how…," Anne touched her chest, which heaved with slow, satisfying breaths, the sensation of drowning a distant memory. A roll of her tongue around her mouth told her that her mouth was full of water. "How is this possible?"

A great many things are possible.

"I don't understand."

Do you need to?

A tentacle came up and wiped one of Anne's red curls away from her eyes while another tentacle cupped her face. Using the tentacles attached to Anne's arms, the woman pulled herself close to Anne.

What do you desire help with?

"I want to… go home. Back… up."

Why? What waits for you there?

Anne opened her mouth to answer, but didn't have one. Contemplation of her life swirled in the dark rainbow of the ocean, those silver eyes drawing every coherent thought from her mind and dispersing it through the water. The tentacles toyed with Anne's t-shirt, gently lifting it from her skin and twirling it between its suckers.

"Who are you?" Anne said, reaching a hand out and pressing her fingers against the woman's cheek.

I am me. And who are you?

"Anne."

Well hello, Anne of the Land. Pleasure to make your acquaintance.

The woman floated backwards, dipping into a floating curtsy. *I am Zelda.*

Anne bowed in return. She was unconscious, or dead, she was certain, but it was lovely. The sensation, the gorgeous array of colours and textures so far below the surface. This impossible reality was magnificent.

You are lost, Anne of the Land.

Anne gazed at the stunning, tentacled beast before her, and her life poured down her on, sinking her even lower into the abyss.

"Yes."

Anne cried. The tears were heavier and thicker than the ocean water. The woman moved forward once more and wrapped Anne in her tentacles.

There, there, Anne of the Land. We are all lost. But we have found each other.

Anne melted into the woman's embrace. She felt amazing, this haunting creature, her smooth skin, the firm, round curves of her body. Anne became acutely aware of the woman's breasts pressing into her own, their breath moving as one. Anne felt a surge of emotion, a ravenous hunger driving her body, her mind. She tore at her clothes, pulling off her t-shirt, wriggling out of her jeans, violently tearing away her bra and panties. Her head fell back as she watched her garments float up towards the pinprick of the moon above the surface.

The tentacles were on her again, coiling around limbs, wrapping around her waist. When Zelda spoke she was so close to Anne that her words pushed water directly into her mouth.

What do you want, Anne of the Land?

"I don't know."

Anne ran her fingers through the mane of indigo hair, pulling Zelda's face to her own. Their lips pressed together, soft peach on inky black, their tongues flicking. Anne held Zelda's face, kissing her hard as tentacles kneaded her back, her thighs, curling around and parting her, penetrating her, gyrating and heaving until Anne gasped and convulsed, every millimeter of her body surging and pulsating with pleasure.

Like a cork jammed in the bottle, Anne's throat closed, the reality of the water suddenly crashing upon her. She couldn't breathe. Water gushed into her airway and she sputtered and gagged. Though she knew she was dying, she wouldn't leave, wouldn't pull away from the tentacle still inside her, from the breasts that were still firmly pressed against her. She sighed, resigning herself to death at the peak of this experience, when the icy cold slapped her across the face.

Pain replaced pleasure, and her hair was hauled over her head, a pair of heavy hands, gnarled and crooked, clawing, grabbing pulling…

"What'd I tell you about the water?"

Anne coughed and vomited salt water over the sand.

With teeth chattering and thick gooseflesh rising on her bare flesh, Anne hugged herself, desperate for warmth. Gasping for breath, she looked around, searching for beauty, dark, greens and silvers and indigos. For Zelda.

What she found was Gwen, kneeling over top of her, a silhouette against the lights of Jutland House in the background.

Gwen covered Anne with a blanket and rolled her onto her side. Anne sputtered out more water as her hands examined her body beneath the blanket, naked and cold, her groin still warm and pulsating.

"Ambulance is on the way. I'd drive you myself, but I don't want my truck wet. Where's the other one at?"

Anne looked at her, head cocked.

"Your sister," Gwen said. "Where's she at?"

Anne didn't answer. All she could think about was

the world below the surface, the beauty, the sensations. Even as the flashing red ambulance lights lit the forest like wildfire, Anne could only think of silver and indigo.

The Goat's Moat was quiet. Charlie wondered if it would be, but didn't really care. She was there to see one person, regardless of how few or many others there would be. When she shut the car door behind her, she raised her chin and breathed deeply, drawing the all the scents into her nostrils. A medley of pine and loam, and the musk of a wide range of creatures. One in particular teased a grin at the corner of her mouth.

"Charlie? I'm glad you popped by!"

Bran came towards her in large strides, slowing as he got close. His eyes dropped to her body, to the sheer red dress hugging her muscular, slender frame.

"Oh… I… did you have a… an event to go to? Party?"

"Nope. Just feeling sassy. Like it?"

Bran's brow furrowed. "I do, but, it doesn't seem like you."

With her face scrunched into a frown, Charlie clucked her tongue.

"No no, don't get me wrong," Bran said, "you look amazing, it's just—"

Charlie stepped forward and took Bran by the hand, leading him along the edge of the parking lot to the nearby hiking trail. Bran looked over his shoulder at the smattering of customers seated at picnic tables, no one taking notice of his departure.

"Charlie, what are you doing?"

"Little stroll in the woods. Romantic, don't you think?"

"Uh, sure, but I can't go far. Or be gone long. I'm working, and I'd love to, but could we wait just a bit. Daytime would be better, anyways. Safer, what with the animals out here."

Charlie stepped in front of Bran and put her hands on his chest.

"Safe?" she cooed, running a finger over his collarbone. "Now where's the fun in that?"

She kissed him, wet and hard. Bran resisted for a microsecond before grabbing her face and kissing her back, their tongues pushing together, their bodies pulled close. Charlie grabbed his shirt and tore it open, sending the buttons flying off and pelting the nearby trees.

"Hey now," Bran said. "I have to get back—"

Silencing him with her tongue, Charlie kissed him while her hands found the button of his jeans, tearing that off too. Bran gasped as she grabbed his cock, pumping it in her hand.

"Wanna stop?" Charlie asked, a low growl under her voice.

"I don't…. know…"

Bran's hips moved with the motion of Charlie's hand, his own hands caressing her body, shy to touch her. She pressed Bran's hand against her breast, her erect nipple driving into his palm. Bran pushed Charlie against a tree and slid his hand beneath the red dress. She arched her back as he thrust his fingers into her, rubbing and pressing.

"Fuck me," she yelled, trying to pull his jeans down but not wanting his fingers to stop.

"Hey, seriously, have you been drinking? I think we need to slow down a bit."

She humped his hand and put her mouth on his chest, dragging her tongue across his collarbone and up to the nape of his neck. When she reached his shoulder, Bran cried out.

"Fuck!"

He pulled away, stumbling back and falling over a large, exposed root and crashing to the ground. Charlie crouched on all fours and crawled towards him.

"You bit me!" Bran touched his fingers to his neck, and they came back covered in blood. Charlie saw the blood, and something inside her twinged—a ping, an odd sensation. She backed away and leaned against a tree.

"What have I done?" she breathed.

"What is… is that…"

Bran pointed a shaky finger the front of Charlie's dress. She looked down, and discovered a dark stain on the crimson fabric, and a dark smear across her pale chest.

Charlie panicked, her hands frantically brushing at the mess. "Is this blood? Bran, what's happening?"

Bran scrambled over to her, looking at her body and his own body. She also searched for the source of injury, finding only a bite mark on Bran's neck with a tiny pinch of broken skin; it was not enough to have produced that amount of blood.

"Charlie, we should call the cops. Where's Anne?"

"I… I don't know."

Both of them jumped when Bran's phone sang out. He pulled it out his pocket, looked at the number, puzzled, then answered.

"Yes?" Bran said, eyes fixed on Charlie. "Yes she is. Is everything all right? Oh my God. Yeah, we'll be there shortly."

Poking the screen, Bran hung up the call and held Charlie by the shoulders.

"Are you okay?" he asked, looking her over again.

"What was that?"

"That was Gwen from Jutland House. Anne is fine, but she had an incident in the water. She's been taken by ambulance to the hospital."

"What?"

Charlie jumped to her feet and looked down at the dress. "Fuck this!"

"It's fine," Bran said. "I'm gonna chase away the stragglers and close up. You grab a pair of sweats and a hoodie from the store, on the house. Then we'll head up to the hospital."

He started back towards the building when Charlie grabbed his arm.

"Bran, I'm… so sorry. I don't know what's happening."

He looked at her, fear and confusion on his face, but leaned forward and kissed her on the cheek.

"We'll figure it out. Let's get moving."

CHAPTER 17

Drip. Drip. Drip.

The sound of the IV was intense, and Anne swore she could feel it pumping through her veins, icy cold fluid straining against her skin. Anne scratched her arm, irritated by the medical tape and all the monitors beeping and clacking.

"Is all this really necessary?" Anne asked the nurse fiddling with the chart at the foot of her bed.

"Gotta be on the safe side, especially with water-related incidents. Aspiration, hypothermia, all that."

"Yes, but do I need the IV? The needle is bothering me."

"It's standard procedure. Get you hydrated, pump some antibiotics."

Anne sighed as the nurse clipped the chart to the bed and came up to adjust her pillows.

"Look, you might as well make yourself comfortable. They're gonna keep you here overnight, poke and prod you a bit, make sure all your tests come back okay."

The door to the hospital room flew open and Charlie came barreling in.

"Holy shit, Anne!"

Collapsing on the bed, throwing her arms around Anne, Charlie sobbed and squeezed her sister so hard both lost their breath.

"I'm sorry, I shouldn't have kicked you out of the car," Charlie blathered. "It was spite, I was hateful—"

"I'm the asshole," Anne said, lifting Charlie away from the many cords. "I was immature, and I lashed out at you. I said so much I shouldn't have…"

Charlie was a mess. Anne took a quick look over her sister, her disheveled pixie, a grey BC Lions hoodie two sizes too large, and sweatpants that pooled on the floor over her feet. The look was a far cry from the outfit she had selected from the boutique.

"What's all this, then?" Anne asked, motioning at the ensemble.

"I, uh, had to change."

"Where did you get that? And change from what?"

Out the corner of her eye, Anne caught Bran lurking in the doorway, studying the laces on his boots.

"Bran?"

"Yeah, hey," he said, running his fingers through his mop of hair. He looked haunted, somehow. Terribly uncomfortable.

"He drove me here," Charlie said.

Looking from Charlie to Bran and back again, Anne smirked.

"It's not what you think," Charlie said. "I was… I had some trouble and stopped into the Goat's Moat. Gwen called there after she found you."

Skeptical, Anne eyed her sister and Bran, and was about to speak, when Charlie launched her inquisition.

"So what the hell happened? Why the fuck were you in the water? Anne, you know the ocean, safety precautions."

Anne looked at her sister, at a loss, her memory hazy and distorted as the ocean.

"Not too sure. I walked home after you dropped me off and took a stroll to the beach. There was…"

Singing. A siren song from the depths.

"I heard something," Anne said, shaking her head.

"Something?" Charlie sat back and crossed her arms. "What aren't you telling me?"

There was a pause, short but full of emotion and

questions. When Anne finally spoke, it came out as a whisper.

"Perhaps the same thing you aren't telling me."

The stare down continued, reanimating the nurse and forcing Bran back to the doorway. Neither sister spoke, just studied faces, body language, both deep in their own thoughts.

"Your blood pressure is still quite low, Anne," the nurse said, ending the standoff. "And your temperature, too. I'm going to page the doctor, see if we should do anything. Can I grab you a warm blanket? And you should try to have a bite to eat. I'll grab you a tray."

"I'm not cold. I'm roasting, actually."

The nurse slid the thermometer across Anne's forehead and scowled, shaking her head at Charlie.

"Nah, you're chilly," the nurse said. "I'm going to page the doctor, just to be on the safe side."

"I'll get you food," Charlie said, maintaining eye contact with Anne while standing from the bed. "And where can I grab one of those warm blankets?"

"Tall cart at the end of the hall," the nurse said, motioning out the door. "Grab a couple, if you plan on hanging out a while. We run the temp cold in here."

"Thanks."

Charlie reached down and grabbed Anne's hand. Anne felt a lump swell in her throat, a growing need to spew a confession, tell Charlie everything and anything that had happened to her. Tonight, beneath that water… when they were younger—the promiscuity, the drugs, the stealing. Always looking for another high, another risk, another fix. It was never enough and never had been. Anne was the one always in trouble, always getting everyone's attention, never satisfied and always searching.

But Charlie needn't worry. Anne was worried about Charlie. Charlie would never be okay on her own. She'd always had Emme to lean on, Emme to make the decisions and take the risks with her. Emme cared not about consequences. Charlie cared too much.

"I love you," Anne said, tears welling in her eyes.

"I love you, too. Again, I'm sorry for all this."

"Me too."

Charlie gave her sister a kiss on the cheek and slipped out of the room.

It wasn't until she was out in the hallway with the door closed behind her that Charlie allowed herself to shudder and shed some tears. She was terrified—for her sister, of herself. She'd lost Emme, and now she'd just about lost Anne, all while she was gadding about in a drunken stupor. She couldn't even look over at Bran, who must think her a complete lunatic.

"Are you okay?" he asked, touching her shoulder. "I mean, of course not, but, you know."

"Yeah. Just embarrassed. Humiliated. My behaviour towards her was shameful, then you…"

"Don't you mind that," Bran said, wrapping his arms around her, gathering her in for a hug. "I know you're both trudging through hell right now. Crazy behaviour is to be expected."

"She could have died, Bran. Because of me."

"Because of you?"

"I kicked her out of the car, made her walk back to Jutland House down that highway. At night. All the creepers on the road…"

In her mind, Charlie saw a flash of red, an image of greasy hair, a yellow-toothed maw, blood…

Bran grabbed Charlie as she swooned.

"Hey, what's going on?" Bran said.

Charlie wiped the front of her baggie hoodie, remembering whatever she had been covered in before going to the Goat's Moat. "I'm fine, just exhausted. And hungry. I'm gonna grab those blankets and some chow, hunker down with Anne here for the night."

"Maybe you should get checked out, too. You look really pale."

"Just the booze," Charlie said. "I'll be fine. If I keel over, I'm in the right place."

Bran offered a weak smile, and Charlie kissed him on the cheek. "Thank you for being so kind."

"My pleasure." Bran gave her a soft but lingering kiss on the lips before turning lobster-red. "Wanna catch the lift with me?"

Charlie answered with a puzzled expression before she realized. "Ah, yes. Cafeteria's on the main floor, I suppose."

Once inside the elevator, Bran reached over and held her hand. Charlie allowed herself to enjoy it, isolated in that elevator, closed off from the world. She was disappointed when the elevator dinged and the door opened.

"This is your stop," Bran said. "I'm one more down in the garage."

Charlie hesitated, and Bran put his hand on the door so it wouldn't close.

"Again, thank you." Charlie said.

"I'll come by tomorrow around noon and take you ladies to your car. Call if you need anything or if something changes."

"Will do."

With feet like lead, Charlie stepped out of the elevator and watched the door close as she waved at Bran.

The cafeteria was just around the corner from the elevators, and it opened out onto a vast seating area that could accommodate the busy rush of staff and patients alike. The hospital was huge, serving all the small coastal communities up and down the island, but at this time of night it was a ghost town. A few orderlies were at a table in the corner, munching on Cheetos, and a cleaner was waxing the floor in monotonous circles, polishing the same spot over and over again while snoozing on the machine.

Charlie wandered past the glass containers, perusing the bare-bones, middle-of-the-night selection of sandwiches and cold entrees, chips and stale pastries left over from the day before. Nothing looked appealing, so she settled on sandwiches—tuna salad for Anne and roast beef for her—and two bottles of orange juice. She balanced her selections over to the cashier who didn't look up from her phone as she rang in the order.

Meals and drinks in tow, Charlie walked back to the elevators, glancing over her shoulder at the seating area. The orderlies had made a silent exit, leaving the cleaner and the cashier as the sole occupants of the area. Charlie pressed the elevator button with her elbow and waited. Sharp dings chimed from the floors above, but the elevator was taking an agonizingly long time to reach the main floor. The whir of the floor waxer got louder and louder until the volume was unbearable, the sound grinding into Charlie's very bones.

Forgoing the molasses-fueled elevator, Charlie pushed open the door to the stairwell and started the four-story climb to Anne's floor. Part way there, after passing the second floor landing, Charlie was overcome with a sudden and overwhelming hunger. Lightheaded and shaky, she slid down the wall and sat on the floor, recognizing the sensation that preceded a fainting spell.

Then came the smell, thick and coppery. Spontaneously, Charlie's jaw slacked and drool poured out like a faucet, soaking the front of her shirt. Whether from nausea, hunger, or exhaustion, Charlie started panting, the sound of her own breath filling the stairwell. Her stomach growled, a noise to rival the heaves of breath coming from her body. The sandwiches and drinks fell from her grasp as black spots floated over her vision, tunneling in, narrower and narrower.

That smell. Stronger now. Charlie looked down at the upset sandwiches on the floor. She lunged forward, balancing on her haunches, and ripped open the roast beef container. Without using her hands, she smashed her face into the plastic, devouring the sandwich in two massive gulps. The tuna sandwich suffered the same fate, this time with a disregard for the plastic at all;

Charlie chewed through the cover, eating plastic along with the actual food.

Once every crumb and piece of meat had been consumed, Charlie sat back against the wall. *Inhale, exhale*, she tried to control her breath, her heart rate, her looming panic. Slowly she calmed, the smell eliminated, the noise of her breath and the distant waxer fading away to nothing.

"I am tired," a small voice echoed from below.

A scream lingered in Charlie's throat, but she didn't relinquish it, logic and reason insisting she stifle it until fear was warranted.

"It is past my bedtime. I am so very tired, and I need to go to sleep."

A quick glance down the stairwell showed Charlie everything she needed to unleash her scream. A pale girl, rail thin, draped in a yellowed ivory nightgown, stood staring up at Charlie through a veil of long, dark hair. Her toenails and fingernails were black and long, like sharp, thick talons. Her skin was a startling white, and her eyes solid black.

Charlie screamed, and the pale girl screamed with her, a horrible, braying noise tangled with a high-pitched giggle. The pale girl laughed and laughed, her body twitching and contorting, her mouth stretching into an impossibly wide grin that revealed a mouth full of glistening, sharp teeth.

Charlie ran. Up the stairs, leaping past landings, the pale girl's voice chasing her up, up, up until Charlie burst through the door of the fourth floor and out into the hallway.

It was quiet—no screaming, no heavy breathing, no giggling demon child. The nurses behind the station were startled by Charlie's sudden appearance, one standing and rounding the counter.

"Are you all right?"

"I'm… there was…"

Charlie opened the door to the stairwell and listened.

Silence.

As she pushed the door shut again, Charlie forced a laugh. "I'm so silly. Too many ghost stories. The elevator was slow, so I took the stairs, and, well—"

"Hospital stairwell in the dead of night?" the nurse laughed. "Yeah, I dare say you were spooked! Plus that cafeteria is like a tomb this time of night." The nurse cocked a brow. "Didn't find anything to eat?"

Charlie touched her face, feeling the damp remnants of mayo on her cheeks. Looking down, she found her hoodie was covered in crumbs.

"No."

It was all Charlie offered before she walked away. Before returning to the room, she fed some bills into the vending machine, selecting an array of chips and chocolate bars to bring back for Anne. As she was about to close the door, she looked down the dark hall, deciphering shadows, and found the pale girl, sitting crossed-legged in the corner, rocking and giggling under her breath.

Charlie entered the room, leaving the girl behind.

THOUGH THE GREEN wool shawl was thick and warm, Isadora was still chilled to the bone.

"Perhaps you's coming down with something." Penny said as she put another log on the fire.

"You are," Isadora corrected.

"What?"

"You *are* coming down with something. Not you *is*."

Penny huffed and left Isadora on her own, staring out the window at the yard below and ocean beyond. It was the dead of night, far later that Isadora cared to be awake, but the air was restless. And once Isadora learned that young Anne had been taken to the hospital, she bid adieu to sleep.

No matter. Sleep had been waning as of late. Something stirred in the corners of her mind, niggling at her peace, waiting to pounce.

"Some tea?" Penny had assumed the answer ahead of time. She carried in a tray with hot water, a cup and saucer, and a pot of honey. After setting it down on the table beside the window, she looked out at the night alongside Isadora.

"What do you suppose Anne was doing out there?" Penny asked.

"Nothing good, that's for certain."

"Why you say that, ma'am? They seem like nice enough women to me."

"Well this isn't your place, is it?"

Though accustomed to Isadora's cruelty, Penny winced, the words carrying a sting. Isadora did not look away from the window, but her eyes dropped.

"What of the other one?" Isadora asked.

"The other one?"

"Charlie, you damn fool. Was she here too?"

"Not that I heard. Gwen didn't say, but I saw them load Anne into the ambulance, and she went alone. The car's not here, so maybe Charlie followed behind, but—"

"So you don't know."

"Guess I don't."

Penny walked away, her footfalls heavy and irate.

No matter. She's just the help. And no help at all, that one.

Isadora poured a cup of tea, dribbled in some honey, and lifted it to her lips, the aromatic steam fogging the window. Before she drew her first sip, the steam dispersed, disturbed by air from a door swinging open.

"What do you want?" Isadora hissed. "I'd like some peace and quiet."

Isadora turned, intending to scold Penny sufficiently enough to scare her away for the night, but the room was empty.

"Hello?"

No answer. Isadora looked at the steam trailing from her cup, then chortled softly. "Old fool, Isadora. Calm yourself."

When she turned back to the window, the steam danced again, this time from her own gasp of air.

"My word!"

On the fogged glass was a handprint, long and slender, perfectly pressed into the moisture. It faded so quickly that Isadora wondered if it had ever been there at all.

"I touched the window. Or Penny did, that's all. Mind playing tricks."

Hot, damp air blew into Isadora's ear, carrying words that sounded a million kilometers away.

Never meant to be.

The tea cup hit the floor with a smash that shattered the quiet of the night, spraying porcelain and scorching water over Isadora's slippers. She shrieked and swiped at the air, backing away from the voice.

The door to the kitchen slammed open as Penny burst into the room, rolling pin in hand.

"What is it, ma'am? What's wrong?"

Isadora stood in place, evaluating the room, then smoothed the front of her dressing gown.

"A careless old woman, is all. Dropped my tea."

Penny sighed and lowered the rolling pin. "Ah, me nerves. I thought we had an intruder. Spilt tea is no big thing, ma'am. I'll clean it straight away. You want another?"

"No, I think not. I'm going to retire, try to get some sleep. My nerves are shot."

"Want something to help you nod off?"

"Yes, please, some medication, if you don't mind."

"Yes ma'am."

Penny scurried off, and Isadora looked at the window where the handprint had been, her heart quivering in fear.

CHAPTER 18

It was just past lunch when Bran pulled his truck into the parking lot of the Goat's Moat where Charlie's car was still parked from the night before. Anne got out of the car and stretched while Charlie lingered a moment, looking over at Bran.

"You sure you're okay?" Bran asked, his eyes wide.

"It's been a lot, but we're fine."

"Not sure about fine, but you will be."

Charlie reached over and squeezed his hand. He leaned across the console and kissed her on the mouth; his mouth was gentle and warm, and she lingered on him for several breaths before Anne knocked on the window.

"Uh, adorable. Also gross. Can we wrap this up

and get moving? Looks like the sky is about to split open and drown us all."

"Drive safe," Charlie said, reluctant to pull away.

"Of course."

As Charlie opened the truck door, Bran grabbed her arm. "Wanna come by tomorrow, have some food? Maybe purchase some more runway fashion?"

Charlie look at her wrinkled, saggy clothes and smiled.

"I'd like that."

As the wheels of the car crunched down the drive and out onto the highway, Anne threaded her arm through Charlie's.

"So, that's a thing now?" Anne asked, smirking.

"He's lovely. He shouldn't get tangled up with the likes of me."

"Don't be ridiculous," Anne said. "He's the lucky one."

The sky growled, and the trees creaked as the wind launched a gusty attack at the forest. In the distance, the light show began, a storming mass of dark clouds floating over the ocean.

"Best be getting back to Jutland House," Charlie said as she pressed the gas a little harder. "She's about to open up."

In a flash, the sisters showered, dressed, and took their perches down in the sitting room to watch the spectacle outside as Penny fussed over them, ensuring their drinks were full. Gwen stood sentry at the window, watching the sisters as much as she was watching the storm outside. Jutland House groaned and complained as the wind battered her walls, creaking her foundation and pelting her with rain and debris from the nearby forest.

"Any worry about the storms?" Charlie asked as she sipped on her glass of merlot.

"It's all talk," Gwen said. "This house is old and solid, and resilient as the forest itself. All have stood for many years, and will stand for many more."

"Storms always seem worse in the wild," Charlie said. "Raw nature, violent and powerful."

"Ooh, you should be a writer!" Penny said.

"I should be many things, I suppose."

"You are more than you think," Anne said, her voice breathy and quavering.

"Anne, are you all right?"

Charlie stood and hurried over to her sister who was sprawled out on the floor by the window, holding an icy mojito to her chest. Her skin glistened with sweat, and her normally pale complexion was scarlet.

"You are running a fever—" Charlie stopped when

she placed the back of her hand on Anne's forehead. "Uh, you're not even warm. A tad cold, actually."

"I'm melting," Anne said, tugging at the collar of her tank top, "but I'll live. This drink helps."

Anne took a hefty gulp of her drink and held the cold copper mule to her chest again.

"I'll touch up the refreshments," Penny said as she exited to the kitchen.

"Go easy on the vodka, honey," Charlie said. "You've just come out of the hospital, for fuck sake."

"I'm obviously invincible, so bottoms up!"

Anne tried to smile, but it came out strained. Tension hung heavy in the air, questions unanswered, stories untold.

"Anne." Charlie was quiet, her eyes unable to lift from the floor. "Something happened to you, on the dive, out there last night. I can tell. I can feel it. I know, because something happened to me too—"

"This place," Gwen said. "I told you."

Penny came in the room with a tray of smoked salmon, cheese, and crackers. She set it down on the table with a bang.

"You ladies decide on another round?"

Lighting ignited the sky, and a vibrating boom came close behind, rattling the pictures on the wall. Penny let out a small yelp and clasped her chest.

"Lord thundering..." Penny muttered as she arranged and rearranged the snack tray.

"Are you all right, Penny?" Charlie asked, watching the nervous young woman twittering about.

"Unsettled, is all."

"I love storms, myself. Beautiful," Anne said wistfully.

"Naw, the storm don't bother me none."

"Isadora clawing your nerves?" Charlie asked.

"Always. But that ain't it, either. Got the news playin' in the kitchen. Never a good thing, I tells myself, but I watches it anyways."

"Something happening?"

"I'd say."

Penny waved the sisters to follow. Charlie stood, but Anne stayed in her seat, fanning herself with a book. Gwen directed her attention out the window, little interest in what was happening outside the shelter of the Jutland House property.

Penny and Charlie walked into the kitchen, the door swinging closed behind them, and Charlie caught the tail end of an ongoing news report:

... one of the most savage slayings the island has ever seen. Investigators are interviewing people in nearby communities, and are asking anyone who has travelled the highway in the past twenty-four hours to come forward if they saw anything unusual.

Penny snatched the remote off the counter and

skipped it back to the beginning of the broadcast, then set the remote down and walked away, busying herself with cleaning counters and drying dishes.

"Had enough of that, I have," Penny muttered. "What kinda lunatic is skulking around out there? This world, I tells ya."

Vomit gurgled in the back of Charlie's throat.

A grisly discovery was made in the early hours this morning. A young couple who had stopped at the side of the highway came upon the half-eaten body of a what appears to be a man.

Charlie braced herself on the counter. Images flashed across the screen of the forest, the highway, and an old pickup truck pulled off to the side of the road.

Investigators say what first appeared to be an animal attack, might actually be foul play. The attack was localized on the man's body, causing him to bleed out. It will be a difficult process to determine pre- and post-mortem damage from wildlife, so investigators are asking for the public's help. If this is murder, it will be one of the most savage slayings…

Penny shut the television off.

"Harriet down the way says the poor man's twig and berries were torn clear off his body and tossed into the woods. The animals left that alone—not even the wolves would touch that wretched package—but the rodents and bugs made a feast of his body, they did. Can you imagine?"

"Do they have a suspect?" Charlie was breathless and sweat formed on her upper lip.

"Naw, they still wonder if it was just an animal. But really? Just the boy business? Why would an animal do that? I get the eating the meat afterwards, but…"

"Who was he?"

"Some pig farmer on the outskirts. Shady fucker, anyways. I say some hooker knifed him when he got too rough. Still, though. Murder."

"Yeah."

On shaky legs, Charlie went back into the sitting room where she curled up in her chair and looked out the window.

"What the fuck was it?" Anne asked, her brow scrunched. "A damn poltergeist?"

"Something like that," Charlie said, her eyes scanning the trees, her fingers tracing her chest where, less than twenty-four hours before, a brown stain saturated the red silk of her dress.

CHAPTER 19

With the excitement of the past few days, and the lack of sleep at the hospital, exhaustion crept up on Anne, slamming into her before it was even nine o'clock in the evening. Charlie didn't protest the early retirement, instead joining Anne in their room where they both cocooned themselves under the shelter of their heavy duvets. Despite the raging storm outside, both sisters were asleep in a matter of minutes.

After only a few hours of heavy slumber, Anne woke in a pool of her own sweat. Charlie was having another fitful sleep, struggling on her back, fighting with the nothing in the air above her. Anne slid out of bed, taking care not to trip up in the blankets she had tossed off herself in her uncomfortable sleep. She fetched a change of clothes from the armoire and tiptoed to the bathroom where she peeled off her wet shirt and panties and mopped herself off with a cool facecloth.

But the more she dabbed her bare skin, the hotter she got, the sweat sticky and infuriatingly uncomfortable. Anne let the cool water run, soaking the washcloth and squeezing the water over her skin.

Not enough.

Turning the shower on—full blast, full cold—Anne sat in the tub and turned her face up to the cool, pelting water.

Still too hot.

And desperately thirsty.

Anne figured it was from all the perspiration, but regardless of reason, the thirst caused her to panic. She lapped at the water, slurping the stream in great gulps.

Not enough.

Anne scrambled out of the tub, gasping for air, for drink, for cooler temperatures. Her brain hot and scrambled, she crawled out of the bathroom on all fours, slithering down the stairs and shambling out the back door to the yard. One, two, ten, twenty loping steps and her feet were in the ocean, then her legs, and finally her chest. A sigh of relief washed away the panic as the ocean engulfed her, its soft waves lapping against her throat and chin.

A tentacle wrapped around her leg and tugged.

Anne closed her eyes and allowed herself be pulled beneath the surface.

The heat was gone. The thirst disappeared. The panic was doused by the cold Pacific. Zelda caressed her, twirling tentacles through her red curls and stroking her face.

There, there.

"What's happening to me?"

You are safe.

"Am I?"

Zelda kissed Anne, their lips pressing together firmly, sending shivers and spasms through Anne's body. Above, lightning danced, the gentle rumble of muffled thunder resonating in the surrounding water.

"I am lost," Anne cried.

You are here.

"What is all this?"

I have found you. You have found you.

"I don't know what the fuck that means."

You will. Or you won't. But I am here if you decide.

"And what are you? What's your part in all this."

I want.

"You want?"

I want. But I need help, as well.

Anne kissed Zelda, her fingers circling her dark purple nipples.

"You have me," Anne breathed into Zelda's mouth.

I have help?

Anne pulled away and looked into the creature's silver eyes. They were pained, full of sadness. Through the caress of the suckers, Anne felt Zelda's despair, her yearning. Her anger. Anne kissed her again, firm, her fingers winding through the mass of indigo hair floating in the water like writhing snakes. Anne's red curls entwined with Zelda's tendrils of hair and the women pressed together, moving inside each other, bursting with pleasure and rage that rocked the Pacific.

CHARLIE STRUGGLED TO BREATHE, the crushing weight on her chest threatening to snap her ribs to splinters.

It's just a dream, Charlie thought as she wriggled the duvet over her face. It moved without resistance. *There is nothing there, you silly girl.*

Yet the weight on her chest remained, pushing against her each time she inhaled. When she tried to roll over, the pressure appeared on her shoulders, holding her in place.

"Anne?"

Charlie's voice was loud enough for Anne to hear, probably loud and panicked enough for Isadora to hear, but she was answered by silence. She couldn't hear her sister's typical soft snores.

It's the storm. I can't hear anything over that drum solo in the sky.

Lightning flashed, bright enough for Charlie to see the flicker from beneath layers of eyelids and blankets combined. As the storm raged outside, terror brewed in Charlie, the weight on her chest becoming unbearable.

She gulped air, stifled by the blanket overtop her face.

I'm suffocating.

Her bones creaked, giving under the weight of the boulder on her chest.

This is a heart attack.

The storm surged, the wind slamming the side of the house.

No, this is a dream. I'm being ridiculous.

Charlie threw the covers back, and her heart lurched into her throat.

Not a dream.

A flickering silhouette against the flashing sky, the pale girl was kneeling on Charlie's chest, her straggly dark hair pooled like ink across the white blanket. She giggled, her sharp teeth shining in the flashes of lightning. Charlie tried to speak, to scream, but the pale girl leaned forward, grinding her knees into Charlie's chest, crushing her words. With her face over Charlie's, the pale girl's hair tickled Charlie's cheeks and ears.

Charlie opened her mouth wide to scream, to call for Anne, Isadora, anyone to come to her aid, but nothing came out. Instead, the pale girl mirrored the action, opening her cavernous mouth wide and vomiting a gush of squirming, crawling, fluttering insects over Charlie's face and into her mouth. Millipedes, tree roaches, slugs, and earthworms filled Charlie's eyes, mouth, nose, and ears. They crawled over her, in her, under her skin and into her organs.

Then nothing.

Charlie sat up, gasping in great breaths of air. The pale girl had leapt off her chest, and was now jammed in the corner of the ceiling like a lurking tarantula, her black eyes glowing and a low giggle rumbling in her belly. Frozen in horror, Charlie watched as the pale girl skittered down the wall to the floor and opened the door.

Anne was not in her bed, and her blankets were on the floor. Peering out into the hall, Charlie could see that the bathroom door was open and the light was off.

Where are you?! I need you!

The pale girl shrugged her shoulders and curled her finger, beckoning Charlie to follow. And Charlie did. Like she was a helium balloon being pulled across the room, she followed the pale girl into the hall, down the stairs, and out the back door. The cool, wet grass felt good on Charlie's bare feet, soothing her panic. No longer able to see the pale girl, Charlie followed the small footprints depressed in the lawn to the hiking trails by the staff quarters.

Like a punch in the face, Charlie was hit with the smell; it was a coppery, burning scent she could taste on her tongue. Drool dribbled down Charlie's chin and she gagged, the stench both delicious and rancid. She trudged forward, her hunger overcoming her senses until she could no longer see or hear, only taste. Soon, she was on all fours, her mouth filled with hot liquid and globs of meat, her belly gurgling with satisfaction.

CHAPTER 20

THE SUN HAD RISEN above the horizon and the morning was red with its early glow. There was action in Jutland House, slamming doors and loud words, rousing both sisters out of a deep slumber. Anne stretched, her body sore and exhausted, but her temperature had improved; she no longer felt like she was going to light the sheets on fire. Charlie was looking at her, eyes glowing a vivid yellow.

"Charlie?"

Anne sat straight up in bed and reached for the lamp, pulling the string and bathing the room in warm light.

"What's wrong with you?" Charlie said, head cocked.

Charlie's eyes were normal, bloodshot and puffy, but not glowing nor yellow.

"Your eyes."

"You're wet."

Anne touched her curls. Soaked, dripping. She touched a ringlet to her tongue.

"Salty."

"You were in the ocean again."

"I don't… and you?"

Anne pointed at Charlie's hands which clutched the blanket up to her neck. Charlie's fingernails were caked in dirt and muck. Charlie dropped the blanket, revealing a white tank top stained brown. Her skin was covered in leaves, dirt, and…

"Is that blood?" Anne asked, voice shaking.

Charlie looked at her shirt, at her hands, then jumped out of bed and examined her body. Anne got up and helped, checking every centimeter of her sister for wounds.

"Charlie, where did you go? What happened to you?"

Fat tears filling her puffy eyes, Charlie looked at Anne, lip quivering. "What about you?"

Anne touched her hair again, then looked down at her own body. She was naked, skin damp and cool. Anne pulled the blanket off the bed and wrapped it around herself like a toga. The sisters sat next to each other on the bed, looking at their feet.

"Charlie?"

"I don't know. It's… impossible."

"Yeah."

"Horrible."

"Is it?"

Charlie looked startled, leaning away from Anne. Before she could respond, the sounds of shouting traveled up the stairs and through the vents.

"Sounds like Penny," Anne said.

"And Isadora."

"Those two." Anne rolled her eyes. "Well, I guess we should make an appearance, try to rescue Penny from whatever that is now." Anne slipped on some clothes. "I'm clean, but you need a shower. And hide those clothes for now."

Charlie stripped and tossed Anne her soiled clothes. Anne opened the armoire and jammed them in the back behind a stack of shirts, and pulled her hand out in slow motion.

"Huh," Anne said, as she dangled her fingers in front of her face. Hair, long and coarse, was tangled through her fingers. She groped in the closet, pulling out more chunks, finally bringing out Charlie runners. They were caked in hair and blood.

Charlie cried out. Anne stuffed the offending

footwear back in the armoire, grabbed some clothes for Charlie, and slammed the door.

"We are leaving here, Charlie. We'll calmly go see what the commotion is, get our shit, and go. Without saying a word, understand?"

Charlie nodded and grabbed the clothes.

"Quick shower, downstairs, poker face. Yes?" Anne instructed. Charlie nodded and left, Anne watching after her, tears stifled until she was alone in the bedroom.

Charlie showered quickly, if you could even call it a shower. She opened the faucet and passed through, just enough to rinse off the grime and look half-presentable. Less suspicious, at least. When the sisters finally made their way down the stairs, everyone was still upset and frantic. Isadora paced in front of the window and Penny was sitting in a chair, head in her hands, tears streaking down her face.

"I tells ya," Penny squalled, "I heard them, squealin' and screechin', but didn't think nothing of it."

"*Anything* of it," Isadora corrected.

"Whatever," Penny snapped. "And how are you so calm?"

Gwen stood, her back to the window, watching as

the sisters entered the room. She was calm but stern, her attention focused at her and Charlie.

"What's wrong?" Charlie asked, walking over to Penny.

"Oh, it's all done gone straight to hell," Penny howled. "First that poor dismembered man in the ditch—"

"Questionable sort," Isadora murmured.

"Be that as it may, ma'am, it's still bloody murder. There's a murderer traipsin' about and you's as cool as a cucumber!"

"She doesn't look so cool to me." Gwen's voice caught everyone's attention. The room fell to silence, all eyes on the woman standing by the window. "Seems the madame might just pace a trench in the carpet, straight through to the basement, and wring those bony hands clear off her wrists if she does not calm down a notch."

Isadora's jaw fell slack as she gasped at Gwen. Gwen walked towards her, muddy logans trodding on the floor, until they were nose to nose.

"All is not right in your world, is it, Ms. Isadora? Something's got you thinking. Rattled."

Gwen whispered in Isadora's ear. "Something haunting you, ol' girl?"

A pause, then Gwen stepped back suddenly, causing Isadora to jump and upset her mug of tea.

"I'll clean that, ma'am," Penny said.

"Jesus Christ, what's going on?" Anne demanded.

"Quite a busy night." Gwen walked to Anne, looked her over, then strolled past Charlie, giving her the once over as well. "Someone broke into the stables last night. Made quite the mess. I think it's animals, same as got that man on the highway."

"Animals?" Charlie said, her voice quiet.

Charlie and Anne looked at each other, and Charlie's eyes flickered to her hands, imagining the death that she had just washed down the drain.

"Do we have anything to worry about?" Anne said, looking at Isadora, who had faded to a sickly shade of grey.

"No," Gwen said, the word sharp and pointed, aimed at both sisters. "You don't."

Gwen took a step towards Isadora, her eyes squeezed into slits, a smile on her face. "But you…"

Isadora looked as if she might faint. She turned to the window and looked outside as Penny fussed at her feet, cleaning up the tea with a rag.

"Ladies," Gwen said. "Let's take a walk."

"What?" Charlie said. "Where? It's not even daylight."

"Follow me."

There was no room for argument. Charlie didn't want to, anyways. She was terrified but curious, and resisting might arouse suspicion. The quicker they took care of this, the quicker they could be out and gone and on their way home. Or at least away from Jutland House.

"You doing okay?" Gwen asked Charlie as they walked out the door.

Charlie did not. She felt sick to her stomach, terrified, angry. She already knew where they were going. And she knew what they were going to see.

"Just a little under the weather," Charlie said, avoiding eye contact.

"And what about you, little ginger? After your dip in the ocean?"

"Fully recovered, but still a little shaky," Anne said. "I'll be fine."

Gwen grunted an acknowledgment and walked across the grass with the sisters at her side. When they had reached the middle of the yard, Gwen pointed at the ground.

"That's where she died," Gwen said.

The sisters stopped.

"Where who died?" Anne asked.

Charlie knew.

"Willow," Gwen said. "Ms. Isadora's sister. Her body was hauled into the woods by the wolves."

"Holy shit, what?" Anne said, her voice rising in pitch. "How did she die?"

Gwen didn't answer or miss a step. She kept on walking, up to the ridge of rocks leading down to the beach. The sisters followed, but Charlie kept looking back at the spot, the very patch of grass where she had fallen her first night there. The pale girl was crouched there on her haunches, naked, mangey patches of fur sprouting over her crooked, bent body.

"And here," Gwen said, pointing over the rocks at the shore below, "is where the other sister met her end."

Anne stepped in front of Gwen and stopped, blocking her path. "Wait a damn minute. What happened to these girls?"

"They died," Gwen said.

"No fucking shit," Anne said. "Are we in danger out here?"

Gwen sighed. "The answer isn't simple."

"Sure it is," Charlie said. "Were they murdered?"

Gwen was quiet, then looked at Charlie. "Yes."

"Goddamit. What the fuck… I knew it! Why weren't we told?" Anne shouted.

"Folks find it's best to stay out of it," Gwen said.

"An RCMP officer that came sniffin around here after the fact earned himself a shotgun blast to the chest."

"Jesus Christ," Charlie said.

"Shouldn't this place be condemned or something? And did they catch who did it? It was Isadora, wasn't it? And we're here, sharing a house with a goddamn murderer… and she shot a cop?"

"Follow me," Gwen said, stepping around Anne.

Charlie walked behind Anne, who followed Gwen, the three women charging forward single file towards the hiking trails. As they approached the barn, the smell of copper suddenly filled Charlie's mouth and nose, nearly driving her to her knees. Anne looked back in time to see Charlie misstep and caught her before she fell.

"Charlie! My god, what's wrong?"

"Keep coming," Gwen said. "She's fine."

"The fuck it is! Look at her!"

"You need to see," Gwen said. She swung the gate to the stables open and walked inside, leaving it ajar for the sisters.

Charlie knew.

As they walked into the barn, their feet crunching on the hay, Charlie knew. She could feel it. That hay had crunched beneath her feet the night before. She could hear it, the sound of the barn door creaking as it swung open on rusty hinges, the sound of the horses fussing as they banged against their gates. It was overwhelming again, that copper smell, that taste that filled her mouth, and drool started pouring down her chin.

"Charlie," Anne said as she helped her sister along. "Are you gonna puke? My fuck, you're drooling!"

"Keep going," Charlie growled. "I want to see."

Though Anne and Charlie saw at the same time, only Charlie knew what it was instantly. Anne looked perplexed another few moments, and a few more after that.

The barn hummed with the drone of a thousand flies buzzing around in glee. The sisters had arrived at the epicenter of the stench, a combination of blood and rancid meat. Gwen pulled a cord, illuminating a naked bulb that hung from the ceiling. The barn ignited in spotty light, the bulb's glow obscured by splatters of blood.

It was as if a bomb had gone off, firing shrapnel of horse around the entire room. Globs of meat and fat and splinters of bone covered most surfaces, some of it still dripping or sticking to the wall. The horses' skeletons were left only partially intact, a bit of gristle hanging here and there, but picked fairly clean.

"Oh…" Anne said, tears streaming down her face.

Charlie saw, but she didn't care. The smell was overwhelming. The glisten of the blood on the hay and the scraps of meat still leeched to bone were driving her insane. She dropped down and loped over on all fours, dragging her tongue up and down an equine rib before burying her face in a pile of leftover intestines. She heard Anne screaming, crying, pleading for her to stop, but it didn't faze her. Only when she caught the gleam of Gwen's shovel in the light from the bulb did she turn her head. Then, with a heavy ring, everything went black.

CHAPTER 21

GWEN'S CABIN was a single room, with a small kitchen, living room, and a corner with a single mattress. Though spacious, it was simple, everything in one place. Anne sat in the corner, eyes fixed on her sister. Gwen brought a fresh ice pack over to Charlie, who was laid out on the sofa, nursing a sizable goose egg on her temple.

"Feeling better?" Gwen asked.

Gwen handed Charlie the ice pack and a mug full of hot tea.

"Yeah," Charlie said, holding the pack to her head and taking a sip of the steaming liquid.

Anne expected to see terror on her sister's face. Or confusion. But rather, she saw despair and guilt.

"I'm not mad at you, Charlie," Anne said.

"What are you?"

"I'm..." Anne stirred her coffee, watching the cream swirl to a mocha brown, looking for answers in the liquid. "I'm confused."

"This place," Gwen said.

"So you've said," Anne said. "And what does that mean, exactly?"

Gwen stood and walked over to a cabinet by the studio kitchen and pulled a photo album out of a cupboard. She flipped it open and set in on the coffee table in front of Charlie and Anne. Inside were pictures of the house, Isadora's parents, and the little girls playing in the yard.

"Lovely family. Pillars of the community, and the girls were sweet as sugar and sharp as glass. Good humans, that lot."

"What happened to the parents?" Charlie asked.

Another page flip. It was the front page of a newspaper, reporting the quadruple murder at Jutland House.

"No one could fathom it," Gwen said. "Rocked the island, that someone so evil could be here in Canada, let alone nestled in the beauty of Vancouver Island. This was a place of peace and nature, not hate and violence."

"They never suspected Isadora?" Anne asked.

"Not for a single second. Investigation went on for years until they finally pinned it on an Asian man, Yip, who had confessed to a killing spree in Vancouver. Timing was right, and Yip ended up hanging for his crimes."

"Poor Isadora," Charlie said. "I feel bad for making fun of her."

A grunt escaped Gwen, followed by a shake of her head. "Don't feel too bad."

Gwen lit another cigarette off her burning filter.

"You came to help Isadora after it all happened?" Anne asked, looking around Gwen's house at the artifacts, drums, talismans, and other cultural collectibles Gwen had gathered.

"No. I did not." Gwen shut the album and placed it back on the shelf. "This place, it… has a way. I like it here, the history, the mythology. I belong here, and I mind it not."

"Even though such awful things happened here?" Anne said.

Anne's stomach clenched. She looked over at her sister, balled up on the couch. She pictured her covered in blood, licking the bones of those poor horses.

What did you do, Charlie?

"Don't be scared of your sister, chil'," Gwen said to

Anne. "She woulda eaten you already, if she had a mind to."

"What?" Anne shrieked, as Charlie sat straight up, a look of shock on her face. "I'm fucking beyond confused here."

Gwen laughed, a loud burst of noise. "Of course you are. Your sister just ate my horses, so that's something new for you."

Charlie sputtered on her tea, and Anne choked out a nervous laugh while Gwen fiddled with her own coffee, giving her words a minute to sink in.

"I… this is unbelievable," Anne said.

But is it really? Anne thought. *Unbelievable?*

Anne thought of that first night, of Charlie on the ground, Of all the weird behaviour and noises and glowing eyes in the dark.

"What happened to you that first night we were here?" Anne asked Charlie.

Anne thought she wouldn't get an answer. Charlie stalled, chewed at her fingernails, looked at the floor. But when Charlie finally looked up, right into Anne's eyes, Anne braced herself for the truth.

Charlie told Anne, sparing no detail, about the lawn, the pain, the eyes and the fur. About the incident in the shower and every odd sensation and sight and occurrence right up until the red dress. She stopped there, not knowing how to continue. The silence ignited Gwen.

"Ain't no shame in ripping off that man's business." Again, flabbergasted, the sisters stared at Gwen who was carrying on like she was discussing the weather. "He would have had his way with you and fed you to his pigs while his seed still squirmed inside you. You did the world a favour, not that you knew it at the time. But you knew danger, so it wasn't malice, if that's what you are worried over."

"I did that." Charlie said it more to herself than the others, an admission and confession that made what she did real. She started to cry, and Anne came to her side and held her.

"It was self-defense, that's all," Anne said. "He was dangerous, like Gwen said. And they can't… they can't prove it, and no one knows…"

"She's right. It does not matter. The blues won't work very hard on behalf of that piece of shit."

"That's why you were acting so strange in the hospital," Anne said. "And why you were wearing those clothes."

"Bran… I went to the Goat's Moat right after, threw myself at Bran. I was feeling… electricity, hunger surging through my body. I wasn't myself, Anne. It wasn't me."

"No shame, chil'. You are right. It was not you."

"Then at the hospital, when I went to get food, there was a pale girl in the stairwell, with black eyes and sharp teeth and the most horrible laugh—"

"Mara."

Gwen's voice was deep and dark, her mouth moving as if the word tasted sour on her tongue. She stopped rocking and set her coffee down. She grabbed a glass vial from the windowsill and set it down on the coffee table in front of Charlie. Charlie reached for it, but drew her hand back. Anne grabbed the vial and held it up to the light.

"The island is full of magic," Gwen said. "Spirits and creatures of myth and folklore leave the pages of storybooks and live in our woods and under our waters."

"A claw," Anne said. "Large and thick, but it's shaped like… a fingernail."

"Can't break that one, though," Gwen said. "Strong as steel, that." Gwen set her cigarette in the amber ashtray and turned to Charlie. She reached out and took Charlie's hands and spoke.

Tears rolled down Charlie's face. Anne rubbed her back and nodded for Gwen to continue.

"The child from the hospital? The pale girl?" Gwen said. "She is Nattmara. Mara, they call them in Scandinavian folklore. In English you'd call her Night-mare. The Mara is both nightmare and wolf, a biped canine, a massive and feral creature of the woods. Female werewolves. They've been known to join our world, seep through our walls and cracks like sand, assume the form of a slender young women and ride people's chests at night, inducing bad dreams. Hence the title Nightmare. Seems one has taken a liking to you."

Charlie sputtered. "Werewolves?"

"Not many, but yes. They reside here. Elusive as the Yeti, and violent as nature itself."

Anne winced.

"Do Mara swim? Under the ocean, I mean?"

Gwen laughed, her cigarette jostling between her lips. "I walk with the land, not swim with the seas. You are a whole other kettle of fish, my dear."

Anger and frustration clenched Anne's stomach, and she balled her fists. Charlie took notice, stepping in and turning Anne to face her.

"We need to leave. We need to go now, get away from this," Charlie said.

"No, Charlie, we have to find out what's going on."

"Why, Anne?" Charlie yelled. "Let's go home and forget all of this bullshit!"

"Really? Can we? Can we just forget everything that's happened here, everything we know and everything we don't?"

Gwen interjected, her voice soft and coaxing. "You

aren't done yet." She walked over and opened the front door, then guided Charlie gently, a hand on her back. "Take a walk."

"Where?" Charlie asked.

"You know where."

Charlie stared at the woman, then stood, nodding as she passed through the door. Gwen reached out and embraced her. "You will be fine, chil'. One way or another."

Charlie lingered in the hug, then kept walking.

Anne stood, and Gwen shut the door. "Not you."

"What? Oh fuck a bunch of that, Gwen, she isn't going out there alone."

Gwen widened her stance and puffed out her chest. "Really? That woman just ate my horses and picked her teeth clean with the bones. What are you worried about, exactly?"

"Mara, actually, if there is such a thing."

Gwen plucked a set of keys off a hook on the wall by the door. "Come on, you fiery beast. Time to go for a ride."

"Hell no."

"You want answers too, do you not?"

Anne hesitated, taking a step back.

"Okay. You don't believe in werewolves." Gwen stepped up to Anne and pulled a tendril of her red, wet curls. "Do you believe in breathing under water?"

Anne hesitated, holding Gwen's stare until Gwen smiled and motioned out the door.

"Just gonna make a quick call. Meet you at the truck. Just follow the trail down to our lot."

Despite all logic, Anne nodded and left for the parking lot.

CHAPTER 22

IT HAD BEEN a long time since Anne had seen the sun rise. It was beautiful, the fog shrouding the grass, the purple glow between the trees. Anne almost forgot what she was doing as she walked along the gravel path towards the road where the staff parking area was located. The trees were alive with the early birds eating their worms and the nocturnal creatures cooing themselves to sleep. And a moan, a grumble from off the beaten path.

"Charlie?"

But Charlie had gone the other way, towards the other side of the property. Anne had watched her go when she left Gwen's cabin. But the sound she was hearing, low and guttural, was human.

"Gwen?"

Anne spied a narrow path leading into the woods.

Not a good idea, you idiot.

In true Anne fashion, she did it anyways, stepping off the main path and into the trees. It wasn't long before she came to a small clearing where the sound was amplified in the basin of trees.

It was straight out of a horror movie. A headstone, crude and overgrown, constructed out of wood and stone, poked out of the fog as if gasping for air. Wilfrid was shuffling about, picking weeds and brushing off the grave, moaning what might have been a beautiful song had he not sounded like a bovine in pain.

"Good morning, Wilfrid."

Wilfrid startled and dropped the handful of weeds on the ground. He stood tall, then bent in half, bowing to Anne.

"Sorry to startle you," Anne said. "You're working early—oh."

Wilfrid was naked, his flaccid penis swinging between his legs, shriveled and grey. More shocking, he was pocked with black patches and exposed bone, his remaining skin stretched tight over his skeletal frame. Though obscured by his massive beard, Anne saw the tease of a massive wound on his chest, his heart exposed, still and black as night.

"Holy fuck," Anne whispered.

Wilfrid watched her, then looked down at his body.

He started whimpering and trembling, his hands covering first his genitals then his chest, and back to his genitals again. He crouched down to the ground, huddling in a ball and hiding himself from Anne.

"Oh… no. No, big guy. I didn't mean to embarrass you. I just… I'm surprised, is all."

Reluctantly, Anne went to Wilfrid and put her hand on his back. His hide was like leather, cold and stiff. He pressed against Anne's touch and smiled up at her like a rescued puppy.

"It's okay," Anne said, stroking his head.

With all his strength, Wilfrid threw his arms around her, hugging her. Her ribs creaked, and she squeaked, trying to endure Wilfrid's affection. When he put her down, her body ached. With a wide smile revealing a toothless mouth, Wilfrid got back to work, tending to the grave.

Like thick worms, his fingers peeled away debris, doting on the headstone with tenderness and care. Anne helped, yanking away weeds and moss, brushing her hand across the stone to read the inscription.

She stared at the word chiseled into the stone in a child's script. A single word, no dates, nothing else.

WILFRID.

Wilfrid used those long worms for fingers to trace the word on the headstone, then he parted his beard, revealing a gaping hole through his chest, his heart, and out the other side of his body. Anne crouched down, looking through Wilfrid at the sunrise on the other side. He looked at her, eyes wide and filled with tears.

"Uh huh," Anne said, undecided whether she should laugh, cry, or scream. "I mean, why not? Werewolves, ghosts. I've gone absolutely mad."

Wilfrid patted her cheek, his hands damp and musty with soil, and continued toiling, beautifying his resting spot. Once it was spic and span again, he got on all fours, curled around in a circle, and nestled in for sleep.

Anne patted the behemoth on the shoulder and stood, backing away from the scene.

"We need to leave this place," she whispered. "Now."

Her stomach in knots, Charlie walked away from Gwen's quarters, her mind muddled and her body aching. She tried to pick sense of it, to find a logical explanation for everything going on.

Mara. Werewolf. This is absolutely fucking absurd.

Charlie's mind swept back, landing on the grass in the night, the pain in her gut, the fur in her mouth. The sensation of being dragged into the woods…

As she passed the stables her belly roiled, drool pooling under her tongue. Quickening her step, Charlie trotted past the gardens and the house to the spot on the lawn where she had fallen that first night. She knelt in the grass, which was now shimmering with light from the sunrise, and put her hand down. As soon as her fingers touched the blades, laughter erupted from the woods.

Charlie raised her head and saw the pale girl standing at the edge of the woods. She was different, longer, her face stretched down to the middle of her breastbone and fingertips touching the ground. The pale girl swayed on the balls of her feet, her hair blowing in the breeze. Long and skeletal, a finger came up, stretching and curling. Not too slow and not too fast, the pale girl walked into the woods. Charlie followed, keeping a safe distance behind.

Over root and brush, branch and rock, they walked as if tethered until the pale girl stopped and turned suddenly. Charlie's heart clenched into a vice, her body telling her to run, to scream, to give up and just die. But she was frozen in that spot, a place she'd been before; a strong sense of deja vu washed over her, bringing with it an eerie calm.

The wind blew, the leaves rustled, and the pale girl laughed, her voice becoming hoarse and weak as she dissolved, crumbling from the top her head downwards, turning to sand and pouring into a mound on the forest floor.

But no. Not just a hill. A pile. Movement. Shifting and growing, then standing, the sand formed limbs then torso, ribcage and skull until what stood before Charlie was not a little girl, but a massive werewolf, contorted, sparse tufts of hair sprouting over its muscular body, snout long and jaw massive and filled with an impossible number of teeth.

"Willow," Charlie said.

"Yes."

"How…"

Willow stepped forward. Charlie tensed but did not step back, even when the Mara was mere millimeters from her face, its hot, rancid breath misting into her mouth. Willow's long, gnarled paws wrapped around Charlie's arms, and the world swayed, swinging and shifting…

Willow. On the lawn. A knife in her belly.

Willow's throat in the jaws of a Mara, biting, pulling her into the woods.

Willow's blood soaking the ground while the Mara licked her, cleansing her, prepping her.

Out of Willow's body came the pale girl, stretching, piling like sand until fully formed, then contorting and twisting until her eyes were glowing yellow, her face elongated, and claws erupted from the tips of her fingers.

Willow's body faded to sand where the newly minted Mara stood, licking its lips and howling at the night sky.

With a blink it was daytime, and Charlie was standing in the woods, face to face with the Mara. With Willow.

"Oh Willow," Charlie said, raising her hand and stroking the beast's face.

I. Am. Sorry.

"No need for sorries. You were taken so young."

So. Sorry.

"What for?"

Charlie's feet were suddenly very warm. And wet. Grinding her feet into the ground, warm forest decay squished up between her toes. Charlie lifted a foot, then realized she had not been standing in the soggy leavings of the forest floor.

She was standing in her own, rotting corpse.

Charlie looked down into her own eyes, her body shredded and torn apart, her throat laying in tatters around her face. All manner of insect crawled in and out of her body, feasting on her blood, her meat, her bones. A heavy paw rested on her shoulder, and Charlie looked up to find fat tears clouding Willow's eyes.

The smell of her own blood was suddenly overwhelming, and drool starting dribbling down her chin. As she fell to her knees, eager to sate her hunger on her own flesh, Willow hauled to her feet and picked her up into the air.

"No."

Charlie sobbed, anger and terror wracking her body. Willow held her against her massive, muscular frame and stroked her hair.

"What am I supposed to be?" Charlie wailed. "What am I supposed to do?"

Willow set her down on the ground. Charlie felt a jab, and looked down to find the hilt of a fillet knife poking her between the ribs, the other end buried deep in Willow's belly. Charlie's hand was wrapped around the hilt. She gasped, pulled her hands back, and held them in front of her face. Hands that weren't hers. Long, skeletal, weathered.

Willow reached out and touched Charlie's cheek.

"Help me," Willow growled, pleading.

Charlie's mind swirled to the past. To the truth. When she opened her eyes, there was no knife in Willow's belly. Not any more.

"Yes," Charlie said, holding Willow's paw. "I will help you."

CHAPTER 23

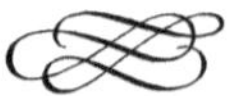

Gwen's rusty pickup hiccuped down the highway, jostling Anne around and upsetting her already tumultuous stomach.

"Why are we here?" Anne asked.

"Gonna pick up some supplies."

Anne pouted, her patience worn onion-skin thin.

"Okay. Why am *I* here?"

"To visit with the locals," Gwen said, motioning to fisherman on the dock, coming in and out of the shop and restaurant.

The truck struck a pothole, and the tools in the back jumped, clanking together and startling Anne. She looked in the backseat, on the floor, and spotted a heavy wooden box, long as the truck was wide, occupying the entire floor space of the back seat. Anne reached back, tracing her finger along the intricate, Native artwork burned into the heavy wood.

"This is beautiful. What is it?"

Gwen took a deep breath as she pulled into a parking lot. She exhaled heavily as she spoke.

"Mine," Gwen said. "Also, none of your business."

And with that, Gwen killed the engine, getting out and leaving Anne behind. Anne huffed and got out of the truck as Gwen walked into the little store.

Though it was early morning on a weekday, the lot was full of cars, and people were lined up at both the boat rental dock and the bait shack. Anne figured that made sense, as fishermen liked to hit the water early; best fishing is in the morning. Beside the dock was a cluster of picnic tables flanked by a little cafe serving breakfast and coffee.

"Good a start as any," Anne muttered, her stomach growling.

Anne made her way inside the smokey little building. A small bell on the door announced her entrance, turning every head in her direction. The clientele were all rough sea men, none less than fifty years old, a pallet of yellow and green rain gear. The air was thick with cigarette smoke, and the building crackled with warmth from the wood stove behind the bar.

"Get you anything, love?" the barkeep asked as

Anne slid onto a seat at the bar and looked at a crinkled menu card.

"Just a coffee."

"Our salmon and eggs are to die for," the man said, giving her a wink.

"Yeah. Can't resist that. Sure, let's do it."

He smiled, flashing a gold tooth embedded in a sea of white teeth, and barked an order to the kitchen. Anne perused the walls, which were plastered in black and white photographs, newspaper articles, and decorative plates. One plate in particular caught her attention: a blue and white plate displaying a scene of Copenhagen from afar, with a mermaid on a rock looking back at the city. As Anne focused on the plate, the world around her faded, the plate brightening to a faint glow. The haunting melody from the water came to life, humming in her head.

"Like that one, eh?" The barkeep lifted the plate off its hangar and placed in in front of Anne. "Little Mermaid. That's a bronze sculpture in a bay off Copenhagen. You've heard the story, certainly."

Anne nodded. "One of my favourites as a child."

"Beautiful one, at that."

"Seems Danish folklore is big out this way."

"All folklore is. The people of the west coast love their stories, regardless of origin."

Anne nodded.

"Wondering how you fit in?" the man asked.

Startled, Anne looked up at the man. He was attractive, tall and sturdy, deep green eyes, thick white hair, and beard framing his chiseled face.

"Pardon?"

"Allow me to introduce myself. I'm Edvard. I'm a friend of Gwen's."

"Ah. She told you I was coming."

"Aye. Called me a bit ago."

"So…" Anne said, placing her hands on the counter.

Edvard fished around in drawers behind the counter, plucking out paper after paper until a bell dinged, and a plate of food appeared at the kitchen window. He snatched it up and set it down in front of Anne, along with the stack of papers.

"Enjoy."

And with that, he walked away, grabbing the pot of coffee and strolling around the restaurant, refilling cups and exchanging pleasantries.

Anne flaked the salmon with her fork, dragging it through the hollandaise sauce before poking in her mouth. As she chewed, she lifted the first paper on the stack. A gossip mag, the National Enquirer of the island, claiming sea monsters impregnated a troop of girl scouts. Next were sightings of a long, prehistoric sea monster—cousin to Ogopogo and Nessie—lurking about Pachena Bay, slurping small pets out of campgrounds at night. Anne snickered, flipping through story after story of all flavours of sea creatures and the impossible.

"Big imaginations out here," Edvard said as he came back and filled Anne's coffee mug to the brim.

"I'd say," Anne said.

"The unknown is fascinating."

"Yeah," Anne said.

"Suppose, though, we aren't the be all end all. Suppose we don't know everything there is to know about life out there."

"We certainly don't," Anne said, scooping another bite of fish into her mouth.

"The ocean is vast and deep, and we only know a small fraction about what resides out there. Scientists will tell you about what might reside in the dark abyss, in the cold pockets unseen by human brains and eyes. So much possibility."

Anne flipped a page and stopped chewing, her food balling in a lump at the top of her stomach.

It was a crude sketch done in pencil crayon of a sea creature, almost exactly like Anne had dreamed.

Dreamed, right?

The creature was naked, perched atop a rock very much like the Danish Little Mermaid, but very different. Instead of limbs she had tentacles, her hair was a massive mane of indigo trailing down her back, she had full female genitalia garnished with a sea-foam green patch of hair. And instead of looking towards a city, she was glancing off the page, right at Anne.

"She, there, is little known folktale. The Vandheks. A melding of mythologies—the love child of the mermaid and the kraken. All their children are female, and have traits of each of the beasts."

"Gorgeous," Anne said, her finger tracing the indigo tresses.

"Quite. But sorrowful. Lonely. The Vandheks are an abomination, an anomaly in the world beneath the surface, and there aren't many of them, the tales say. Once in a blue moon does the kraken love the mermaid, thus not many of these creatures are spawned. The only ones who will befriend them are the octopuses, and that relationship is limited. Octopuses have a lifespan of a mere three years, where it is said this lass lives eternal."

"And what do they want?"

"Want? Nothing. Just to be, I suppose. Like any other creature. And connection. It is said they take those who drown in the ocean, but are never satisfied with their catch."

Anne slid the drawing back into the papers and pushed the stack away. "This is ridiculous."

"How so?"

"How do you even know this? How can people be sure? These are silly campfire stories."

"Indeed," Edvard said. "I never said the Vandheks were anything more than folklore. We were just yarning about old tales, were we not?"

Anne pushed the food around her plate with her fork, then scooped the last bite into her mouth, contemplating. Edvard perked up when the bell summoned him to his next delivery, a plate of crepes and Saskatoon berries. When he went to deliver the fare to its customer, Anne slid the picture of the sea creature out of the papers and looked at it, the silver eyes, the sorrowful face looking off the page, a slender hand reaching for her…

"Take it," Edvard said. "I have copies."

"Where did you get it?"

"An old fisherman drew it one night in a drunken stupor. Said he'd seen some things, but could never quite articulate what in words. Ol' island whiskey sparks an active imagination, I guess."

Whether it the thought of whiskey or the insanity of the creature, Anne's stomach did a flip, and sweat beaded on her skin. She rubbed her temples and held her head in her hands.

"You all right?" Edvard asked. He reached behind the counter and poured up a glass of ice water, setting it in front of Anne.

With trembling hands she raised the glass, drinking the water in great gulps then holding it to her chest.

"Fine. Hot. Hormones, I guess."

"Yeah," Edvard said, his expression communicating his disbelief.

"I should go," Anne said, pulling her wallet from her pocket.

Edvard waved a hand. "On the house."

"No, why?"

"My treat. I insist."

Anne tipped her head and stumbled off the stool, rushing to the door. She hadn't the time nor the will to argue. She was burning, her tongue thick and dry with thirst.

It's just panic. Get yourself together.

Bursting outside, the air was cooler, hopefully cool enough to get her back to Jutland House in one piece. Gwen was loading bags of soil into the truck along with sacks of horse feed.

"What's that for?" Anne asked, talking over a sandy tongue.

"Horses."

"No shit. But… what horses?"

"There will be more. Horses are important for Jutland House. Tourists love them, as do I. Horses soothe restless souls. I will adopt more as soon as you are gone."

"Why do you need to wait until…"

Anne paused as they made eye contact.

"Oh. Yeah. When we're gone."

Without another word, Anne boarded the truck. The women spent the trip back in silence, Anne holding the drawing of the Vandheks tight in her grasp.

CHAPTER 24

THE HEAVY DOOR CROAKED, grinding on its hinges as Charlie snuck back into Jutland House. She had no desire to speak to anyone. In her room, under her blankets, alone with her thoughts was the only place she wanted to be. Luck was not on her side, she realized, as she heard the heavy clip clop of Isadora's shoes.

"Did you see it?" Isadora said, her words sharp, eyes accusing.

"It?"

"The… stables?"

"Oh. Yes. I did."

Isadora stared, waiting for more, but Charlie didn't give it. She stared back as long as she could before dropping her gaze to the floor.

"Did you see it?" Charlie asked, not looking up.

"Heavens no. I have no desire to see such carnage. Gwen will tend to that, set traps for the wolves or cougars that did that, and we'll go about our business."

Charlie nodded and turned to the stairs.

"Heading upstairs?" Isadora asked, stepping in Charlie's way. "Any plans for the day?"

Charlie shrugged. "Not sure yet. Has Anne come back?"

Isadora's eye twitched. "She is not with you? You went to the barn together, did you not?"

"Yes, but… I went for a walk. The blood made me queasy, and I needed some fresh air."

"Hmmm." Isadora tapped her cane on the ground. The soft rattle made Charlie flinch. "No, I didn't see Anne return, but I might have missed her, if she scurried up to her room as you intended to do. You sure are a skulking couple, aren't you?"

"Suppose so," Charlie said, then motioned to the stairs. "May I?"

Isadora watched her, searching her face and body. After a moment of contemplation, Isadora gave a single nod and stepped to the side.

"I will go lay down for a spell, then," Isadora said. "Will you ladies be around for dinner tonight?"

"Yes. I'll speak with Anne when she gets back."

"I'll have Penny prepare something."

As Charlie climbed the stairs, Isadora disappeared

into the house, clucking her tongue. Charlie opened her door and went inside, bolting it locked behind her. When Anne returned, she would let her in, but she didn't want to be disturbed by anyone else. After taking a seat on the bed, Charlie thought about everything: the woods, the Mara, her own changes… Emme. She dropped to her knees, reached under the bed, and pulled out a small suitcase. As if someone would hear, and hearing would mean anything at all, Charlie quietly unzipped the suitcase, revealing a burgundy velvet bag with a gold string. She pulled it out and held it her her chest.

"Oh Emme," Charlie said, her voice breaking. Her tears started to flow, dripping on the bag. Charlie pulled an intricate, emerald urn out of the bag and traced her fingers over the gold etchings. "I miss you Emme. And I don't know what to do. With anything. Any of this, my life… anything. My life is like a side-scrolling video game, and I'm just trying to get to the end." Charlie gulped, swallowing a sob. "Is that how you felt?"

Charlie hugged the urn before setting it on the floor. She lay beside it, staring up at the ceiling, her hand wrapped around it. "And now this. You should get a load of this Mara business. You would never believe. I want to say I don't believe, but… I do. I can feel it, I *know* it, nonsensical as it is. You'd love it,

Emme. As horrifying and bizarre as this whole change is, you'd find something magical in it."

Charlie turned on her side, confronting the urn face on. "But I don't know what to do, Emme. You were supposed to be here, helping me."

Anger overwhelmed Charlie. She hugged her knees and cried, cursing Emme for leaving her alone, for showing her there were no other options. If Emme couldn't sort her shit out, certainly Charlie couldn't either.

A loud bang at the door startled Charlie, and she sat up. The second bang vibrated the floor, and a third summoned a yelp from her belly.

"Jesus! Who's there?"

No answer.

Charlie tucked the urn back in its velvet bag and pulled the drawstring tight, then secured it in the suitcase and shoved it deep under the bed. Before she had a change to stand, the knocking began again—forceful, frantic, hard enough to buckle the heavy oak door. Charlie covered her ears and squeezed her eyes closed, a sudden fear of what was in the hallway, waiting for her to open the door so she could be torn to shreds, consumed, digested, and shat out as something horrible and unnatural.

When the knocking stopped, Charlie could still feel it in her chest, pounding back against the pulse of her heart. She gave it a minute, then a minute more before finally standing and braving the journey across the room. As her fingers pressed the cold, iron handle, Charlie closed her eyes, bracing for the worst. She opened the door, just a sliver at first, then wide. Charlie found nothing but hallway, and no sounds from beyond. All quiet on the stairs, all quiet down below, no movement in sight.

But then a knock. Four knocks. Distinct but quiet, coming from downstairs. Charlie took her time sneaking down the stairs, not eager to find out what in the fresh hell the noise was. The kitchen was empty, as was the dining room and the sitting room beyond. The yard was unoccupied, bathed in the hot rays of the beating sun, not a soul in sight.

Knock, knock, knock, knock.

Louder than before, but still far away. Below.

Oh good. In the basement.

They had been given the tour after they arrived, a brief perusal of the mansion and its amenities, but hadn't ventured to the basement. They had been told it contained paper goods, bedding, and a wine cellar, but little more. Now Charlie doubted that. She walked down the hallway to the basement door, contemplating what excuse she would have for Isadora if she was caught snooping about the house.

Well, she didn't say not to go to the basement.

Charlie descended, pulling the light cord as she went and flooding the staircase in light. At the bottom of the stairs was a switch which lit a few bulbs hanging from the ceiling. The basement was musty, dark, and crowded with boxes and supplies. There had to be a year's worth of paper towel and toilet paper—thank you, Costco— and shelves along the wall stacked with bedding. The place looked fit to serve a full hotel rather than a bed-and-breakfast.

At the back of the room, behind rows of boxes, was a narrow door tucked in a corner. Charlie peeked in the door, squinting in the dark until she saw the brass cord hanging from the ceiling. One tug, and the room was illuminated, the bulb casting red, dancing shadows off the walls. It was the most beautiful wine cellar Charlie had seen. Packed dirt floor, dark walls, walnut shelves—and hundreds of bottles of wine from all over the globe. She walked up and down the rows, fingers caressing the bottles, the light from above twinkling off the glass.

Click.

Charlie stopped, thought, then lunged for the door. When she pulled on it, it didn't budge.

"Hello?"

No amount of pulling, prying, or rattling would move the door even a millimeter. It had no lock, but somehow, it was locked from the outside.

Tink.

Something tapped on glass across the room.

Tink, tink.

A fingernail, perhaps. Charlie didn't turn around. She rested her forehead on the door, willing it to open.

Knock, knock.

From the other side of the room, off wood this time.

Charlie walked, despite all logic and sense of self-preservation, to the source of the sound.

Knock.

Down an aisle, to the far wall…

Knock, knock,

The sound was coming from behind a rack of Cabernet Sauvignon. Charlie pulled down bottles, one by one, setting them in the dirt. After the rack was empty, she shimmied it out of the way, revealing a plank door with a hammer hanging on the wall beside. Charlie pressed her hand against the door and waited.

Knock.

She felt it, that single knock, from the other side of the wood. She worked on a loose board, working the nails with the hammer until the board was free, then another, and another.

It was a small room, a closet, virtually empty. But there was a box. A small box covered in intricate carvings of totems—wolves and cephalopods—nailed shut.

Charlie knelt down in the tiny space, in front of the box, and worked out the nails with the hammer, delicately, as if there was fragile treasure within.

The box seemed to sigh when Charlie lifted the lid off. The first thing, set on the top, was a picture in a frame. Charlie stared at it, running her finger over the image, then sifted through the rest of the box.

After examining the contents, she closed the lid, hammering in just two nails to keep it in place, then squeezed out of the room, the box in her arms.

She knows.

The voice startled Isadora out of her nap. She rubbed her eyes, squinting though her lace curtains at the afternoon sun.

"Oh my," she said, disorienting by her deep, midday slumber.

She stood and straightened her gown, then sat at her mirror and got to work replacing her hairpins, ensuring that every strand was in its place. A bit of rouge and a touch of lipstick later, she was satisfied and ready to face the remainder of the day. She stood and examined herself in the full-length mirror beside the door, smoothing out a few ruffles in her skirt and adjusting her collar, when a pair of hands curled over her shoulders.

Isadora screamed and spun around. It was a woman, her skin grey and face gaunt. Her eyes were red and oozing with blood. She blinked, splattering blood over the front of Isadora's white gown. When she spoke, thick black sludge dribbled from her lips.

She knows. Soon they all will. And you will, too.

Ariculating the last word, green and black vomit poured from the woman's throat, coating her bones and her body and pooling on the floor, splashing over Isadora's feet. Isadora grabbed her cane and ran for the door, throwing it open and flapping out into the hall. When she turned to slam the door, to close the evil inside her room and lock it away there forever, she found nothing but white carpet and linens, sunshine and mirrors. The room was empty, the floor clean. Isadora stared, straightened her gown, then shut the door anyways, barring in the vision still fresh in her memory.

"It's nothing, you crazy old bat," Isadora said, fumbling with her hairpins. "Nothing at all. Nerves, is all, from these wretched guests."

Isadora spent a full minute shaking her cane, listening to the soothing rattle within the wolf's head to calm herself until she noticed the door to the basement was open. Isadora didn't miss a beat before cursing Penny.

"Damn, good-for-nothing fool."

She marched down the stairs, looking over her shoulder. When she reached the basement, she immediately saw the open wine cellar. She investigated there, and found a shelf along the back wall had been stripped of all the wine, the bottles strewn haphazardly about the floor.

"That bloody imbecile," Isadora muttered, her face red. "What in God's name did she do?"

Isadora picked up a loose board and tossed it aside, then noticed the exposed closet behind the bare shelf. It was empty, but not undisturbed. There were footprints in the dirt, and a rectangle where something had been sitting on the floor but had been removed.

"Stealing from me, are you? I don't know what it was, but it was in my house, so it belongs to me!"

Isadora took a step into the closet, but was overcome with pain, her heart pounding and lungs struggling to function. She backed away and leaned against a wine rack, peeking into the closet from afar.

"I should not be down here," Isadora said to the room, her voice filled with terror. "The help. This room, this basement. It's meant for the help and only them."

She didn't know where to look. Up the stairs to her

ghostly assailant, or into that closet, a room filled with pain and death.

"Your imagination, you loony crone," Isadora muttered to herself. "Get ahold of yourself."

She tried again, stepping one foot into the small closet when the sound of broken glass rang out behind her.

"Who's that!" Isadora screeched as she backed out of the closet again and pressed her back against the wall beside. From her vantage point, she could see nothing awry. Slowly, she walked across the room, looking up the aisles of bottles until she found a smashed red, its contents seeping into the dirt. With caution she approached the spill, crouching over it until she could see her reflection in a large shard of glass. But it wasn't her. The eyes, they were her own, but her face was distorted, suffocated, as if encased in a caul. She attempted to stand, but she found herself wrapped in the tight, stretchy sheath that had spread over her whole body, shrinking down until she was restrained in the fetal position.

Screaming and thrashing, Isadora pushed and rolled across the floor, slicing herself on the glass and banging against the walls, but the caul would not split open. She fought and struggled across the floor until she worked her way into the closet. Her fingers peeled moist hair away from her face, which she tried to put back in pins. Her elbow brushed against her own skin, and she grimaced, realizing she was naked in the caul, wet and sticky. Never one to leave the confines of her bedroom with a single hair out of place, Isadora felt the wrath of shame and humiliation, and she panicked.

"Help!" she cried, but her mouth was full of liquid, and no words would form.

HELP HELP HELP, her mind screamed, but her fingers no longer had the strength to move or her body the strength to fight.

Like a slice of moonlight through a dark sky, a glimmer of silver hovered over her face, a scalpel slicing through the material of her containment. Rotting fingers pushed through the caul, peeling it to the side, freeing Isadora. She scrambled back against the wall of the closet, pulling at the stretchy, gooey material that had held her captive, but found nothing there. Nothing but the dead woman floating in front of her, smirking, dark vomit covering the front of her naked, rotting body.

This is where you belong, Isadora. This is what you were meant to be.

With a blink, the woman was gone. Isadora held her breath, waiting for another assault. When none came, she stood, stepped out of the closet, and brushed herself off.

"Mad, I am mad. And it's all Penny's fault. And the sisters."

She snatched a wine bottle off a nearby rack and threw it at the wall, the red wine spattering back and showering her in crimson and glass.

"You will not take this place from me!" she screeched, spittle flying from her mouth and tears of rage streaming down her face.

With a scrunch of her brow and a huff, Isadora stormed out of the cellar, through the basement, and up the stairs.

By the time Gwen pulled into the drive, Anne was sure her blood had boiled and she would spew fire if she opened her mouth. The heat was excruciating, and sweat soaked her clothes and her hair. Gwen said nothing, just pulled her truck alongside the house and rolled to a stop. Anne jumped out and ran into Jutland House before Gwen even had the truck in park.

Taking the stairs two at a time, Anne sprinted down the hall and locked herself in the bathroom. She didn't want to see anyone or answer any questions. Fully clothed, she jumped in the shower, turned the spray on full blast on cold, and lay in the tub, gulping the water as it hit her face. She peeled off her clothes and rubbed her skin, which itched like a sunburn. She scratched harder, clawing at her thighs until her skin peeled, shreds of flesh tearing off under her fingernails. Anne looked down at the flaps of skin hanging from her fingers and held them up to her face. With the amount of flesh hanging from her nails, Anne expected the tub to be full of blood, but it wasn't. There was no blood at all—not in the tub, not on her. Only silver.

The gouge marks Anne scratched in her thighs revealed iridescent silver skin beneath, rainbow scales that glittered in the light. Anne touched the raw, red skin on her abdomen, rubbing until her own flesh sloughed away, revealing the diamond skin beneath. Anne closed the faucet, stepped out of the tub, and wrapped herself in the robe hanging off the hook on the door. She tied her dripping hair in a knot behind her head and leaned into the mirror, examining her eyes. Her eyes were bloodshot, burst vessels webbing over the whites of her eyes, and her left iris and pupil had gone completely silver. She smacked her lips together and they split, dry and crusted with blood. She wiped them with the back of her hand, revealing black skin beneath.

Anne left the bathroom and strolled out the front door. Gwen was unloading the last of the dirt and looked up as Anne passed. Anne turned her head, and they made eye contact for a brief second before Gwen nodded and went about her business. Anne rounded the house and walked towards the water, dropping her robe on the grass when she was halfway across the lawn. She reached the shore, and, without hesitation, dove in and disappeared beneath the sparkling surface.

CHAPTER 25

ICE CUBES JINGLED in the glass as Charlie sipped her drink, the liquor sliding down her throat, soothing her nerves. Bran joined her with a drink of his own, taking his place beside her on the log and wrapping his arm around her shoulders. The Goat's Moat was busy, almost every table full, and for that Charlie was thankful. Too quiet and her mind would work overtime. She needed the noise. The distraction.

"I appreciate you," Charlie said, "and everything you've done."

"I've done nothing," Bran said. "I like you, Charlie. You are a beautiful person, in so many ways."

"You barely know me."

"I know you enough."

"You have no idea."

Bran took a swallow of his drink and traced his finger along Charlie's hand. "Look, you're going through shit. I get that. Just because you aren't at your best doesn't mean I'm going to run screaming. I want to hang with you. Keep in touch with you when you go. Where is home, again? Where are you going?"

Didn't matter. None of it mattered.

"I don't know where I'm going."

Bran was quiet, rolling his drink around his glass. Charlie watched him, his eyes, full of life and kindness. He lifted his head and looked at her, and a smile spread across his face.

"Why are you staring at me?" he asked.

"You're beautiful, too."

Bran turned red and stroked his beard. "Hey, have you ever considered staying?"

"Where?"

"Here. The island."

"And what, buy a house?"

"You've got money, haven't you? You could get a job anywhere. Hell, I'd even hire you."

"Slinging drinks. Life goals."

Bran laughed, and they clinked their glasses together, toasting a moment of cheer in the darkness. Charlie slugged back the remainder of her drink, then leaned in and kissed Bran. She held him there, holding her hand on his cheek, feeling him, pressing into him, taking him all in. When she sat back, there were tears in her eyes.

"I should go," she said, standing from the bench.

"Charlie, what's wrong?"

I will never see you again.

"Nothing. Isadora is having dinner prepared. She gets upset if we're late."

Bran wrinkled his brow and stroked her cheek. "You sure that's all?"

Charlie smiled and kissed him, a quick brush of her lips on his before walking away. He held her hand, stalling her briefly before she wriggled free and walked to the car, not looking back so Bran wouldn't see her cry.

Gwen sliced her steak, tossing the meat in her mouth and savouring every morsel. Once Edvard had a few minutes of downtime, he sat with her at her table in the corner, bringing two shots of whiskey with him.

"Busy night tonight," Gwen said, nodding at the full restaurant.

"Sure is. You aren't gonna be there at Jutland House tonight?"

"No sir. Staying out of that one."

"Proper thing."

She chewed, and he looked out at the stars that were already shining bright in the dusk sky.

"What do you suppose will come of all of them? Of all of this?" Edvard said.

"Been a long time coming, this has."

"Sure has." Edvard took Gwen's hand, and looked at the ornate box under her feet. "Why do you stay, Gwen? I could take care of that for you."

She looked down, patting her foot on the lid. "I know you would. But I'm happy. And I'm not ready. Never will be, I imagine."

"Well, I won't last forever," Edvard said, winking.

"Perhaps that will be my time to go, too."

They smiled, and Gwen pulled his hand up, resting her head in his palm.

"Who will come out on top?" Edvard said.

"Who can tell? But my bet is on the sisters."

"Which ones?"

Gwen smiled and raised her glass. Edvard raised his, as well.

"May the best beast win," Gwen said, and they clinked their jiggers together, toasting the end.

THE SUN WAS low and red, obscured by the nearby hills when Anne emerged from the ocean, her skin cool and refreshed and her thirst quenched. She stood in the waning shreds of daylight and looked out over the water, watching the ripples, sparkles dancing here and there. She closed her eyes and imagined the colours below, the beauty, the calm, the serenity of Zelda's touch, the haunting, moving melody of her song. Anne opened her mouth and sang out to the bay, notes she didn't think she had in her, a melody sweet and melancholy.

Below the crystal waves of salt
A pool of tears amongst the drought
A land of beauty down below
Into the depths of life I'll go.

The sea birds cawed in unison, a harmony to Anne's sultry tones. The water stirred, fish and critters dancing in the slight surge, twirling and whirling to her tune. The cold air licked at Anne's flesh, but she was not cold. The depths of the Pacific were much colder than anything above.

After enjoying the ocean much longer than she should have dared, exposed and naked as she was, Anne strolled up the lawn, scooping up her discarded robe and draping it over her shoulders. Charlie got out of the car and met her at the front steps, and they entwined fingers before entering Jutland House one last time.

CHAPTER 26

THE TABLE WAS SET with the best silverware and china, a meal of freshly caught fish and moose steaks were cooking in the kitchen, and Penny hustled about, polishing glasses and arranging flowers. Emotions were running high, the importance of the meal unknown but emphasized, nonetheless.

Isadora lingered in the music room, sitting on the couch and wringing her hands. She stared at the violin on the wall, her body shaking and brain screaming until she took the instrument off it's hooks and smashed it against the piano, over and over and over, wood splintering and strings twanging out in pain.

Anne and Charlie were together on Anne's bed, laying down, fingers entwined, silent, staring at each other.

They knew. They knew the importance of what they were about to do, and were prepared, at any cost, to get it done.

"DINNERTIME!"

Isadora's voice rang through the house like a bell, summoning everyone to the dining room.

"The table is set, and the food awaits!"

Charlie and Anne sat up in unison, their eyes fixed on each other. When they opened the bedroom door, music wafted through the house, the crackle of a Scandinavian opera. The sisters walked to the stairs, side by side, but Charlie went first, pulling Anne behind her as they descended to the main floor. Candles were lit along the way, in sconces on the walls and in the centerpiece on the hallway table. When they walked by the kitchen, Anne sniffed the air and salivated at the aroma of lemon-butter salmon simmering on the stove. She looked over at Charlie, who was swallowing hard and looking away from the kitchen.

"The smell bother you?" Anne whispered.

"The blood. Sets me off."

"Ah."

They entered the dining room, which was decorated with flowers cut from the gardens that day, and took their places at the table, side-by-side. After they were seated, Isadora floated in the room dressed in a lavish, gold gown.

That's different, Anne thought. *But familiar.*

"Well, I do say, very well done arriving promptly for dinner!"

"Yes." Anne and Charlie spoke in unison, their voices monotone and low.

Isadora appeared not to notice, her eyes darting around the room, searching the corners and flickering at the shadows thrown by the wavering candlelight.

"Feeling all right?" Anne asked, her head cocked.

"You seem on edge." Charlie said, the corner of her mouth upturned in a devilish grin.

"I am quite fine," Isadora said, fiddling with her pearl necklace. "This house has… unsettled me today. It will pass."

Isadora sat at the head of the table and rang the bell on her belt. Penny came in the room immediately, wringing her hands.

"Yes ma'am?"

"It is shocking that I would need to summon you to bring wine. The moment our guests arrive they should be offered refreshments."

Penny bit her lip. "Yes, of course. I apologize."

Penny gritted her teeth and went back to the kitchen, Isadora watching her the whole way.

"You should be kinder," Anne said. "She is doing a good job. Besides, this is a bed-and-breakfast, not a fucking castle."

Isadora glared at Anne. "What did you say?"

"Kinder," Charlie repeated. "There's no need to treat her like a servant."

"Well she is," Isadora said. "Staff, servant, all the same. There is a hierarchy here, girls, like it or not. I expect a certain level of quality when it comes to my home."

Without Isadora's hands moving, the bell on her belt rang, and the old woman screeched.

"I… do apologize. It's been… acting up, the house has."

Penny came back into the room with two bottles of wine. "I do apologize," Penny said, corking both bottles. "Which would you prefer?"

"Red," Charlie said.

"White," said Anne.

Penny poured up the glasses, glancing over at Isadora who was watching her like a hawk. "Would you like me to leave the bottles?" Penny asked.

"No, it is quite crude to have those sitting on the table. Besides, you will pour for us, so you can carry them back in."

"No," Anne said. She took the bottle of white from

Penny, and Charlie followed suit, taking the red and putting it in front of her place setting.

"We will keep them here and refill our glasses ourselves," Charlie said, glowering at Isadora. "We are completely capable, and not so entitled that we can't pour a glass of wine."

Penny froze, caught in the stare down between the sisters and Isadora, then backed away and left the room.

"So," Isadora said as the sisters sipped their wine. "Have you recovered from seeing the stables earlier? I do apologize for such a horror. My guests should never have to experience something like that."

"No worries," Charlie said, licking her lips. "It's the circle of life."

"Indeed," Isadora said, watching Charlie closely. Isadora was disheveled, her gown wrinkled and her hair falling out of its pins. Her eyes were red, darting around the room like prey, watching, anxious. "And where did you ladies goof off to today? See any sights?"

"We had a visit with Gwen in her quarters," Anne said. "Then she drove me to the supply shop. I had a bite to eat there, visited with Edvard."

Isadora scoffed. "That old fool? I remember when he used to come around here, trying to fish off my waters. I told him where to stick it. Haven't seen him since."

"You know what I think, Isadora?" Anne downed her wine in three gulps and grabbed the bottle, filling the glass to the rim while Isadora looked on, shocked. "You think everyone is a fool. Everyone but you."

Isadora's mouth hung open, but no words came out, anger reddening her face.

"I'm just messing with you," Anne said, forcing a laugh that came out as a child's giggle.

Isadora forced a giggle too, trying to regain her composure. She sipped her wine, then took a large swallow, her hands shaking. "And you, Charlie?"

"After I left Gwen's, I took a stroll through the woods."

"A terrible idea," Isadora scolded. "It is dangerous out there in the woods."

"Why is that?" Charlie said. "What is so dangerous out in the woods?"

"I… uh, the animals—"

"What animals?"

"You saw those horses."

"I did," Charlie said.

"And that man that got attacked."

"I saw him, too."

Isadora stopped. She set her wine down and her breathing stilled. She and Charlie stared at each other, and the bell came to life again, ringing so hard that it detached from Isadora's belt and rolled across the floor. Isadora covered her mouth, stifling a scream, then fiddled with her hair pins and put her hand atop her cane.

"Someone messing with you?" Charlie asked.

Penny came in carrying silver domes of food, setting one in front of each sister. She lifted the domes, revealing a feast of salmon for Anne and venison for Charlie.

"Anything else I can get you?" Penny asked.

"God no," Anne said, as she flaked her fish apart with her fork.

"Looks amazing." Charlie said. She picked up the venison with her hands and gobbled into it, blood dribbling down her chin. Penny did a double take, then walked slowly back to the kitchen, watching Charlie as she devoured her food.

"And what about you, Isadora?" Anne asked. "What did you do today?"

"Me, well I…"

Charlie finished off her piece of meat and started on the mashed potatoes, scooping them up with her fingers and stuffing them into her mouth.

"…I took a nap, then—"

Penny came back with a single silver dome, placing it in front of Isadora and lifting it in one motion.

"Good?" Penny asked, abrupt.

"Fine," Isadora said waving her away.

Penny went back to the kitchen, and Charlie sat back, plate in her hands, licking it clean.

"That is enough!" Isadora slammed her hands on the table and sat forward. "You ladies are swine! I know you are trying to get a rise out of me, and a rise you shall get. You have been here long enough, and you have been disrespectful, so I suggest you tend to your business and move on."

"Oh we are," Anne said, delicately placing flakes of fish on her tongue and sucking them down. "Say, what shall you do, Isadora, once we've left?"

"What do you mean?"

"Once we're gone," Charlie said as she set her plate down on the table, "and the next guests are gone, and the next. What are your plans? Live out your days here in Jutland House until your dying breath?"

Isadora straightened in her chair. "Yes. I will be here until the end. This is my home, my property."

"This is your parent's house," Anne said.

"It is not!" Isadora said. "They didn't deserve it. Didn't care. They were going to sell it, leave everything we had."

"So what?" Charlie said. "Families do that all the time. Home is not about houses and possessions. Home is family. Where your people are."

Charlie's tongue curled over her lips, licking away blood and mash. She leaned forward, her yellow eyes boring down on Isadora. "But that's the thing, isn't it? All you have is this place. Without Jutland House—"

Penny came in, carrying a bottle of vintage merlot. "You wanted this, ma'am?"

As Penny approached the table, her foot snagged on the carpet and she came crashing to the ground. The bottle of wine smashed on the table, the merlot spraying over Isadora, soaking her hair, face, and the front of her gown. The air sucked from the room, everyone stunned, then Penny started rambling.

"Holy shit, no," Penny mewled. "I am so, so sorry. I can't even believe I did that. I can clean this. I can, I'm sorry…"

Isadora's face was dark and steady, staring down at Penny in disgust. She plucked a few shards of glass off her ruined gown and flicked them at Penny, striking her in the cheek and nicking her skin.

"Hey, you old bitch! It was a goddamn accident!" Penny stood from the floor, untied her apron, and threw it on the table. "I've had enough of your shit. I quit. This job don't pay me enough to put up with your—"

In one fluid movement, Isadora picked the broken bottle neck off the floor, stood, and swiped it across Penny's neck, severing her throat. Penny was shocked, her fingers finding the gash as a geyser of blood poured down her shirt. She crumpled to the floor, her last words an incoherent gurgle.

Isadora smoothed her gown and sat back down.

"Enough of that unpleasantness," Isadora said, not looking at the sisters. "Finish your meal and enjoy it, for it will be your last here, you ignorant buffoons."

Charlie and Anne looked at each other. Anne set her fork down on her plate while Charlie tilted her head back and forth, cracking her neck.

"You are absolutely right, Isadora," Charlie said as she cracked her knuckles. "That's quite enough of this unpleasantness."

After standing and taking a few steps back from the table, Charlie lurched forward, bending at the waist, and let out a blood-curdling growl. Her hair swirled, shifting, pouring like lines of sand as it cascaded down her face, taking her skin and clothes with it. When she straightened her spine and stood tall, she was at least nine feet, maybe ten, with bulging muscles and patches of fur over her nude body. Her skull transformed, creaking and snapping while bones separated and fused, reshaping and lengthening into a long snout.

Isadora's chair tipped back as she jumped from the table and ran for the main door. She had her fingers around the handle and the door opened halfway when it slammed shut. A gagging sound erupted behind her, and the splashing of liquid. Isadora turned, pressing her back against the door which had been slammed shut by a thick, writhing tentacle. Anne was still sitting at the table, coughing, copious amounts of water spewing from her mouth over the table cloth. When she was done purging the fluid from her lungs, she wiped her mouth with another tentacle and stood. She still had her legs, though they were shining silver, but one arm had been replaced by two tentacles, coiling and feeling the table, the air, one holding the door and one fumbling with Isadora's hair.

"Hell has come to swallow this house," Isadora gasped.

"Better than you having it," Charlie said. She snarled at Isadora, then lifted her head, puffed her chest, and brayed out a hoarse, guttural howl. Anne coughed again, producing more water that sprayed across the room at Isadora. When they were done howling and coughing, Anne spoke. The words came out of her mouth, but the voice was not her own.

"What's the matter, sister," Zelda said through Anne's lips. "Didn't think you'd hear from us again, did you?"

"Monsters," Isadora said, her voice a spasming whisper.

"No," Willow growled through Charlie's jowls. "You are the only monster here."

Isadora moved suddenly, with speed surprising for a woman her age, and grabbed the broken bottle neck from the table, brandishing it at the sisters.

"You will never take this place from me," Isadora screamed, "or me from this place! It is mine!"

She swiped, slicing the closest tentacle, and blue blood poured out on the carpet. Anne cried out, but quickly composed herself, the wound healing in a matter of seconds. Charlie jumped on the table, balancing on her haunches and rocking, posturing to attack. Isadora slammed backwards into the kitchen and propped a chair against the handle. As she ran for the other entrance to the kitchen, the sisters ran for the main entrance of the dining room.

They burst into the hallway, and Charlie reached the kitchen door in two strides. The room was empty. Anne's slender, glowing legs carried her into the music room, her tentacles opening cupboards and closets as she passed.

"She can't get away," Zelda said through Anne. "Too many years she's gotten away with this."

"We'll get her," Willow growled through Charlie's teeth. "She's old and feeble. Time has not been kind, and we are powerful."

Charlie cocked her head.

Knock. Knock. Knock. Knock.

"Did you hear that?" Charlie asked, looking at Anne.

Knock. Knock. Knock. Knock.

"The basement!" Charlie yelled as she trotted around the corner and hit the stairs at a sprint. Anne followed behind, gliding to keep up to her sister.

The basement was cold, dark, and damp, but that did not trouble the sisters. The part of Anne that was Zelda was accustomed to the frigid temperatures of the deep Pacific, as well as the darkness so far below the surface. Charlie's sparse fur left her a little more chilly, but the dark was her friend; her eyes glowed yellow even in the absence of light. Anne lingered at the bottom of the stairs as Charlie sniffed the air, licking boxes as she passed and hunching over to sniff the ground.

"She's here," Willow said.

"But where?" Zelda asked. "She's not so small that she could fit into any of these boxes."

Charlie recalled a distant memory of a recent path and cautiously approached the door to the wine cellar. She sniffed, but shook her head.

"Not there," Willow said, but Charlie opened the

door anyways, needing to confirm that Isadora wasn't in the only other hiding space in the basement.

Knock.

The sound came from the other side of the room. Boxes had been moved aside—recently, from the look of the displaced dust—revealing an opening and short staircase leading to a door in the ceiling.

"A cellar door?" Anne said.

Charlie came over and sniffed the steps, then growled. "Yep. This way."

Charlie shoved past Anne, climbing the ladder first, but the door didn't budge when she pushed on it. Anne helped, and with all their force they pushed against the door, then slammed against it, but it stayed firmly in place.

"She's locked it from the other side." Charlie growled.

Knock, knock, knock.

The sisters backed away as the iron lock on the other side of the door rattled, then clanked. The door flew open. A figure floated there, glowing in the night.

"Emme," Charlie choked.

"Come on," Emme said, reaching for a tentacle and a paw. "It's time to be finished with this and move on."

CHAPTER 27

ANNE LOOKED up at the stars, both her and Zelda wishing they were below the waves.

The night was clear, the grass a shimmering blue, just like when they had first arrived at Jutland House. Owls and crows conversed through the trees, their songs complimentary and lyrical. It was not hard to find Isadora. Old as she was, she must have just made it out of the cellar and locked it before the sisters discovered where she went, and was only halfway to the woods.

"Nowhere to go," Willow shouted though Charlie. "Might as well give up."

"Never!" Isadora screamed.

When she turned to them, Anne could see she was

brandishing an axe, its blade gleaming in the moonlight.

"You haven't the strength to wield that, old woman," Zelda said through Anne.

"You won't take it," Isadora said. "It's mine, and you will leave me be! Leave me here with the house!"

"You started this, Isadora."

Emme floated forward, necrotic organs hanging stagnant beneath translucent flesh. "Pleasure to formally make your acquaintance, Isadora. I am Emme. The third sister."

"Hell you are," Isadora said. She hoisted the axe above her head and swung with every bit of strength she possessed. The blade sliced right through the middle of Emme's head, splitting through her body and landing squarely in Isadora's own thigh. Isadora shrieked in pain, but her face contorted in laughter. "Got you!"

The two halves of Emme had been separated, but floated together like fog reconnecting until she was whole again.

"The creatures here have quite the tales to tell," Emme said, looking at the woods and the water. "About your family, about you, about what you did." Emme motioned back to her sisters. "I met your sisters. Bloody shame, that. A tragedy all around."

"But how… this is nonsense," Isadora said.

Isadora wiped the front of her gown, but couldn't fix it. It was stained with Penny's blood and torn where the axe had ripped through the fabric. Her fingers meddled with her hairpins, trying to tame the mess upon her head. "No, all nonsense. I've gone a touch delusional, must be the THC that helps calm me to sleep."

"Enough of this," Zelda said through Anne as she marched forward, tentacles whipping through the air. The flesh on the tentacle shimmered, and turned from silver to red with anger. "I watched you murder Willow right on this spot! Isadora, how could you! I hate you!"

Anne wrapped a tentacle around the handle of the axe and pulled it from Isadora's thigh. It came out with an audible squelch, then made a soft thud when Anne swung it, burying it deep in Isadora's throat.

Isadora gasped and sputtered, then fell back on the ground, landing in the very spot Willow had that fateful night. Anne watched as she thrashed around, moaning and clutching her neck and thigh.

"We got her, Willow," Zelda said, crying. "She finally got what she deserved."

Anne looked at Charlie's face, but didn't find elation, as she had suspected.

"That won't do it," Emme said, looking at Charlie.

"What? Why?" Anne and Zelda said.

Anne's attention shifted to Isadora. Impossibly, the

old woman had sat up, and was trying to pull the axe from her throat. Anne walked over and dropped to her knees, using her tentacles to pull the axe loose and toss it on the ground. Isadora's fingers groped her throat, her thigh. She pulled up her dress, revealing skin so bare it looked like it had never been touched, let alone sustained a wound from an axe.

"There's no blood," Isadora said, fumbling at her throat. "You can't kill me!" she said, a maniacal giggle encasing her voice. "I'm one of you freaks! You can't get rid of me!"

"Nothing to get rid of," Charlie said. "You're already gone."

Confused, Anne watched as Charlie ran into the woods and reemerged with a small wooden box. It was very similar to the box she had seen on the floor of Gwen's truck—intricately carved with symbols and animals. Charlie set the box in front of Isadora and pried it open, revealing the contents.

"Such a tragedy," Charlie said. "With Willow's guidance, I came to understand how old you really are." Charlie pulled the photograph from the box. The photograph was of an infant, swaddled in a golden shroud—the same as the gown Isadora wore this very evening—face puffy and eyes fixed open. Beside the infant in the photograph was a silver rattle with the head of a wolf and the base of an octopus."

"My cane," Isadora said, touching the photograph.

"Back in your day, some found it custom to photograph the dead to preserve their memory. Your parents decided to take it one step further."

Charlie pulled a crimson blanket out of the box and gently unwrapped it, revealing the skeletal remains of a small infant. Isadora gasped and took the body from Charlie's arms, cradling it in her own and rocking it back and forth.

"You were stillborn, Isadora," Emme said.

"I knew when Emme led me to the box in the wine cellar," Charlie said. "There were never any pictures of the three sisters together, because there was never a third sister. Not in the flesh, anyways."

"Children are more susceptible to seeing spirits," Emme said, "so your sisters believed you to be real. Never told your parents, though, for the risk they might be accused of telling tall tales."

"But..., Isadora stammered, "I killed..."

Emme moved closer and re-pinned Isadora's flyaway hairs. "Specters can be quite dangerous, especially when their existence is threatened."

"Mom and Dad wanted to move," Willow said quietly with Charlie's voice. "They were talking about getting rid of you. You overheard them discussing it. I remember, you were very angry."

"Yes," Isadora said, tears rolling down her cheeks.

"They were going to take me away from the house, put me somewhere."

"A cemetery," Emme said. "They were finally ready to let go. But you weren't. In your rage, you destroyed everything that threatened your existence."

"Without this house..." Isadora looked up at Jutland House, her eyes wide, "... I am nothing."

"There are many reasons that people don't move on..." Emme looked down at her sisters for a moment before continuing. "But if you don't choose to move on, you are tethered to your body, and must stay within range or you will be forced to move on."

A tear formed in Anne's eye as she thought of the intricately carved box on the floor of Gwen's truck. As if summoned, Gwen appeared, hands in her pockets, watching the scene unfold. Beside her was Wilfrid, dressed in his old RCMP uniform, a singed hole through the center of his chest. Isadora pointed at him with a trembling finger.

"But... but I shot you, you oaf! For nosing around where you didn't belong!" Isadora screeched. "Too smart, you were, and you almost had me, didn't you! But I got you first!"

Wilfrid growled at Isadora, his toothless maw wide as a cavern. Gwen put her hand on his chest, and he leaned into her, resting his head on her shoulder. Gwen looked at Isadora, hatred in her eyes.

"I didn't know where your damn body was," Gwen said, nodding to the infant, "Or I'd have fed it to the wolves decades ago."

Anne walked over and pried the infant's skeleton out of Isadora's weakening grasp.

"No!" Isadora shrieked.

She scrambled to her feet, pressing the infant to her chest, trying to hold the bones together and run. But time had made the bones brittle and delicate, and the tiny skeleton crumbled apart, the bones scattering on the ground.

"Leave me be!" Isadora cried. "You'll never take this place from me! This is my home!"

Crows descended from the trees in a flurry of feathers, plucking bones out of Isadora's grasp and off the ground then disappearing into the night. They came down in flapping droves until every ivory bone was gone, destined for new and separate homes over the island.

Isadora cried, the tears peeling skin as they rolled off her cheeks. Her quaking wails rattled the flesh off her body in clumps, her breasts, stomach, and buttocks dissolving into slick powder. The thighs and the arms were the next to go, crumbling to dust, leaving only a spine, ribcage, and skull.

The jaw moved, words coming out of the nothingness of the hollow ribcage. "Some things were never meant to be, I suppose," Isadora said, punctuating the last of her words with a click of her teeth.

The remaining bones crumbled into a pile of dust on the ground. The wind picked up, the spirit of Isadora carried off in an ethereal breeze, away from Jutland House at last.

CHAPTER 28

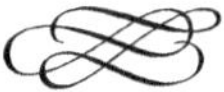

ANNE RAN a tentacle through the grass, drawling mandalas that were quickly ruffled away by the breeze off the ocean. Charlie was curled up, still in Mara form, her head rested in Anne's lap, Emme's urn tucked into the crook of her leg.

"Won't she still haunt this place?" Anne asked.

"No," Emme said with confidence. "She's gone. There's nothing left to tether her here."

Anne was quiet. She looked down into Charlie's eyes.

Sister, Zelda said.

Sister, Willow answered.

They embraced, tears flowing.

"Go on," Emme said. "You are not lost to each

other. You will always be together, one by land and one by sea. Let go of my sisters."

Anne's body lurched, her back arching, and a glowing mist seeped out of her pores, rising into the air and hovering above the sisters. Her tentacles twirled together, forming back into an arm, and the silver of her skin warmed to a soft pink. Once human again, she reached out, swirling her hand through the iridescent fog.

Thank you, Zelda said to Anne. *I love you.*

Anne nodded, her words confined within a sob, and the mist dispersed over the ocean, falling beneath, rippling the reflection of the moon.

"Do not cry, little sister," Emme said. "She will return to her body, to her home. You helped her a great deal, you know."

"This has changed me," Anne said, looking out at the ocean. "All my life I've been searching. Lost. I've never quite been able to find my place."

Emme nodded, and touched Anne's cheek with a wispy, ethereal hand.

"Some things were never meant to be," Emme said, "but some things were meant to be something else."

Anne smiled. Emme floated forward and kissed Anne on the lips, then nodded to Charlie.

"What?" Charlie said. "What's going on?"

"Walk with me," Anne said, grabbing Charlie's paw.

The sisters walked hand in hand to the rocks, Anne humming the melancholy tune she'd learned in the ocean. When they reached the water's edge, Charlie looked at her, smiling, tears pouring down her face.

"I know," Charlie said. "I know what you're doing. Are you sure?"

"Quite."

"I'm glad," Charlie said, but her eyes were sad.

"I'm not like Emme," Anne said, stroking her sister's fur. "It's not an end. This is something different."

"Finally. You've found yourself," Charlie said.

Anne nodded.

"I will always be here. With you," Anne said.

With nothing left to say, Anne and Charlie embraced, crying into each other. When they pulled apart, both were smiling.

Anne turned and walked into the water, wincing from the cold. Once she was waist deep, a tentacle reached up and coiled around her arm. Anne walked backwards, watching her sisters as she descended into the ocean, deeper and deeper until the colours returned, her breath was new and steady, and the world around her came alive.

Anne's pink flesh sloughed off, revealing sparkling,

icy-white scales, her limbs separating and contorting and softening into majestic tentacles. Her red curls erupted into a mass of fiery snakes, entwining with Zelda's indigo hair, swirling in a soft cyclone above their heads.

They kissed, and Zelda pulled back, pure joy on her face.

"Welcome home," they said to each other.

"What now?" Charlie asked

Charlie stood at the edge of the forest next to Emme, who hovered a foot in the air.

"You move on," Emme said.

"To what?"

"What do you want to move on to?"

"Guess I'm Mara now. Anne seems happy, so…"

"Convincing," Emme said, rolling her eyes.

Emme floated down to eye level and put her hands on Charlie's shoulders. "I was lost, too. I made a bad choice, but I was blind. It is what it is, and now I move on. And I've learned something. There's always something different."

"I just never saw myself spending eternity chasing squirrels and licking my ass."

Emme laughed, a sound like chimes. Charlie couldn't help but smile.

"Why did you do it, Emme? Why did you leave me?"

Emme grew quiet, her eyes closing. When she opened them, they were blue and glowing with tears. "I didn't leave you. I got scared. Any choice I had seemed impossible, so I left me. Me, not you, not anyone. Just me."

"I'm sorry," Charlie said.

"Me too," Emme said.

They embraced, cried, then Emme pulled away. "All right, enough of that. Let's get moving on, shall we?"

"I guess I go find my pack, then."

Emme gave Charlie a hard look. "Remember what I said. Choices. Options."

Charlie embraced her sister one last time, then opened the urn and poured it over the yard. The crows descended once more, flapping through the ash and upsetting it into a glittering cloud that floated upwards, leaving Emme's voice ringing in Charlie's mind.

Things are meant to be whatever you want them to be.

And with that, Emme was gone, her trail of dust floating up on the wings of the crows. Charlie watched, marveling at their beauty, then walked down the forest path.

CHARLIE STOOD over top of her corpse, looking at her tattered throat, her bones that had been picked clean by animals and insects, and the rest of her rotted from the elements. She thought of Emme, of Anne, of Bran. She imagined the life she'd lost. But then she imagined the life she could have if she wiped the slate clean, began again and took risks, went with her gut, sunk her teeth into what she really wanted to be.

Go ahead, Willow said inside her head. *I will leave you.*

Slowly, little by little, the Mara disintegrated in two. Half the sand reconstituted into a Mara that stood tall, watching. The other half of the sand sifting down into the corpse below, filling organs, bones, closing wounds, thickening and melding and conforming until Charlie's body was whole and clean, her heart beating and blood flowing through her veins. She gasped, sucking in her first breath, and her eyes opened.

CHAPTER 29

"STRAWBERRY LEMONADE, ANYONE?"

Charlie picked up the pitcher and poured up three glasses, lining them up along the picnic table.

"Later, Mommy! I'm winning right now!"

A little girl with curly red hair ran towards a makeshift goal created from hockey sticks and duct tape. She crossed the goal line and danced, chanting about being the ruler of the universe. Midfield, Bran fell to his knees, cursing his loss with exaggerated emotion.

"Foiled again!" he hollered, rolling on the ground. "C'mon sweetie, let's go grab a bite to eat then I'll kick your bum in another round."

"Mommy! Daddy said bum!"

The sun was high, almost cresting the peak of

Jutland House. The yard was in full bloom and the water was alive, splishing and splashing abound as birds and boats mingled about, fishing and conversing, enjoying the ocean and her spoils. It was perfect—a painting come to life. Charlie smiled as Bran tossed Luna on his shoulders. As he crossed the grass, Charlie marveled at their beauty, their happiness. The pure joy of her life.

"Want me to throw some dogs on the barbecue?" Bran asked.

Charlie grabbed his face and kissed him, long and hard. He held her, then rubbed her swollen belly, his face practically splitting from the size of his smile.

"Ugh! Stawp!" Luna whined as she shimmied off Bran's shoulders. "You guys are gross."

"Listen here, pipsqueak, how do you think we made you?" Bran said.

Luna cocked her head, thinking, and Charlie punched Bran on the shoulder.

"Magic," Charlie said, articulating the word.

"Ah yes," Bran said, winking. "Magic."

"Mind if I snag a glass of that lemonade?" Gwen said as she sauntered around the corner, dressed in muddy jeans and a flannel shirt.

"How are the horses?" Charlie asked.

"Brats, those horses," Gwen laughed as she poured

herself a lemonade. "Emme's been eating my fence again, and Anne keeps kicking over the water trough."

"Sounds about right," Charlie said, smiling.

"I'm gonna go grab the mustard," Bran said.

Charlie nodded, and Bran disappeared into the house. Rubbing her belly, Charlie released a sigh, satisfied. She closed her eyes and heard her family—the laughing of Luna, the crows cawing in the trees, a haunting melody floating in off the ocean...

"Good home you've built here," Gwen said, raising her glass in a toast. "Good life."

"It's perfect," Charlie said.

They clinked and drank, smiles and contentment across both faces. A crack drew their attention, and they looked over to the side of the house where Wilfrid was chopping wood for the stove. He looked up and wiped his brow, then smiled large and loud at the ladies before continuing his work.

"Gentle soul," Gwen said. "He's so happy here, now. We both are."

"You miss them?" Gwen said, looking out at the water.

"Always," Charlie said. "But they're here. And they are happy. Just different."

Luna tugged at Charlie's shirt and patted her belly. "Mommy, I left Zelda somewhere!"

"She's there," Charlie said, pointing across the yard.

"Oh! I see her!"

Luna ran off, red curls bouncing off her shoulders as Charlie watched on, her heart full.

"THERE YOU ARE, YOU SILLY THING!" Luna grabbed the old doll in the gossamer dress and clutched it to her chest, soothing it with hugs and kisses. "The woods is no place for an old dolly," she scolded.

Deep in the forest, the leaves rustled and a branch cracked. Luna walked closer, until her toes crossed the line between yard and forest.

"Hello?"

The wind swirled, the birds fell silent, and a low growl came from the deep within the forest.

"Luna!" Charlie called. "Come, honey, it's time for lunch!"

Luna turned to go, but looked back into the woods, her eyes glowing yellow.

AFTERWORD

SPOILERS AHEAD! READ THE BOOK FIRST!

There are many ideas all mashed together in The Sisters Three. Here are some fun little easter eggs I threw in to amuse myself, but that might also be of interest to the more curious reader:

• I was born in Victoria, on Vancouver Island in Canada. The area this story takes place, though specifics are fictional, is north of Sooke, British Columbia on the west side of the Island. The Goat's Moat is a fictional business, but loosely named after my favourite restaurant on the island, Old Country Market, affectionately known as Goat's on Roof. It is a restaurant and store with, literally, goats on their grass roof. Look it up. You won't be disappointed.

• Jutland House, the bed-and-breakfast, is named for the town my mother is from—South Jutland in Denmark. My mother and her family immigrated to Canada in 1942, landing at Pier 21 in Halifax, the same pier Isadora's parents landed on when they immigrated here. Thanks for the story fodder, Mom.

• I named Wilfrid, the hulking staff who we discover is a former RCMP officer who was shot by Isadora at Jutland House, after the Prime Minister of Canada in 1896, Sir Wilfrid Laurier. Laurier wanted to reduce and eventually disband the North-West Mounted Police. Thankfully, they were needed to police the Klondike Gold Rush, and in 1904, King Edward VII conferred the title of Royal Canadian Mounted Police, and the rest is history.

• The Mara is actually a creature in Danish folklore. Mara, or Nattmara, is a race of female werewolves spawned from the souls of restless children. They are in constant werewolf form, other than when they seep through the cracks of houses as sand to terrorize those who are sleeping, but manifesting as pale girls that sit on chests.

• Can't find mention of The Vandheks in your folklore Google search? That's because the Vandheks is my own creation. I adore the Giant Pacific Octopus, and also mermaids, specifically the one depicted on the rock offshore Copenhagen. My mom has the image of that sculpture on a blue plate hanging in her kitchen—as Edvard does in his restaurant—and I always had a soft spot for it. The name Vandheks came from the melding of two Danish words—Vand is water, and heks is witch. The water witch is a combination of these two ocean creatures that I find both gorgeous and haunting.

• Speaking of Edvard, he is named after the artist who created that iconic bronze statue of the mermaid on the rock by the waterside at the Langeline promenade in Copenhagen, Denmark. The artist's name was Edvard Erikson. I do not know if he was in love with a ghost named Gwen.

• As for the sisters, their names come straight from the literary world. Anne, Emme, and Charlie are named after the Bronte sisters, Anne, Emily, and Charlotte. The similarities end there, of course, but I liked these sisterly, literary names. Arnold, which is Anne, Emme, and Charlie's last name, is the last name of my auntie Darlene, who lives on Vancouver Island. Carsten,

Isadora's last name, is an abbreviated form of my mother's last name, Carstensen. Oh, and Bran? He's named after the fourth Bronte child, Branwell Bronte.

• And finally, the idea for this story came from an odd place, one not associated with the tale itself. In a moment of being homesick—of which I have many—I was looking through old photographs and came across one of me and some friends of mine in Banff, Alberta, hiking, the Three Sisters mountains in the background. The Three Sister, I thought. And thus, a story started to brew in my brain. I reversed the name, calling it The Sisters Three, as it sounds like a folk tale.

Thanks for indulging me and reading my tales.

Jae

ACKNOWLEDGMENTS

Thanks to my critique group. Jess, Amber, Roger, Diane, Ethan, and Nikki— you were all a huge help with this book.

Thanks to my mom, who received many FaceTime calls about Danish facts, words, and descriptions.

Thanks to wine, coffee, and late nights.

ABOUT THE AUTHOR

Jae Mazer is a Canadian who was born in Victoria, British Columbia, and grew up in the prairies of Northern Alberta. After spending the majority of her life battling sasquatches in the Great White North, she migrated south to Texas to have a go at the armadillos. She is a connoisseur and creator of horror, speculative fiction, and fantasy. Many moons ago, a rampant love of reading led her to believe she could weave a good tale herself, and now she is an award-winning author with eleven novels under her belt, as well as stories published in various anthologies.

ALSO BY JAE MAZER

Landing in Eden

Delivery

Pal Tailor

Gahl's Door

Chrysalis and Clan

Crone

Beautiful Beasts

Tales from the Den: A Collection of Dark Fiction

Also written by Jae, under the Pen Name J.M. Adler

Notch

Jae Mazer has short stories included in the following anthologies:

Eclectically Heroic, by Inklings Publishing

Hair Raising Tales of Villainous Confessions, by Mad Girl's Publishing

www.ingramcontent.com/pod-product-compliance
Lightning Source LLC
Chambersburg PA
CBHW071155100726
47908CB00002B/388
9781733613224